Your Own Kind

Linda Fagioli-Katsiotas

The characters and events portrayed in this book are fictitious.
Any similarity to real persons, living or dead, is coincidental and
not intended by the author.

ISBN: 13:978-0989219433
ISBN-10:0989219437

ACKNOWLEDGMENTS

With love and gratitude I thank my family, especially:
My husband, Nick,
Jim and Carol Fagioli,
Bob and Anne Fagioli,
and Cousin, Linda Taft-Fagioli,
for their hours of editing, advice
and for their endless encouragement.

"LET YOURSELF BE SILENTLY DRAWN
BY THE STRANGE PULL OF WHAT YOU REALLY LOVE.
IT WILL NOT LEAD YOU ASTRAY."
-- RUMI, PERSIAN POET

CHAPTER 1

Everyone was asleep when the Turk's son came looking for Sarah that morning. With a thick willow branch tucked under his arm, he walked on the edge of the dirt road with long angry strides. The sun had just become a thin red line in the east and the bitter smell of wet reeds was coming off the marsh near the lake as he rounded the corner and made his way to the front of the Middleground Boarding House. Mrs. Middleground was the first to hear the commotion, awakened by the thuds of the branch hitting the windshield of the red car. As the shards of glass fell against the metal hood, she raced to the window, her sluggishness momentarily forgotten. She'd fallen asleep in the chair the night before. The magazine she'd been reading had slid to the floor and lay with its spine open—the cover showing its beaten state—torn and creased, last year's edition of *The World in Pictures:1974*.

Ordinarily she wouldn't have thought much about seeing the Turk's son outside her window, especially in the morning. That was the boy's usual routine after his newspaper deliveries. He always appeared on foot at the front of the boarding house, meeting with Sarah to do whatever it was they did together. And then they'd drive off in that blue Impala of hers. Well, in Mrs. Middleground's opinion—and she had many of them—he was much too young for Sarah. Three or four years can be an enormous difference in age, especially at that time of life. She peered through the lace curtains and shook her head. That boy couldn't have been more than thirteen or fourteen.

Mrs. Middleground was a woman with many philosophical principles for life, though they changed more often than her boarders. The fishermen were her steady renters but the young people who were there to work during the summer season would come and go like a stubborn rash. They all seemed to follow the same foolish path — living an entire lifetime in that short three month period before leaving East End with nothing to show for it. Or at least that's how Mrs. Middleground saw it, and she figured the reason the Turk's son was hanging around that year, was because he'd just gotten old enough to know there were girls at her boarding house. But now as she held open the curtain in her trailer window, watching him swing the branch at the red car with such venom, she was caught between intrigue and genuine fear.

Sarah was lying in bed, suspended between a dream and reality when the noise started. She heard the shuffle of feet in the hallway and opened her eyes to see Alexandros fighting to get his arms into a tee shirt. In an instant she was behind him, following him out to the yard. She pushed her hair away from her face but it fell back into her eyes as she came up next to him and saw his damaged red car.

"Kareem, What are you doing?" she cried.

Sarah was the only boarder who knew the Turk's son by name. To the others, Kareem had always been no more than a moving piece of the background, an early morning paperboy who threw rolled up newspapers onto lawns while balancing on his bicycle seat. It wasn't until he'd started coming around the boarding house that they'd heard Mrs. Middleground refer to him as *The Turk's Son*. And there he was, on that unusually warm spring morning, having fully emerged from the scenery with all the fire and rage of a real live person.

Kareem's insults hit Sarah like a blow to the head and it took her a second to realize that the crumpled paper he was thrusting into Alexandros' hand was actually a photo. Her heart pounded into her ribs as Alexandros looked at it and then at her — his expression impossible to read. By then, the sun was already sitting on top of the boarding house, its heat pushing through the elm branches and burning holes into her back. She wanted to grab the photo from Alexandros and explain, but there were no words and then Kareem was gone, disappearing into the brush around the lake and a police car was pulling up onto the dirt.

It was all a mistake—a terrible misunderstanding, but how could she stop the movement of a boulder falling from a cliff? She knew—though she tried to convince herself otherwise—if she hadn't stayed in East End, none of this would be happening. Those were the thoughts that pushed her as she ran to the blue Impala and got in, hoping to get to Kareem before the police. She at least owed him that, and she made it half way to Main Street before the vibrations hit the side of her car and a deafening blast slapped against her face through the open window. Her body went ice cold, the chill starting at the base of her spine, running up her back and stopping at the nape of her neck. She knew—without knowing—it was over. Nothing would be the same after this.

She pulled to the side of the road when she saw the line of police cars blocking the intersection, and she left the Impala to join a small group of onlookers moving toward the ocean, toward the tower of black smoke that was billowing above the dunes. As her pace quickened and she broke from the group, a cop with a walkie-talkie grabbed her by the elbow, the static buzzing from his hand and voices spitting commands out of the small gray speaker. His thick fingers pushed against her skin, but she'd already gotten as far as the IGA and there was something lying in the street—something that made her want to yank her arm from his grasp and run to it. But his grip was too tight.

"Move back. Crime scene."

He ordered her back to an invisible line where others had gathered.

"Move back. C'mon, move!"

The smoke was starting to turn a light gray; a strong sea breeze smeared it across the cloudless sky, shading the sun with an artificial twilight. Sarah listened to the hum of conversation around her, not really hearing it until a hand on her shoulder startled her.

"Sarah?"

It was Oscar. So much time had passed since the last time they'd seen one another, she almost didn't recognize him with his crew cut. But with Karen Marie there, standing beside him, Sarah knew who he was, and in a flood of relief, she folded herself against his chest and let the tears come. Karen Marie put her arms around them, so Sarah was in the center of the embrace and couldn't see the red car parked across the street with its front wheels sunk into the sand, or Alexandros, who had been running toward her, suddenly stop. She simply closed her eyes willing herself to be back in time, back in Owl's Head with her family, back to the general store. But the past is a closed door, though Sarah longed for it anyway, pressing her eye lids tightly together until she could see herself sitting on the stool behind the dated wooden counter beside the old brass register. And she was home again.

CHAPTER 2

Owl's Head, New York: 1974

Sarah Petit held one of the little crunched up paper balls she'd made from the wrapper of a straw. With her thumb and middle finger, she flicked it into the air and watched it fly to the glass door of the small refrigerator built into the opposite wall. Its items — the staples of life that the nearby neighbors came to buy when they didn't have time to go to Edward's Supermarket up on Route 21 — were blurred by the condensation collecting on the glass. Some of the little paper balls had landed on the shoulder-high shelves in front of the refrigerator and were lying against cans and boxes of food that sat like her dreams, carefully arranged to hide the empty spaces between them.

A damp breeze from a passing storm pushed through the open door and blew some of her hair into her eyes; its heavy scent of wet dirt mixed with the old wooden smells inside the store. It was always like that in the mountains, during the summer. The clouds would blow over, turning purple with anger and then empty out in torrents, leaving the people below wet and sticky.

"No more rain, please," she whispered.

But she could see more clouds building in the distance and she knew there would be more. She slid from the stool and reached on the floor for the metal clip that had fallen from her hair. Grabbing it, she pulled her hair back from her eyes and reattached it as she kicked aside the candy wrappers that littered the floor around her feet. Then she reached down to the space under the counter and pulled her spiral notebook out from the dust. She slapped it onto the counter next to the neat assortment of junk — candy, chips, gum — that was mostly there to attract the neighborhood kids who also came to buy cigarettes and beer *for their parents*. And at that moment, Sarah heard the creak of the front porch and looked up to see one of them making his way into the store. She smiled at Oscar as he walked through the door with something that resembled a rolled cigarette tucked behind his ear, half hidden under the long strands of his hair.

"Got a light?"

"What took you so long? Thought you weren't coming."

"And miss your birthday? No way."

Sarah threw the notebook back to the floor and kicked it under the counter.

"Close the door."

The general store was housed on the ground floor of a two-story blue house, which sat on the corner at the end of First Street in the sleepy town of Owl's Head, a town tucked deep inside the Adirondack Mountains of New York. It was a place where old-style homes cluttered together near Main Street and then slowly dispersed into random dots as they reached the foot of Owl's Head Mountain and disappeared under the blanket of pines.

The porch on the blue house still had the brace in the ceiling where the swing had hung generations before, and the neighbors would come to sit and chat with the owner, Anne Petit, Sarah's great-grandmother. It was the house where she raised her children after her husband had been killed in the logging accident in the north woods. The store on the first floor had ensured her survival through the hungry years and her sanity through the lonely ones. But it was also a beacon of light for the townspeople who were paralyzed by snow in the winter months and tranquilized by boredom in the summer. It was the heart that pumped life to the body.

Slowly though, like a light mist drifting over the mountains, the valley was dusted with droplets of change. Grandma Anne watched some of the boys leave for the war in Vietnam while others headed to the Canadian border a few miles north on Route 21. Then there were the hippies. The ones who thought they had it all figured out when they ventured through the mountains and stopped at the general store, but all they ever brought with them was life—the same life that existed in Owl's Head. Grandma Anne would recall her own youth whenever one of those young women came into her store. She'd look down at her great-granddaughter and say something like: *everything changes, my dear—but nothing is ever different,* to which Sarah, just a small child at the old woman's side, would agree to with a nod. But Sarah didn't really believe it as she looked in awe at the flowers in the young woman's hair or the smooth string of beads that disappeared into the neckline of her flowing dress, a dress that ended at the wooden slats of the floor with dirty toes peeking from under the ragged hemline. To Sarah, this was different—very different.

But in a town as small as Owl's Head, such difference was discouraged because people in such a small town knew that there rarely existed permanent escape from decisions made in youth. One's past was forever etched in the air that the townspeople breathed.

So a person could attempt to reinvent himself by moving to a city and making new memories. Then he could take a break from that successful business he'd created from dust, to bring his beautiful family for a short visit back to his hometown because like it or not, the instinct to return is hypnotic. And though he'd since graduated from an ivy league university top in his class, invented Velcro and become a millionaire, cured cancer and won the Nobel peace prize, back in his hometown he'd still be the guy who climbed the water tower in January and pissed on the mayor. So before joining a Hari Krishna troupe or hitchhiking to California to live on a commune, a kid from Owl's Head knew he'd better take a moment or two when deciding on a direction, no matter how trivial the move might seem, for he had only to listen to the stories of the previous generation to know his actions would be among the archives for the next.

Edith and Ron Petit had been grateful during those turbulent years that Sarah, the older of their two children, was tucked safely away from adolescence with Grandma Anne in the general store. But now that Grandma Anne was gone and Sarah was old enough to be there alone, many of her summer days were spent hanging around the store in the guise of work.

After Edward's Supermarket was built on Route 21, the number of customers dwindled to just a handful a week, leaving Sarah with endless hours inside the store working her imagination for possible escape routes from the boredom. But on that day, in the summer of 1974, the day of her seventeenth birthday, if someone had happened by a little before noon, Sarah would have been otherwise occupied and the customer would have found the door locked.

Sarah's mother, Edith, holding the hand of her five-year-old son, Earnest, walked the two blocks from their house on Church Street and approached the store with a crumbling piece of coffee cake in a napkin. Earnest had reminded her, repeatedly all morning, that it was his sister's birthday. So finally, Edith had rummaged through the pantry shelves and found the half-eaten cake, grabbed the lighter from her cigarette case and a used-candle from the junk drawer and ventured down to the store, expecting a quick visit and then a return to the house. The two tiptoed up the front steps and stopped at the closed door. Earnest wiggled in anticipation, not experiencing the same irritation as his mother at the sight of the unopened door.

He held his finger to his lips and looked up at Edith, the excitement showing in every movement of his body, the floorboards creaking with each light step.

"Light it, mom," he whispered. His hand covered his mouth trying to suppress a giggle but it escaped from between his fingers.

Edith pulled the lighter from her pocket, lit the candle and whispered, "one, two, three." Then she grabbed the knob as Earnest cried out.

"Surprise!"

But the door did not open and her body hit against the glass, jostling the cake, sending it to the wooden floorboards, the flame dying. And Earnest's smile was replaced with a look of wonder as a blurred figure caught his attention at the corner of the house near the rose bushes. He ran to the end of the porch expecting to see his sister, but still attending to his mother's actions, lest he miss the festivities he had convinced her to initiate earlier while following her around the house clutching his G.I. Joe figures.

"What the heck?" Edith jiggled the doorknob, then pounded on the glass, "Sarah! Are you in there?"

She cupped her hands and pressed her face to the window, trying – with no success – to see within. Sounds of movement on the inside floor brought Edith's voice to the pitch of fury.

"Open this door right now . . . Sarah!"

Her anger was bubbling to a boil when she heard someone calling her name from behind and turned to see Mr. Durea leaning on his cane under the drooping leaves of the elm. He tilted his head toward the end of the porch and pointed his thumb in that direction giving Edith the chance to see the figure run from behind the store toward the mouth of the wooded area. And Earnest, though not what he had expected at the onset of the morning diversion, was delighted to see a real live G.I. Joe—camouflage and all—disappear into the trees.

Sarah opened the door and an aroma wafted out as she offered her mother a glassy-eyed greeting and a smile.

"Enter," she pulled the door further inward and back against the wall.

"Hello Mr. Durea!" Sarah gave him an exaggerated wave as if she were flagging down a rescue ship. The old man shook his head slowly, and then called to her mother.

"Edith, it was that boy. Oscar."

"Thank you," she called to him while putting one hand on her daughter's forearm and pushing her into the store, the two disappearing within and Earnest galloping after them.

Moments later Oscar was falling across the width of his bed, listening to music as he stared at the black vinyl disc spinning on the turntable that sat on the floor. The beat bounced between the slanting ceilings of the attic bedroom he shared with his brother.

No.

No brother.

It was his room. Alone.

Daniel had come home in a body bag last fall, only a few months before the cease-fire was signed, ending the war. It was hard to swallow that information and he often forgot that his brother was gone. The house held its breath in expectation, waiting for the return. And the silence echoed with a deafening intensity as Oscar tried to breach the chasm that widened between his parents with each passing day but it simply swallowed him into its depths. And then his mother left. Gone while he sat staring out the window in eighth period English class. No good-bye. But what about him? He was still there. Alive.

His head and his arms hung over the sides of the bed and his eye caught some movement in the rug beneath. He focused into the shaggy shafts of the rug. One strand in particular was bending with the weight of an ant on a mission. A crumb – a boulder – from the half eaten sandwich on the desk above, lay inches away on the top of a crumpled sock—Mount Everest!

The ant ascended the next strand in the rug and then continued on, up and down as he made his way over miles of terrain. Oscar watched in a deep concentration of lost time.

"C'mon little guy. You can do it."

He thought about moving the sock closer, to shorten the journey, but his hands did not move. The ant reached the base of the sock to begin his climb upward, in and out and around the folds of cloth like a runner on an obstacle course, over each crease until he had his prize between his feelers. Then the ant's descent from the sock began just as the bedroom door crashed open and hit against the wall, the knob leaving an indentation among the scrapes and holes of the plaster behind it.

"I said to keep that racket down!"

Oscar's father hovered over the bed, breathing fire toward him. He stumbled forward and then stopped, frozen, his upper lip in a curl. This son. Why this one? The boy's face enraged him and then he saw the fatigues.

"Hey! Those clothes . . . I told you."

He swung and missed as Oscar rolled onto the floor, eye-level with the ant who was unperturbed by the chaos above as he continued down the sock—until a mud-covered boot came down hard and the sock was flattened, the ant gone, and Oscar's lip was raw with blood.

"They ain't your fatigues." He grabbed the shirt. "You got no right."

The buttons became launched missiles as Oscar was pulled from the shirt. Bare-chested, the boy felt a blow to the ribs. He got to his feet, gasping, and caught the next swing of his father's arm, pushed it away and ran for the door.

"Bastard. Worthless son of . . ." the man's slurred words were drowned in the whine of the hinges as Oscar ran through the front door, jumped from the porch steps and disappeared into the fading light.

And at that moment, Sarah's mother tried to reign in her own anger.

Edith was sitting on the closed toilet seat talking through the mist as bursts of water were hitting the shower floor.

"We can send her to live with your brother on Long Island."

"Send our daughter away?" The soapy water dripped into Ron's eyes as he squeezed them shut. "Edith, I can't."

"I can't raise these kids alone, Ron."

"Edith, I'm not out drinking or gambling." He turned the water off. "I put food on the table and a roof over our heads." He pulled the shower curtain and it scraped along the metal rod stopping at the damp wall. "Gimme the towel."

She reached for the towel on the floor. "I can't keep her away from that boy. She's like a bitch in heat."

"Edith! Geez—"

"Well, she wears those shorts. Her cheeks are sticking out like a little whore."

Ron cringed. "How can you say that crap about our daughter? Stop it. She's just a kid, and so is Oscar."

Edith handed him the towel and he wrapped it tightly around his torso. Then he shook his head hard from side to side, the droplets of water spraying out at her like a garden sprinkler.

"Ron, she's the same age I was when I had her."

"Edi, it's not like that with them. She and Oscar grew up together. They're like brother and sister."

"You don't know what you're talking about."

"He's a good kid Edi. There's no harm in it."

"Are you insane? They're not little kids anymore. You don't see the stuff I see."

"What do you mean?" Ron was wiping his hand across the fogged mirror and suddenly stopped, his hand pressing a halo into the tiny droplets of steam, then slowly sliding to his side. "What kind of stuff are you talking about?"

"The way they look at each other—it's a look—well, you know."

Ron stared into the mirror, past the streaks of wet lines. He swallowed hard and his voice dropped to a whisper. "Maybe you're right, Edi." He picked the comb up off the side of the sink and pushed it slowly through his hair, his eyes still facing the mirror but he seemed to be seeing something different, something far inside his reflection.

He sighed. "But Edi, with Mikey? What's she gonna do down there with him? He can barely take care of himself. It'd just be more trouble, different location."

"She could work. A job. Start her life."

"What about school? She's only got one year left."

"What good is school if she ends up stuck here?"

The words slapped him hard. "Edi, she's not you," he said.

"I'm not saying that she is me. I just want — she needs a chance."

"This is her home, Edi. This is the only place she knows."

"Exactly! That's what I'm worried about."

"She has to finish school."

"She can work with Mike at the cannery and learn responsibility."

"She's got a job in the —" Ron's words were swallowed by his thoughts. "Why doesn't she apply at Edward's?"

"Everyone in Owl's Head has applied there. Anyway — how is that different from your grandmother's store?"

"Really? You need me to tell you that?" He turned back to the mirror and combed hard into his scalp while Edith deflated with a long steady exhale.

"Well that's my point. There is nothing here for her."

"Okay, Edi. Just give me a little time to think. I don't want to send her away."

"Listen Ron, she was all flushed when she opened the store door. I don't know what they were doing but I can guess. Don't take too much time to think or —"

Earnest's muffled voice broke through the steam. "Hey. What're you guys doing in there?"

"Flushed?" Ron asked. "What do you mean?"

Edith looked at his reflection in the mirror and said nothing.

He slowly shook his head. "Give me a chance to think. I'll come up with something. Maybe I'll talk to the kid's father."

"Oh, what good will that do?"

"Hey, open the door." Earnest's pleas ended the conversation.

*   *   *   *

It was almost dark when Sarah heard something hitting her window. She was lying on her bed, her spiral notebook open on the pillow.

"What rhymes with *need*?"

The pencil eraser was in her mouth as she cocked her head deep in thought and stared off into the air at nothing.

She nodded.

"*Bleed*, that's good."

She pulled the pencil from her teeth and heard a pebble hit against the window screen. She knew it was Oscar. She wanted to tell him to go home, not to provoke her parents but when she pulled back the curtain, she saw the battered half of her whole. Oscar stood there shirtless, shivering in the cool air, his mouth swollen. She had to let him in. She couldn't disappoint him.

"Wait by the kitchen door. I'll be right down."

She closed the spiral notebook and threw it under her bed, then tiptoed down the stairs. Her mother was sitting on the sofa with Earnest, his head resting in her lap as he fought sleep. Both were mesmerized by the blinking images on the television screen, its volume set to a point that offered insurance against the detection of Sarah's movements. Her father provided more cover, lying prone on his worn recliner, his mouth open wide with the angry growls of snores pulled deeply from an exhausted body. Sarah knew where to place her feet on the wooden floorboards to avoid the creaks. She made her way toward the kitchen quickly and silently, testing out the wooden planks with her toes before putting her foot down. The old floor was a minefield. Gingerly, she put one foot in front of the other—left, right, left—until she was safely entering the kitchen. But when she reached the kitchen door and pulled Oscar inside, she didn't think to look out to be sure there was no one watching.

Once inside the warmth of Sarah's room, Oscar's body began to relax. With a sweeping movement, he flicked off her light and sank to her bed. In the dim evening light that glowed from the window, Sarah looked at his swollen face.

"Your father?" She stroked his cheek.

He nodded.

She pushed the stuffed animals from her pillow and pulled a blanket up from the foot of her bed.

"Come on, get under here. You're cold."

The boy closed his eyes and allowed Sarah to mother him, fighting the tears that threatened to reveal his thoughts.

"I'm okay." He rolled to his side, looked up at her and patted the pillow. But when he tried to smile, the movement caused him to grimace and he inhaled hard.

"Poor baby." Sarah slid under the blanket and pulled his head to her shoulder. Her nose rested in his hair. Its damp sweaty smell, like wet woolen mittens, reminded her of those winter days when he used to catch her and push the snow into her face and the scent of wet wool would linger for a moment or two. Back then, they were just two little kids, unaffected by the icy air around them, and they'd have to be pulled apart and dragged home before frostbite set in.

Oscar was the sullen boy two doors down—familiar, comfortable—the kindergarten classmate who slowly evolved into something more, simply because he was there. In a matter of days, by some trick of nature, his childhood veneer was pulled back and a playmate was suddenly a virile knight in shining armor— Sarah's first kiss, after her first beer behind the cemetery. Yes—the cemetery—though regarded by most as a final destination, it was the place of many *firsts* for the kids of Owl's Head. Boredom, adventure, and challenge pulled them like a magnet to the empty field behind the gravestones. Dares were played out and time was passed.

But at that moment, in her childhood bedroom, Sarah lay with Oscar whispering in the dark, lost in her own reality that kept her from knowing that those were their last moments together for a long time. As they lay, enveloped by the dim light, sharing the comfort of each other, Sarah's father, half asleep, was shuffling across the kitchen floor to answer the knocking. And as he conferred with Mr. Durea in a hushed voice, holding the kitchen door slightly open, Sarah pulled her childhood friend closer, into the warmth of the blanket.

Ron ascended the stairs.

Sarah listened to Oscar's serenade. He whispered his own version of a song.

"Saraaaaah, You're beautiful . . ."

"Sh." She put her hand to his mouth. "They'll hear you." Then she pulled the blanket over their heads and he lowered his voice but he continued to sing.

"All the dreams we held so close seem to all go up in smoke. Let me whisper in your eaarrr . . . "

Ron hesitated outside his daughter's bedroom door. He heard Oscar's muted voice from within and reached for the knob.

"Saraaaah, Saraaaaah, where will it lead us from herrre?"

Sarah felt the sudden movement in the room before Oscar did, and light flashed onto the other side of the blanket as she yanked it from their heads and was momentarily blinded while her eyes tried to adjust to the change. Her father stood, framed by the doorway, his hand hovering over the light switch.

Ron wanted to shoot across the room like a deadly bullet, grab Oscar by the hair, yank him from his daughter's side and drag him across the floor. But instead he held tightly onto the knob of the door as he took a moment, bracing his free hand on the wall above the light switch. Taking in his daughter lying intertwined between her white sheets with the bare-chested Oscar, the rage he had initially felt slowly melted into fear. Through a clenched jaw and the slightest quiver in his voice, he addressed Oscar who was already pulling himself from beneath the cover.

"Say good-bye to Sarah," Ron said.

He was relieved to see Oscar emerge with pants on, and to Sarah he said, "We're going downstate tomorrow to visit Uncle Mike."

"Dad, we uh—" She knew there were no words. Her father's eyes silenced her.

Ron walked into the room toward Oscar, kicking a stuffed animal with such force it ricocheted off the wall between the dresser and the closet. Oscar took a few steps backward and blinked wildly like a trapped animal, putting his arm up to his swollen face.

"I'm not going to hit you, Oscar." Ron said, noting the swelling below his eye and the first hint of purple above it. He put his arm around Oscar's shoulder and led him into the hallway. Ron had sympathy for the boy, maybe even a little regret.

It wasn't clear where Oscar slept that night, though the words Ron spoke to him on their way down the stairs and the few moments they spent on the front porch together, insured that he was not nearby the next morning when the Petit family packed the station wagon in the dim light of dawn and started down the road to Route 21. Neither Sarah nor Earnest questioned the unusual circumstance of having their father suddenly available midweek for what was being billed as a vacation. Nor did they know of the stir among their neighbors, hours later, as the news of Oscar's departure became known.

"That poor boy. Lost his brother, then his mother." No one in Owl's Head could fathom how the boy's father could have signed the waiver for the age requirement, discarding the only family he had left as Oscar took the bus south, the forged papers neatly folded in his jeans pocket, finally making things right—on his way to boot camp.

Sarah's guilt kept her quiet in the back seat for the beginning of the trip.

"*I'll call Oscar as soon as I can,*" she thought, watching the electric poles whizz by. Her father would forgive her—he always did. And everything would be back to normal by the time they got back from their vacation.

Somewhere past Latham, at a rest area that looked like all the others before it, the family spilled out of the car with a cooler and sat at a wooden picnic table that was peppered with smears of sap from the pines overhead. They ate hard-boiled eggs and buttered rolls in silence. As Ron emptied a paper cup of its last drop of orange juice, a light tap from Edith's foot beneath the table nudged him into action.

"Uh, Sarah." He cleared his throat and looked across the table at his daughter, "I uh, well—the reason we're going to see Uncle Mike is, well—I need to tell you something and—"

Edith abruptly stood from the bench and grabbed Earnest a bit more roughly than she had intended.

"C'mon Earnest, let's go to the bathroom."

"Wait, I wanna hear what daddy—ouch!"

Edith couldn't quite dislodge his twisted legs from the beam that attached the bench to the table, but she continued to yank as

Sarah looked at her questioningly, and Earnest began to howl.

"Hey, that hurts!"

"Mom, his legs are stuck. What are you doing?"

Earnest was suddenly dislodged and he fell to the ground.

Edith looked at Ron and then her daughter.

"We're going to the bathroom. Get up Earnest."

Earnest, though a bit shaken and hurt, knew that the picnic table was the place to be at that particular moment as he craned his neck, his mother pulling him forward faster than his legs could go.

"I don't have to go yet. I'll stay with daddy. You go."

Edith didn't answer him. She continued her path toward the small cement restrooms, her grip like a vice on his wrist. She slowed her pace as they approached a group of women on the same path, which allowed Earnest to see his older sister throw a half bitten roll into his father's face just before Edith pulled him into the ladies' bathroom, an embarrassing situation for a boy of any age, which made him forget his desire to know what was happening under that pine tree where he'd just finished his eggs.

But as they approached the parking lot a few minutes later, his curiosity was renewed. His father stood next to his sister outside the closed back passenger door. Her face was streaked with tears. Her hand was welded to the car door and his father's hand was on top of hers, prying her fingers loose from the metal handle.

"No, I'm not going."

"Let go of the handle, Sarah!"

Other travelers were parking their cars and some were making their way to the restrooms but their eyes were glued to the scene being played out next to the station wagon.

"This is bullshit!" Sarah cried.

Earnest gasped. "Mom!" He looked up at Edith, not quite sure of the events unfolding before him, but certain that the ache in his stomach was something he wanted someone to stop.

The shock from the sting of her father's hand across her cheek jolted Sarah away from the car door as she brought both hands to the side of her burning face. The car door was opened and she was pushed inside. Earnest, wide-eyed, grabbed the inside of the door to help himself climb up next to his sister.

"You sit up front with us, Earnest." Edith said.

"I wanna sit back here."

Earnest figured if there was going to be hitting, he wanted to be as far away as possible from the hands that perpetrated it.

"Now!"

Ron's voice had the intended effect. Earnest backed out of the seat and went to the front where he was planted between the adults, his sister quietly crying behind him.

"I'm not staying there." Sarah's voice came between quiet sobs.

She laid her head down on the seat and stared at the cracked vinyl, picking at it with her finger as her tears pooled against the bridge of her nose and overflowed down into the foam that was protruding from a small hole she had created.

"I'm not staying there," she whispered.

After a few minutes, Edith turned to her daughter.

"Sarah, you don't have to live there. Just see how you like it and maybe you can stay for the rest of the summer."

Ron looked at his wife. His face was hard.

"She'll stay for the rest of the summer. Period."

Sarah sat up.

It seemed that the proposition was changing. Moments before, under the pine, Sarah had heard that her fate was to live and work with her uncle. Within only a few minutes the duration of her sentence had been decreased to a month. Perhaps as the journey continued, the punishment for her crime would be more parole-like and she would return to Owl's Head after a short visit with Uncle Mike.

The radio buzzed between mountain static and music as Sarah's father restlessly played with the dial.

"Before we hit the city, I wanna stop for gas," he said.

The gas station was close to the exit. As the family waited for the attendant to pump the gas into the car, Edith suggested they use the restrooms. Sarah noticed a telephone booth at the back of the building near the ladies' room. She narrowed her eyes to get a better look at it before she left the car, but as she got closer to the restrooms, she realized that she wouldn't be able to slip into it, unnoticed.

Hours later, as the car passed through the toll lane at the foot of a sprawling bridge, adrenaline pushed Sarah forward to the edge of the seat so that her chin laid on the cool vinyl and the top of

Earnest's head brushed her lips. She watched New York City hug the edge of the black river that lapped below the bridge. It grew larger in the windshield as they moved forward.

"Mike's a little further out." Her father glanced sideways at her. "He's not inside the city."

Sarah was silent as the city loomed large before her and then rotated to the side windows as the car made the climbing turn to the middle of the bridge. She sat back and watched through the passing iron girders as the tall buildings, like a painted mural on the side of a wall, slipped into the back window and became smaller. Ahead, over the bridge, the bustle of the city remained as they passed through an outer borough that was just as elusive as the Manhattan skyline behind them. Earnest's excited chatter filled the spaces between the family members as they sped along. From the height of the highway, Sarah watched a train passing along an elevated track in the distance.

She imagined herself walking on the streets below, eating in restaurants, dancing at discos, talking to the people in the crowd. But the vision faded as quickly as the train blended into the buildings, vanishing as if it had never been there. She sighed loudly, so that both parents could hear, and then she slid back against the seat.

"Mike's a little further." The back of her father's head turned and she saw the look on her mother's face.

The numbers on the dashboard clock clicked onward until there were mostly trees on either side of the highway, and that's when they stopped for lunch at a small diner close to the exit ramp. Ron made several trips to the lobby pay phone, all resulting in a sullen face as he returned to the table and answered his wife's questioning eyes with a slight shake of the head.

Sarah had also seen the pay phone.

"I'm going to the restroom," she said as she slid from the booth.

"I'll go with you," Edith stood next to her daughter. "Come on, Earnest. Come with us."

"I'll go with daddy later, right dad? I don't have to go now." Earnest looked at his father. "Dad, right? I'll go with you?"

His father was looking down at the crumpled paper he kept taking out of his pocket.

He mumbled quietly, "Okay."

As Sarah left the table with her mother, she turned to Earnest.

"I'll take you for a gumball in the lobby when I get back," she said. And Edith liked the idea as much as her son as she saw a chance to talk to Ron without the kids listening.

In the lobby, Sarah gave her brother a handful of pennies—a fortune! Then she went into the phone booth. As she put a dime in the slot at the top of the phone and dialed, Earnest began by putting the first penny into the slot at the top of the gumball machine. He turned the handle and opened the metal cover; one gumball rolled down the chute and into his hand, which he promptly put in his pocket. He looked at his sister.

Sarah was sitting on the little seat inside the phone booth, the door ajar. She was holding the telephone to her ear and staring at the round dial.

Earnest slowly put the next penny in, glancing again at his sister. She didn't look at him, so he continued. Then, when he heard the clank of the dime as it fell to the coin box in the telephone and more clanking as more coins were put in, he put the next penny into the gumball machine. And he worked like a robot on an assembly line, getting as many gumballs into his pocket as he could, before his sister realized the error of handing a five-year-old a fistful of pennies and placing him in front of a gumball machine.

"Hi, this is Sarah. Can I speak to Karen Marie?"

Earnest heard his sister's voice wafting from behind the half-closed door. When his pockets were full of gumballs, he began putting them in his mouth until he was startled by the sound of his sister kicking the side of the booth.

"What?! Are you sure? No way—you're wrong. He would've said something to me. How do you know?"

And as she put the receiver back in its cradle, Earnest watched her put her head in her hands and whisper, "oh God."

"What?" he asked, but the word was indecipherable with his cheeks puffed out from a wad as big as a Ping-Pong ball, saliva running down the corner of his mouth.

"Spit that out," Sarah said quietly, "and chew one at a time or dad is going to take them away."

They went back to the table where their parents sat.

Edith nervously played with the knob on the small jukebox attached to the end of the table. It obstructed the view out the window.

"Have any quarters?" she asked Ron, "let's pick some songs."

"I wanna do it." Earnest wiggled over Edith to get closer to the machine. He rolled the dial and the metal plates with the song titles flipped open like pages in a book. "I'll put the money in."

"What did you say to Oscar last night?" Sarah demanded as she slid next to Ron.

"That's none of your business," her father answered.

"It *is* my business and I wanna know."

Earnest felt that bad feeling starting in his stomach again and he wanted to explain it to the three older people at the table but all he could think of saying was, "Give me the money! I wanna put it in the slot!" which came out louder than he had expected and a little bit like the squeak of a rusty hinge.

"Behave." Edith said it loudly so the people around her would know she was a good mother, which she emphasized by squeezing her son's hand — hard.

"Ouch. That hurts"

"What is your problem?" Sarah's voice rose above the clanking of dishes. The conversations at the tables nearby stopped.

"Check please." Ron waved to a waitress walking by.

*   *   *   *

Blinding white light. That was the town of East End, a huge blank canvas of bright white flatness on all sides of the car. Thick rays of sun, without anything to stop them — no hills, no trees — shot light into the back seat as the car moved forward. The rays bounced off the white sand of the dunes, and the ocean that lay just over those dunes should have been a sea color but the sun's reflection on the rolling brightness, reflected more white into the car.

Sarah and her family were at the furthest end of Long Island and she decided, as she looked out the windows of the station wagon, that Owl's Head was actually bigger. The car crawled down what appeared to be a main street, past a drugstore on the corner, past the parking lot of a long two-story hotel, and Sarah noted that instead of the surrounding Adirondack Mountains, this town was encased by inescapable water. The Atlantic Ocean roiled its white foamy waves into the dunes on one side of the car while the sparkling water of a large lake blinked on the other side. Ron steered the car and turned left at a small square building with front windows sporting pink curtains and a hand-painted sign that said, *Pancake House*. They were following the only road in town, making their way to the bay at the northern end, the ocean and lake disappearing behind them.

Sarah watched a small motel pass by her window. Six little doors were embedded in a brick façade close to the road, just behind a sign that blinked in neon: *vacancy*, but the first three letters were unlit. A larger sign affixed to its roof had *Romance Motel* painted in faded black letters. It was the kind of place that had been built long before there were other choices for vacationers, long before vacationers thought to go out that far. It was a motel that was neither on the ocean nor on the bay, in a town so small that it was hard to find such a piece of land and undoubtedly had been built by someone who feared the water but feared leaving East End even more.

The car approached the bay and more whiteness slid into the back seat from atop the flickering current of calmer waters. High tide pushed the boats in the marina up against the pier. The water gently licked the pylons before curling back into the current on its way to the eastern tip of the town where two bodies of water, bay and ocean, met and crashed against a rocky buttress. A lighthouse stood high above East End at the furthest tip of the island—a dead end. This was a town with three sides of water and the way Sarah saw it, unless you were a fish, there was only one way out.

Owl's Head, on the other hand, had Route 21, a major highway that could take her north or south away from the mountains and toward any destination she perceived as freedom. And if she were so inclined, there were plenty of foot trails to take her through the mountains. Escape was always possible, even if it was only a perception. But East End had only that one small road in and the same small road out—a road that was an hour drive from the highway, the highway being the only escape off of that God-forsaken island.

As Ron pulled up to the marina, he realized that they had seen all of East End, so he made a U-turn in the parking lot, narrowly missing a dog that was lying in the shade of the entrance sign. His window was open and the perplexed look on his face prompted the attention of an old man standing a few feet away with a hammer in his hand. He was about to replace a piece of fence in front of a motel. The motel had a large shamrock over the entrance. The old man squinted his eyes and brought his free hand up, making it a visor over his eyebrows.

"Hey there, friend, need some help?" He called out to Ron as the car pulled slowly into the street. He had the slightest hint of an Irish brogue and Earnest thought he sounded like a leprechaun.

Ron stopped the car.

"We're looking for the cannery. You know where it is?" He knew that Mike would be at work by then.

"Right behind you." The old man walked up to the driver's side and put his hand on the car above the window, peering inside as if he were greeting friends.

"Right there. That building next to the pub."

He was pointing with the hammer to a building that was not much bigger than Grandma Anne's general store.

"If you need a place to stay, this here is a fine family hotel." He pointed over his shoulder to the motel with the fence that needed repairing.

"Uh, no thanks. We're staying with my brother," Ron said, but he made a mental note of it. After all, they'd been driving since before dawn and it was late afternoon. He had misjudged how much distance there was between the two small towns, and there were most likely other factors in that unplanned trip that he might have misjudged. He wondered if Mike would have room for them. He'd have to think it over—spending money on a motel—but right then, at that moment, he was eager to see his younger brother.

"Thanks anyway," Ron said as he pulled away and turned back to the marina.

Ron told the others to stay in the car after he parked at the side of the cannery. It wasn't the type of place they could all go traipsing into. But when he went inside and was told that his brother had been fired months ago, he made his way back to the car as his uncertainty cemented into a full change of heart. There was no way he'd be able to leave Sarah there.

"Mike's not here today," is all he said as he got in and turned the key, the engine giving him a tired whine. They drove back down toward the ocean and Ron pulled up to the phone booth on the corner in front of the drugstore. He unfolded the crumpled paper with Mike's phone number and address as he got out of the car. Then he walked into the booth, closed the street noise behind the door and began to dial. Still no answer. He stood there with the phone receiver pressed to his ear and wondered. Well, he would have had to come down and make sure his younger brother was okay, so the trip was warranted, even if he had no intention of leaving his daughter there. That is what he told himself as he walked further into the drug store and showed the address to a clerk and then returned to the car, Sarah smoldering in the back seat. He opened the driver's door and slid in, completely unaware of the flame he had ignited or the fire that would rage.

And at that moment, his younger brother, Mike, was sleeping the heavy sleep that comes from an overexertion and abuse of the body. He had worked the night shift at the yacht club, parking cars into the early morning. Then he had gone with the other bellhops to the bar on Main Street. When it closed, he had moved with the other partiers to the sand dunes with a case of beer and the cocaine that Surfer Jim brought.

No one was quite sure of Surfer Jim's real name, but he was an older leather-faced guy who was there every summer, seeking out the younger crowd and believing that they accepted the discrepancy between his age and theirs because, as he put it: *age is not relevant. It's your inner soul that really matters.* He ignored the obvious—that they simply wanted the free drugs he provided.

He was just another shadow in the background for the three-month tourist frenzy that rained down on the small town, and Mike was becoming dangerously close to looking like him, except he had been there for two winters, at which time the town shrunk to its actual size with the local businessmen, the fishermen and the families of both. So Mike naively perceived himself as a *townie*, not a loser like Surfer Jim, in a place where those businesses remained in the same family for generations.

The party in the sand dunes had lasted until late morning when the tourists began to come onto the beach and then Mike, with a few partygoers, found his way to the house he shared with several other younger bellhops. They stumbled off the sand and piled into cars to weave through the morning traffic back to the house. And a few hours later, he was completely unaware that his brother was there, standing with his sister-in-law, his niece and his nephew, at the front door of that house.

Ron, seeing that there was no movement about, cleared his throat loudly as he stood with the others on the front steps. He hesitated and then knocked lightly on the weather-beaten door. Still no one came, so he coughed as though he were clearing a giant hairball from his throat, waited and then knocked harder. But the knock pushed the door open, creaking as it slowly inched inward, just enough to see Mike coming forward, hopping as he fit one leg into his cut off jeans and then the other, and then zipping up as the door slowly squeaked to a halt, fully open.

Edith gasped.

Earnest exclaimed, "hey, that girl is in her underwear!"

He was pointing to the sofa, and only because his limited height had not allowed him to see the other disheveled bodies strewn on other furniture pieces.

"It's a warm day." Edith grabbed him and pulled him back toward the car.

"But, but, but—" His neck craned back, squinting to get a better look. "You're not suppose to wear just underpants in the living room. You said. Remember?"

Sarah remained next to her father, her lips curved into a slight smile.

"This is a great place for you to leave me, dad."

"Huh? What?" Mike pulled the front door closed and walked into the sunlight, but his eyes—swollen with sleep—clenched shut as both hands came up to shield them.

"Go back to the car with your mother," Ron said to Sarah and then he turned back to his brother.

The three onlookers leaned against the car watching the two men talking quietly in the shade of a tree and they had no idea that they were all being carefully observed.

CHAPTER 3

Mrs. Middleground stood at the window behind the lace curtains, her hand holding the sill for support as she poured the scotch into the teacup. She was watching the family across the street at Hensen's house as she opened the top of the stereo console and returned the bottle to its place, then gingerly cupped the saucer in one hand and sipped from the delicate china with the other.

The mother was with an adolescent daughter and a smaller son leaning against the car in the street, but Mrs. Middleground couldn't quite see the two other figures that she mistakenly believed to be the older son with his father, standing a few steps from the entrance. There seemed to be so much age difference between the three children. But she knew how that could occur.

A woman falls in love, marries and expects the next step to be a child. But sometimes that child can take a long time to come. Sometimes there's bad luck and the woman is left childless. But she keeps trying as the years slip away. There are all sorts of reasons for those spaces between a woman's children. Ruth Middleground knew that. Stanley used to say, "*You cannot question the will of God. He has a reason for everything.*" But Stanley was a fool, and he didn't have much to say about *God's will* the day he'd come home unexpectedly and found her with George.

A long sigh escaped Mrs. Middleground's lips as she brought the teacup to her mouth and drank deeply, then placed the saucer on top of the closed console.

"Oh, George," she whispered. "There's another one."

George was hanging on the wall within several different frames around the two-room trailer but the one Mrs. Middleground was addressing at that moment was next to the window as if it had been hung there so that he could accompany her on her daily watch.

It showed an old black and white photo of a young man, bare-chested except for some tight-fitting suspender straps. He had black boots up to his hips and was holding a fish across his forearms, the head and tail hanging, and the weight of it pulling him to one side. Behind him was a boat pushed at an angle as if it were caught by the camera in a momentary bob of the water, the name clearly painted on its bow, *Ruth*, coming from behind the young man's hip.

"Look at them, George."

Mrs. Middleground touched the surface of the glass in the framed photo.

"They look like a lovely family, don't they?"

George Theodore, was actually a restaurant manager down by the ocean, and the worn photo was one of several that had been taken some twenty years before. The boat had been a gift and he was a man who had certainly needed one, for he lived his life adrift in churning waters—being pulled from one deadly mass of white water rapids to another, tossed about, almost drowned but somehow remaining afloat. He was there in East End in the summer of 1974, being carried by an unusually smooth stretch of current which brought him a peace he thought was real—like an unsuspecting moth feasting on the nectar of a Venus flytrap. As George floated passively along, purposefully forgetting the turmoil he'd already sailed through, he had not one inkling of the deadly falls that lay ahead as Sarah, a young girl he had not yet met, was poised to jump in beside him. And the roar of the falling water, was left unheeded.

*   *   *   *

After World War II, young George Theodore had returned home to his neighborhood in the Bronx amid a flood of ticker tape raining down from the sky. Those floating pieces of paper pumped dreams of grandeur through his veins and fueled feelings of euphoria that would be short-lived.

The war was over! Or so he thought.

But every night as he closed his eyes on the sofa in the tiny family apartment, away from his mother and sisters who slept in the two bedrooms, he would return to the battle and smell the fear as it collected like rainwater in the gullies along the camp. Each night he'd hear that the marching orders had come once again and a paralyzing terror would cement his feet to the ground, making them as immovable as an oak tree—his feet becoming roots digging deep into the earth. But as the platoon marched in formation, he found that his legs were able to pull up from the ground, moving forward, following the steps of the soldier ahead of him. First one foot, then the other—he became a tiny moving part within the machine. He could feel the tanks rolling beside him and the earth trembling underneath his feet as they grew louder and harder until he awoke to find his limbs entangled by damp sheets wrapped around the sofa cushion, the passing train pounding a beat into the brick wall at his head as the EL passed outside the living room window.

The nausea that wracked his body was dulled by a few glasses of wine from the bottle that his mother always kept on top of the refrigerator, until he found that keeping a bottle of scotch under the sofa was faster and more effective.

His older sisters did not understand. He was home. He was alive. Stop brooding and start living. But Katerina felt her son's pain. She inhaled it from the air around him until it became her own so that the ache was felt in every movement of her body as George descended further into the fog.

Katerina thought of her husband, Dimi. If only he were there to help, he would have known what to do. He always had. But he was gone, and she was alone.

"It will get better," people had said at his funeral. "Time heals all wounds." But it did not get better and the wound never healed. She knew her children were feeling the same, especially her son. And it was true. George did long for his father as he tried to reenter his former world after the ticker tape had been swept away.

Dimi had been a man of great strength and George had grown up thinking his father was invincible—a giant. He remembered being carried atop the man's shoulders seeing the world from a height that only a young child would consider tower-high. Dimi was a hero—his hero, without flaws and with the super-human strength of every superhero he'd seen on the covers of the comic books in the corner drugstore. Yet, it was just a tiny pebble, a miniscule splinter that took his father down.

A sliver of semi-hardened plaque broke away from the side of an artery wall one afternoon as Dimi brought plates from the restaurant kitchen to the table he was serving. It floated on the current, rushing toward his heart like a broken branch in a river and that small fragment of near-nothingness rendered Dimi helpless, snuffing out his life in an instant—a life that had endured and overcome trials of monumental size.

Dimi had come from *the old country*, from an area that was in dispute for centuries—violence and suppression in the name of religion. It was called Asia Minor when he grew up there, later renamed Turkey, but George would only learn of that from history class as his father rarely shared the pain of his memories.

Dimi had been forced with his own father to work in a Turkish labor camp alongside the other Greek Orthodox men of that area, leaving his mother and his grandmother to work the farm. He'd tried several times to unfold his past for his son—leaving out the heartache and trauma—so that the boy would appreciate what he had in America but it always ended up sounding like an adventure—something a young boy, bred on radio shows like *The Lone Ranger*, would never understand.

Katerina, however, knew of it all. Late at night as her husband came exhausted from his job at the restaurant, he would sit with her at the kitchen table as the children slept. Slowly, he'd untie his shoes caked with bits of food and grease, pull his swollen feet from them and rub them gently, wincing as he pressed against the aches. Katerina would take the bottle of wine down from the top of the refrigerator and pour a bit for each of them. They would talk, first about nothing—the broken cabinet handle, the butcher's new wife—then as the wine loosened his tongue, Dimi would draw out the fantastic future he had planned for their lives and the success of their children. He saw it more clearly with each sip as he created the picture for his wife who sat listening, sometimes nodding her head in agreement, always knowing it was the only road that led her husband to sleep. Their son, George, would go to an important university, one with a big name, but—no it didn't matter, he changed his mind—the name was not important, as long as the boy stayed close to the family and as long as he became an educated man. Yes, yes—they agreed—he would be an educated man and never need to be part of this restaurant business. The girls would each bring home a good son-in-law. They'd marry good Greek men, men who loved their wives and loved their in-laws too. There would be many grandchildren. Dimi knew a few games from the old country that he would play with them and he would teach them how to fish as his uncle had taught him. Yes—his uncle, such a good man. The mention of him would bring a shine to his eyes, and with one more glass of wine, there'd be tears, as the pieces of his past would flow from his lips like blood from an open wound.

He spoke of his grandmother and her visits at the labor camp. She was bent with age, with a voice as feeble as a blade of grass, so the guards never suspected her as she brought them all bread warm from her oven—a mother's bread. After all, a soldier is just a boy with a gun, longing for his own mother. Naturally, the guards began to look forward to her visits and they'd let her in to whisper quiet words of comfort into her son's ear and bring her grandson a few moments of relief. What harm could it do?

When she returned from those visits at the camp, Grandmother spoke with her neighbor, Kareem. The Turks perceived him to be one of their own kind because he was Muslim so they allowed him to travel freely in that controlled area. But his true alliance was with his neighbor. It was she for whom he risked his own safety, carrying her letters to the postmaster when he went to market near the sea in the port to the south. She was the woman— the only one of his Christian neighbors—who had heeded his cry as his wife lay bleeding in childbirth. His own son, his first child, was born into her hands, a son strong and healthy because of her quick mind and skill. He thanked Allah for such a gift and it mattered to him not at all, which deity she prayed to.

After each visit to the port, he would return to the village and visit her house to see that all was in order in the men's absence. Sometimes he'd bring a small gift of cloth for her to sew a dress, a hidden letter tucked inside its folds.

Then one moonless night, Dimi and his father escaped. They were led by one of the guards to the outskirts of the camp under the black sky, the boy's heart racing, believing that they were being led toward death. But instead, the guard, Kareem's cousin, delivered Dimi and his father to freedom.

"Go," he whispered, "may Allah be with you."

Was it Allah who had freed them? The thought passed quickly through Dimi as they ran toward the brush. They made their way to the cave at the foot of the mountain where the spring water fell into the canyon, the place Grandmother had instructed his father to go. From there, the family travelled together toward the sea, but not to the port where it would not have been safe for the Orthodox Christians. They went further north like Uncle's letter had said, so that he would be able to sail from the island and they would be able to board his fishing boat without detection. The meeting place was the same landing where Dimi's mother had said goodbye to her sister when she had married the fisherman.

They travelled only after dark, and were unaware of the Greek fleet that had come to liberate their people by way of the port city to the south. On the last night, they came atop the final ridge and saw the black Aegean Sea blinking below them under the light of a half moon.

"Look, down there; It's Uncle's boat," said Dimi's father.

Dimi heard a gasp before he saw the sparkle of the knife blade across his father's neck, and a strange stare—not fear or pain—but confusion in his father's eyes. Shadows moved quickly between them, barking out strange words of a language that Dimi had heard in the labor camp, but never quite understood. His arms were suddenly pinned behind him by hands as rough as tree bark but he thrashed wildly about until he broke free just at the moment a burning sensation ran from his ear to his jaw and a warm liquid spilled from his chin.

He had already been running for several minutes, breathing in hard deep gasps, before he realized he had been moving at all. And he was alone, the cries of his mother behind him, long whining cries like that of a wounded animal. The warm flow of blood spilled down the side of his face but he continued down the ridge, over rocks and through wild brush, falling and returning to his feet barely aware of his movements until his uncle's arms

31

fought to contain him, pulling him into the boat. And they were far from shore when the cries of the women were replaced by the lapping of the water against the stern.

Uncle began wiping the blood from Dimi's face. He pressed hard on the slash that ran from somewhere below the boy's ear, but his hair was matted with the sticky blood and it was difficult to see from where it came. And Uncle's eyes were blurred by the wetness of tears.

Dimi was brought home to the small fishing village. He was Auntie's only living relative, the only remnant left from her home in the mountains and she nursed the heartbroken boy, as if he were a newborn lamb. Dimi slowly came back to life and he became the son that the older couple had longed for. He fished in the sea with his uncle, made friends with some of the boys in the village and those friendships kept him occupied. But Dimi looked out over the straits everyday, the sea breeze so warm and soothing, yet his thoughts so dark and cutting. He knew he could not stay, and so he planned his departure. He never understood his connection to that land, that he was a link in an unbreakable chain that would keep him tied to those mountains across the straits. His spirit would remain there forever, and his descendants would be as tightly connected as he, to those towering peaks and their azure-blue skies.

With some saved up drachmas from his aunt and uncle, Dimi thought he was escaping. He had the address of the butcher's cousin's friend who had settled in a city called Philadelphia so he made his way to Athens and found a job on a ship after a few days in the port of Piraeus. And two months later, he stood on the deck of *The Goddess Eris* looking out at America. But when he jumped into the New York harbor and swam to a dock, pulling himself from the water, wet and exhausted, he hadn't realized how far apart America's villages were or how big her city of New York would be. He also hadn't anticipated the difficulty of being in a place where no one knew his language. After walking for two days, tired and dirty, each street looking like the others, he heard what sounded like a beautiful melody. His own language.

Esi eisa kala?

"Are you okay?" It reached his hungry ears as his eyes drank in the kindness of the compatriot who offered him help. So he pulled a knotted handkerchief from his pocket from which the Philadelphia address emerged on a paper that was torn and streaked with bleeding ink, completely illegible except for a few random letters. The Good Samaritan looked at it with serious eyes and Dimi barely felt the first blow as the fist knocked him to the ground. He was too weak to defend himself. He lay in the mud and felt another blow to his head before he disappeared into unconsciousness. The stranger stole the drachmas from the handkerchief that Dimi had pulled from his pocket and he left Dimi bloody and broken in the alley. The policeman, who had been called to the scene, discovered the crumpled paper with some strange writing—the only identifying information—and he guessed that it was Greek. It seemed to match some of the store signs he'd seen while walking his beat past the Greek neighborhood. So he brought him to Kostas Bakery where the owner, remembering his own days of hardship, took the young man in. His wife nursed him back to health. She broke pieces from the aloe that sat in a pot near the bakery window and rubbed the healing sap on the angry red scar that went from his ear to his jaw before she realized it was an old wound. And their young daughter, Katerina, looked on with curiosity.

When Dimi had fully recovered, the older man gave him work as a baker's assistant and let him sleep on the sacks of flour in the bakery basement where Dimi would grow strong—eating the day-old bread and the meals the wife brought him. His body strengthened with the heavy sacks of flour he carried back and forth, working from dawn until late into the night. Every penny he earned was saved behind the loosened brick near the storeroom.

He listened to the customers as they interacted with the baker's wife for he knew success lay in knowing those American words. He smiled at the customers and practiced what he'd heard, "Hello, how are you?" beaming like a proud child when the customers responded, though he had no idea what was said.

Dimi looked forward to the baker's daughter returning from school each afternoon as she stopped in to help her parents and somehow always arrived when her father was in the basement working with Dimi. The baker mistakenly thought it was her arms full of books that Dimi seemed to be always gazing at and he encouraged Katerina to teach the young immigrant some helpful phrases in English.

Perhaps Dimi would be able to help the baker's wife behind the counter on busy days. He was such an amicable young man and the baker saw how the old ladies gave him a few coins when he carried the bags to their apartments. If he could learn a few more words, maybe the baker could improve the delivery service, maybe even expand further than his cousins' restaurant. He was not a competitive man but he would have enjoyed having a few more American dollars than they had, especially on one of those rare visits back to the old country.

The baker became so wrapped up in his desire to outshine his cousins, that he did not notice the innocent brush of skin as his daughter bent to retrieve the pencil she had dropped, her warm cheek sizzling over Dimi's arm. And he did not see his daughter reach across the kneading table to get something that she had let roll there—clumsy girl— her breast mistakenly brushing against Dimi's reddened face. Nor did the baker know of Katerina's frequent visits to the basement after hours when he and his wife had retired upstairs to their apartment. But when his daughter's belly began to swell, it was deemed more beneficial to move along with a wedding rather than the beating he had begun, when Dimi convinced him that Katerina's child would need a father, and she, a husband.

Thus, the baker provided a modest wedding and the assistant became the son-in-law, settling with his new bride inside the living room in the baker's apartment. But when Katerina was pregnant once again, before the first grandchild was able to crawl, the baker begged his cousins to take the assistant into their restaurant to make more money for the growing family, admitting the inferior state of his bakery, but mostly so that he would not have to look into the face of that man who had deflowered his innocent daughter and who seemed unable to keep his hands off of her.

Dimi was quite happy to leave his father-in-law's employment and get away from his accusing eyes. His father-in-law seemed to despise him until Dimi provided the older man with a grandson, little George, the third grandchild, his namesake. Then Dimi became a man of importance and he was rewarded with a lump of money to rent the apartment across the street from the bakery, close to his in-laws. But not too close. And the cousins gave him a promotion that lifted him from the hot underground dishwasher station to the clean dining room to be a waiter, as his English had so improved with his studying, and not at all because they wished to show Dimi's father-in-law their superiority.

But poor Dimi was gone before the age of forty, dead from a heart attack the year George turned fifteen. In one gray afternoon, everything changed. George had come home from school to find his mother and sisters crying. He had been with his class—that very afternoon—on an outing to the Museum of Natural History. He would not be able to step foot into that museum ever again. It was the place he had been horsing around while his father, balancing plates of food in one hand and clutching his chest with the other, had staggered through the dining area until he fell to the restaurant floor, the dishes crashing into pieces around his body. George had been laughing, enjoying the day, teasing Toula Glikoula, hoping to get a kiss behind the Tyrannosaurus Rex—while his father was dying. So at that soft age of fifteen, he was left with his mother, his older sisters, and a few relatives peppered among the neighbors. They came to console him, to show him the face of stoicism—to carry on.

When George got his draft notice a few years later, he knew that he could defer his deployment as the only son of a widow. But he did not share that information with his mother. She and her daughters were working so many hours to make up for the loss of her husband's income, none of them thought to investigate that fact.

So, there he was back from the war, lost in his own sorrow. Katerina felt helpless as she watched her son suffer. She searched for an answer among her friends who also had sons returning from the war, and she remembered Dimi's dream for his son to be an educated man. There was something called the G.I. bill. President Roosevelt talked about it on the radio and Tasia, at the vegetable market, told her how her own son was using it to become a teacher. A teacher—imagine that—a profession among the most respected. Katerina spoke to George about it. Mr. Roosevelt's G.I. bill—that would save him; she was sure. So, George did as his mother suggested. The university experience had long hours of study which distracted his mind. In some of his classes, he found a few other men who had served in the war in the same places he had. They were men who understood him and they often went to a bar or two after class to talk about their time in the war and the bizarre nature of returning to civilian life, expected to put aside their experience, their fear, their sadness—as if it required no more than the simple turn of a page in a history book.

When it was over, George collected his diploma and proposed marriage to Toula Glikoula because she was of his faith and that was what his community expected. The other young men his age were doing the same, so like the soldier he had learned to be, he simply followed those in front of him and moved forward, suppressing the impulse to save himself. Next in the sequence of the forward march was a move to Long Island where he accepted a position as an English teacher and brought his wife to a Levitt house.

But the war continued to rage. The night terrors and bouts of crying were not what Toula had wanted. Her neighbors and friends were pregnant. In the supermarket their bellies hit the handles of the cart. She could do her duty and accept that sniveling man-boy as her husband; she could accept his drunken stupors and the occasional outbursts, but she expected to at least have one child. She coaxed him into bed but he lay as limp as wet paper no matter what she tried. So she left, back to the Bronx to find a real man.

George was relieved to be left with his bottle of scotch and lost moments of time—day and night were interchangeable. But the principal could not cover for him anymore after he drove his car into the bicycle rack in front of the school. So it was unemployment and foreclosure that awaited George, rather than jail time. Though George would have told anyone who asked, that jail would have been an easier stint than the torment he was sentenced to with the devil that imprisoned him.

But nobody asked.

So as the sheriff came to put his belongings on the curb in front of the Levitt house, and the neighbors stood in circles discussing the tragedy, only eighteen-year-old Stanley Middleground walked across the street to help George Theodore, his former English teacher. Mr. Theodore was, at that moment, shuffling among his possessions on the curb, looking for the fishing rod his father had made for him. And young Stanley, never having learned to swim, jumped head first into the churning waters that surrounded George.

CHAPTER 4

Earnest was the first to see the woman as she made her way to the public mailbox on the corner in front of their car. He watched her inch her way slowly, as though each step caused her pain, like an old woman, a grandma he thought, though she was around the same age as his own mother. The woman's eyes remained on Edith, and Earnest's remained on her. The squeak of the mailbox cover as it opened, caused Edith to turn toward the woman just as Ron was making his way down the lawn toward them, Mike disappearing back into the house.

"Hi there," Mrs. Middleground shuffled toward them. "See you're having some trouble with your son, there. Happens all the time. It's a wild house, that one," and she pointed her chin toward the front of it.

"He's not their son." Earnest answered before anyone else had a chance.

"Good afternoon." Edith was polite, but wanted to be rid of the woman quickly so she could hear what Ron had to say.

"I'm Ruth Middleground. That over there is my boarding house." She pointed across the street past her small trailer that sat beside a forest of tall reeds near the lake. There stood a long one-story building that seemed to have been a home at one time, but had acquired various additions to it over the years so that there were different appendages running off of a central square structure. The yard around it was mostly dirt with a few tufts of long green grass that had pushed up around the foundation and were brushing against the shingles of the house. There were several cars parked on top of the dirt, two of them under an overgrown elm whose branches clung to the roof at one end of the house and whose roots pushed up through the dirt, looking like pieces of brown pipe protruding between the two cars.

"Nice to meet you," Ron said as he walked toward the driver's side of the car without looking at Mrs. Middleground, which seemed to get the others in motion toward the other car doors.

"I run a strict house over there," she said, "none of the shenanigans that go on over here."

Edith looked at Ron over the top of the car, and then turned to Mrs. Middleground. "Do you live on the premises?" Edith's eyes went back toward Ron.

"I sure do. I supervise everything." Mrs. Middleground lied. "Would you like to see inside?"

"We were just leaving." Ron had one hand on the car door.

"I would." Sarah said.

"Yeah. Why not," Edith added, " — let's have a look, Ron."

"We have a long ride back."

"We're going back already?" Earnest cried. "I wanna go to the beach. What about the waves? I thought we were gonna play in the waves. Dad? You said."

Ron exhaled loudly, "Okay. Let's look — just look."

The small entrance to the house had a low ceiling and even though Ron was not a particularly tall man, he had to duck his head a bit as he walked through. It led into a small vestibule with gray peeling paint that had once been white. On the right, there was a tiny kitchen where a sink overflowed with dishes that had brown and gray clumps clinging to them. A small table sat near the sink and had several mismatched wooden chairs around it. On the left of the vestibule was a sitting area, smaller than the kitchen. A sofa was pushed against a large bay window where lacy curtains hung, their ends crushed between the top of the sofa and the window. The small rug on the floor covered only the space in front of the sofa and the broken floorboards beneath it. There were two giant beanbag chairs; one had a small hole in it where some beads were pushed out as the young girl who was sitting there, shifted her weight, lifted her head from the book in her hands and gave them a nod. Ahead of the vestibule was a central hallway with rooms on each side that just fit two twin beds and two small dressers but not much else. A closed door at the far end of that hallway housed the coveted single room, a bit smaller than the rest so that only one person could live there, but that room was taken. There were four other hallways that shot off of that first one with identical rooms in each, an exit at the end and one shared bathroom.

"Oh my," Edith said as she looked around, her hand resting on her chin with a few fingers covertly covering her nostrils.

Ron said nothing but shook his head lightly.

"It stinks in here!" Earnest said. And Mrs. Middleground countered him with, "Oh that's the humidity, dear," and with a quick step she placed herself in front of him and looked at Sarah.

"I'd be able to get you a job in town at the Atlantic Palace Hotel if you're interested, and if you want to defray the cost of rent, you could clean once a week. I happened to have just lost the lovely girl who usually does it. It's her room you'd stay in too. She moved back home to care for a sick parent." Lies flowed easily from her lips like water over a fall.

Ron and Edith exchanged a look.

But Sarah was enamored by the idea of independence. This was where she belonged. She felt it. She was seventeen now, and with all the optimism and inexperience of a seventeen-year-old, she knew the energy she had longed for back in the general store was here among these walls. She felt it as they walked through the hall, peeking into the bedroom doorways. The flash of a guitar leaning against a dresser, the bouquet of wilted flowers on a windowsill, a fat volume of poetry lying open on an unmade bed, and the warped tennis racket propping open a window – these were some of the sights that captured her imagination as they passed the open doors and returned the greetings of those who acknowledged them. Sarah felt what she believed to be the powerful winds of freedom, though like a hatchling at the bottom of a nest, she was only able to guess at how that might feel. She was sure the scent around her was her long-awaited self, waiting to be claimed. Her parents, however, were honing in on some other pungent smells and it was experience that correctly identified them. For Edith, it was the familiar odor of unwashed clothing and moldy food, while Ron fought with a strong whiff of sweaty testosterone.

"There are boys living here?" He asked.

"Oh, sure," Mrs. Middleground answered quickly. "I know each one of them very well. All good boys. And of course, they stay in the boys' part of the hallway."

"I think it's cool, here," Sarah added.

"I have only college kids." More lies. "They're a very good bunch."

"They'd be a good influence on me." Sarah helped Mrs. Middleground.

Ron and Edith conferred quietly and Mrs. Middleground stood a few feet away pretending not to listen. Sarah joined her parents and tried to point out the positive aspects of allowing a seventeen-year-old to experience responsibility for a few weeks.

"I'd never stay here," Earnest added his opinion, "You won't like it Sarah. You'll miss us." But no one heard him.

"I don't know," Ron said, "Let's go have a bite to eat. I need to think about it."

Edith looked at Mrs. Middleground, "I think we're going to discuss it a little more. We'll be back later."

"Well, of course. Take your time. I can't promise to hold it for you though. These rooms go pretty fast."

"Oh." Edith looked at Ron who shook his head lightly.

"We'll see you later." Ron said and walked toward the outer door.

In the interest of saving money and in satisfying Earnest's plea for some time in the ocean waves, Ron and Edith decided they'd eat lunch on the beach. They bought ice for the cooler and filled it with a few items from the only supermarket in town, a small IGA by the ocean. Edith grabbed the old blanket from the back of the station wagon, as Ron hoisted the cooler to his shoulder and they all followed Earnest as he ran onto the sand.

Earnest had seen the ocean on television but he'd never had the chance to experience it—until now. As he stepped onto the sand, his eyes widened at the height of the rolling water and he watched a wave curl its head upward and swallow the blue horizon. The round tip of the moving wave reached forward, slowly becoming a white mountain before it curled into itself and crashing down to the wet shore, sending bits of shells and floating debris to lick the sand in front of his feet. He looked around and saw others in the waves, some as young as he, and they were laughing and screaming with delight. That was the only information he took in before he threw his sneakers in the sand next to where his parents and sister were busy setting up camp, and then he ran straight into the surf. The shock of the ice-cold water threw him off guard and then a force like a punch knocked his feet from the sand sending him down into the iciness as the water spun over his head and pulled him in all different directions. His nose and mouth filled with water; wet sand found its way into his shorts. He was spinning in the cold darkness, the burning salt rushing into his nose and down his throat, when he felt a hand on his legs and then his arm and he was pulled from the water as he coughed violently, forcing the salty water from his lungs and clinging to his father's torso.

That was his one and only encounter with the Atlantic Ocean for he made a life-long decision at that moment, one he unwaveringly kept, deciding that he preferred the lakes and rivers of the Adirondacks to all other bodies of water and he would never again enter an ocean.

As Ron comforted his son, patting him on the back and holding him against his chest, Edith spread the blanket onto the sand. It was the same blanket that Ron used when he laid under the car in the driveway and changed the oil so she folded it in half, putting the oil spots against the sand. Then she ripped open the pre-packaged bologna and slapped the pink slices between two pieces of bread after dipping her finger into the mustard and wiping it on one of the slices.

"Stop crying; you're a big boy. Here, eat this."

She handed Earnest the sandwich as Ron put him on the blanket, and he took it with a sniffle and began eating. Edith continued making sandwiches until each of them had one. Then she made two more with the extra bologna and tucked them into the plastic bag with the loaf of bread and put it into the cooler.

After a few minutes of sitting on the blanket, Edith turned to Sarah.

"Why don't you bring Earnest to the water to look for shells."

"I don't need any shells," Earnest said nervously.

Sarah looked at her brother, "It's okay, buddy. I'll watch out for you."

She was able to coax him back to the water's edge and instead of collecting shells, which just seemed pointless to Earnest, they began building canals for the water. That seemed more productive to him, as though they might be able to tame the wild sea. He cautiously watched the remnants of the waves inch up the sand to fill the narrow gullies that Sarah was digging. Then he bent in the sand and with one eye on the surf, he began helping his sister.

Ron and Edith remained on the blanket, watching from afar.

"This seems like the perfect solution," Edith said to Ron. They were talking about Sarah. "The woman has experience. She's been running a boarding house for years. I think that much is obvious from the condition of that house."

Ron chuckled, "Geez, did you smell that place?"

"I still smell it," Edith said, "but you don't die from living in an old smelly house. If you did, half the people in Owl's Head would be dead by now." She shook her head and sighed. "I think it'll be good for her, Ron. Let her see what life is really like. She wants to stay there. Let her."

"Maybe you're right."

"It's only for a few weeks. The summer is almost over."

"Hm. I don't want to get her away from Oscar and just hand her to some other guy in that boarding house."

"What are you talking about? She's not a piece of pie. You're not *handing* her to anyone. You heard what the woman said. She knows them all. She supervises everything."

By the time Edith had folded up the blanket, and Ron had hoisted the cooler back onto his shoulder, the decision had been made. Sarah would stay for the rest of the summer, provided that Mrs. Middleground actually did have a job for her as she'd said. The sun was getting low in the sky when Ron decided that they'd better head back to the bay and see if they could get a room in the motel they'd seen earlier. It looked like something they could afford.

The next morning, Sarah prepared to say goodbye to her parents and her little brother after a brief visit back to the IGA for some shampoo and soap and a few cans of food that she could eat until she got paid at her new job. Mrs. Middleground assured them, she'd have one by the end of that day and Uncle Mike promised to watch out for her.

So that is how Sarah began her new life, though none of them knew it was a new life. She, herself, expected to return to Owl's Head at the end of August and resume being a teenager in high school where she would wait for Oscar to finish his stint in boot camp. He would no doubt become an officer with his wit and personality. She could close her eyes and see them living happily ever after in the exotic places around the globe that the army would take them.

Ron counted out the first week's rent into Mrs. Middleground's hand and helped his daughter pull her overnight bag from the mess in the back of the car. Sarah stood in the vestibule waving goodbye to the retreating station wagon, then turning, she walked past the bean bag chairs, one being occupied by the same girl they'd seen the day before, though she no longer had the book. Instead she was lighting a cigarette and sucking the smoke deep into her lungs. Sarah gave her a quick nod and headed down the hall to room four, her room that she now shared with a girl named Emily.

Emily was indeed a college student. She was attending a university not too far from Owl's Head but that is where their commonalities ended. Emily's former roommate, a friend from college, had left to get an abortion and had decided not to return after being fired by the father of her baby, a guy named Andreas, the nephew of the owner of the Atlantic Palace Hotel, and he happened to be visiting Mrs. Middleground a short while after Sarah's parents had begun the long drive back to Owl's Head. Sarah was summoned to the trailer to meet her new boss, Andreas.

There he stood, beside Mrs. Middleground, like a perfect Greek sculpture, the god *Adonis* reincarnate. His blue eyes of glass peered from behind wavy chestnut hair that fell in long ringlets to his bronze shoulders, their bulk barely covered beneath a loose fitting tank top. He smiled a big white *Adonis* smile and nodded a greeting.

"Hey," he said with a nod.

Sarah, did not know how to react so she smiled back and mimicked his nod.

"Hey."

And if not for the roommate's story that she had heard moments before, she might have examined the flutter inside her chest, rather than ignore it. Her face flushed pink with uncertainty. This was not one of the boys from Owl's Head.

"You're looking for a job." It was not a question. Andreas' eyes burned her skin and her hand absently felt for the buttons at the top of her blouse.

"I own the hotel on the ocean and the restaurant next to it." He was only a few years older than she, maybe twenty-five or twenty-six, which is a chasm of enormous measures to a teenager. But not the owner of anything, not even the car that he had parked on the dirt outside the trailer.

Sarah breathed in deeply, "oh."

"You'll work for me. Have you ever waitressed before?"

"Um." Sarah suddenly noticed her mouth was dry and she was so thirsty. A small sip of water was all she needed. She looked up at the young man. "What did you say your name was?"

He laughed. "I'll take that as a *no*. And my name is Andreas. Okay, fine. You'll be a maid in the hotel."

Sarah heard herself whisper, "okay."

"Go get in the car, I'll drive you there and show you around. You'll need—"

Mrs. Middleground's voice interrupted, "Ahem, don't you have something for me in that car of yours?"

"I'd rather come by tomorrow, if that's okay," Sarah said. And she added, "My uncle lives across the street. He can drive me."

"Who's your uncle? I know everyone in this town."

Again Mrs. Middleground tried, "Andreas, uh, my – you know." She nodded her head toward the door.

Andreas ignored her.

"What's his name?"

"Michael Petit. You know him?"

"No.

Andreas put his hand on Sarah's shoulder and let it slide down her arm, where it rested on her wrist.

"Okay, I'll see you tomorrow. Come around ten in the morning. Ask for me."

His electricity had her paralyzed—a stone statue glued to the trailer floor. She did not answer, but watched his tight jeans turn and push through the door, and it wasn't until the screen slapped shut against the doorframe that she saw Mrs. Middleground watching her.

"Oh, he's a sweetheart, that one."

Sarah moved quickly from the trailer, back to the safety of the boarding house and turned to get one last look just as Andreas closed his car trunk and walked back toward Mrs. Middleground who was then standing in the doorway, her body pushed against the screen, keeping the door open as the young man handed her two glistening bottles of scotch.

"What'd that sleaze want?" Emily asked as Sarah came through the front hallway and Emily pushed the sitting area's curtain back in place.

"He's got a job for me."

"Yeah. I'll bet he does."

"Really. I just need the money. I don't care about him."

Emily didn't answer.

The two spent the rest of the day setting up their room. The other housemates wandered in and out, occasionally stopping to chat with the new girl.

But as the evening approached, Emily left for her job at the yacht club and the house grew quieter as most of the other kids that Sarah had met, also left for work in the bars and restaurants. Sarah's stomach began to growl. She rummaged through the bag of groceries her parents had left her and found a can of spaghetti. She held it in her hand and stared at the label wondering how to open it. They hadn't thought of a can opener. But the community kitchen probably had one and she was also curious about what else she might find in the cabinets of that kitchen.

When Mack, one of the fishermen, heard the movement in the kitchen, he assumed it was the new girl he'd heard about. Who else would be rummaging around at that hour? He was a person who knew every knock and creak of that old building, a man in his late thirties who travelled from port to port, a man without much thought for the future, as he lay shackled to the past. So he made his way down the hall to investigate the creaking of hinges and the closing of cabinet doors.

"Listen."

He startled Sarah as he came into the room and she slammed a cabinet door a little harder than she had intended, but he seemed not to notice.

"Could you use a broom instead of that goddamn vacuum when you clean?" He lit a cigarette and threw the match into the sink. "That other one didn't give a crap who was sleeping. College kids don't have no sense."

Sarah thought she had met everyone who lived in the house.

"Who are you? Somebody's father?"

He laughed. "Well, I'm somebody's father but that don't got nothin' to do with you. You're the new girl, right?"

She nodded.

"I'm Mack. I live in the fish hallway."

"The what?"

"Goddam. Didn't nobody show you around? The fish hallway with the other fishermen. What about your roommate? Didn't she tell you nothin'?"

"Emily? Yeah. She told me a few things. Don't worry. I know what's going on."

"I doubt that," he said as he pulled the cigarette from his mouth and held it between his thumb and forefinger, coming close enough for her to smell the aftershave on his face. Mack squinted at her, his eyes becoming two small slits, and Sarah turned her head downward nervously, but she continued to glance up at him through the hair that had fallen to her eyes, and Mack continued to stare.

He wondered about Belle. Would she have the same look as this girl? Frightened eyes, prey for the predators. But this girl was as white as ivory, blank white linen—unlike Belle's sweet mahogany. He let out a long sigh. He wouldn't know Belle if she passed him on a quiet street. She'd only been six years old when he'd left and that was all of ten years ago or was it eleven? The years had a way of piling up while his back was turned.

When he'd met Belle's mother, he'd only been first mate on *The Hope* for a few months. The trip to Trinidad had been his first after he'd landed that job—barely qualified—a mere year after learning to be a crewmember. A few summers before, he and Randy had seen a paper nailed to the wall of the pub down near the pier. They were only out at East End for the weekend to pick up girls and have some fun. The handwritten notice, *First Mate*

Wanted, was just a joke for them, an enticing way for two eighteen-year-old boys to bring back to their city neighborhood a weekend story that was different than the others. With one look at the skinny pair, the captain laughed and let them aboard mostly to amuse himself, knowing they'd spend the day retching over the side as the fishing boat went out before dawn to skim the waters of its fish. Randy did exactly as expected, vomiting off the side of the boat until his stomach was raw. Then he crawled under the life raft and lay there, waiting to be brought back to port. But young James MacDonald quite enjoyed the sea and its rolling waters. The captain was amused by his enthusiasm.

"Get over here MacDonald and clean that puke up." He gave him jobs mostly to entertain himself but by the end of the day as young James walked off the boat supporting the weight of Randy who was green with exhaustion, the captain yelled to him.

"Boat goes out at four, tomorrow morning, Mack!" to which Randy groaned and James shouted back, "I'll be here at three-thirty."

Mack had no idea back then, that so many years later, he'd still be working on the same boat with the same captain, paying rent to the same landlady whenever the boat was in East End. And there stood another one of those young girls—but this one was a little different.

Sarah wasn't sure how to react to this older man who came too close to her when he spoke. He was looking at her so intently; she took another step back and bumped into the side of the sink. Mack saw the change in her expression but he didn't move. By now, his little girl was probably close to this one's age. He opened his mouth and artillery shot out at Sarah as he slowly tried to mend the tiny whole that her presence in the kitchen seemed to have created in the walls of his fortress. His tone got a little rougher, his stance a bit further, his shoulders a little wider as he defended himself from the enemy, the incoming bombardment of feelings that landed like shards of broken glass against his skin.

"You're not no college girl. That's for sure, huh? Not one of them. Your roommate's got no time for you?" His eyes brushed from her head to her feet in one quick sweep.

Sarah stayed silent.

"What the hellaya doing here? Whattaya? Sixteen? Seventeen?

This is no place for you." He returned the cigarette to his mouth and inhaled deeply.

Sarah grabbed the edge of the sink and said nothing.

"Are your parents nuts?" Smoke escaped his mouth as he continued, "leaving a little girl like you here? You're a baby."

"I'm seventeen. I'm just staying for a month to make some money. Then I'm going home." And she added as a protective measure, "My uncle lives across the street."

"At Hensen's place? Wild bunch over there."

Sarah nodded and quickly brushed past Mack.

"See you later."

She rushed to her room, closed the door and locked it, but didn't think of closing the window until Uncle Mike's face was framed by it, his voice coming from the other side of the screen, startling her.

"Hey, what time did you say you need a ride tomorrow morning? Oh, sorry." He saw her jump as she turned toward him. "What's the matter?"

"Nothing. I just sneezed a few times. I guess it's the dust. Making me a little sniffy." She wiped her nose with her hand. "Uncle Mike, can I come to work with you? Uh—I'm bored."

"Well, you'll be a lot more bored there. Don't worry you'll make friends. Wait till you start working. I'll see you tomorrow."

And he was gone.

When Sarah made her way across the street at ten minutes to ten the next morning, there was no movement at all in the Hensen's house. She let herself in through the unlocked front door when no one answered her meek knock.

"Uncle Mike?" She whispered as she tiptoed toward his room.

His bedroom door was also unlocked and the stench that assaulted her as she pushed the door open into the dark room, smelled of sweat and cigarette smoke.

Again she whispered. "Uncle Mike?"

There was a groan from the bed and she saw the outline of more limbs than should have been in one person's bed.

"Oh damn." It was her uncle's voice, "Sarah."

She stood frozen to the floor.

"Take my car. The keys are in my—uh—pocket. My pants are—" She waited. She heard the light breathing of sleep resume, and then fished around on the floor for his pants.

Sarah sat in the car looking down at the stick shift. She'd driven her father's car around Owl's Head but never out onto Route 21 where the state police might have stopped her and asked her for a license. Her father's car didn't have a shift, though. It was easy to drive, as long as no one was in her way. She put her hand on the stick and looked at it for several seconds, contemplating.

"How hard could this be if that fool can drive it?" she thought.

But after some embarrassing crunching noises, the car began to roll backwards into the street, narrowly missing a boy on a bicycle who had just thrown a rolled up newspaper into the yard of the Middleground Boarding House, his neck craned to see inside the car as it came to a stop. The car's back bumper rested in the dimple it had made in the side of another car parked in the road. No doubt the owner of that other car slept soundly somewhere inside the boarding house, knowing he'd parked away from the drunks who came back in the early morning hours and drove haphazardly up into the yard.

"Are you okay?" The face of a young boy was peering into the window. He was a black silhouette against the early sun behind him. His fingers gripped the top of the passenger window as he looked in at her.

"Oh, I uh." The lump that was forming in her throat threatened to bring tears with it. She swallowed hard, "I'm supposed to start a job today. I just, uh need — "

"Ya want me to show you how it works?" He puffed his fourteen-year-old chest out a little further, "I can drive a shift."

Sarah laughed uncomfortably and joked, "I'd rather use your bike."

"I'm almost done. Wait a second." The paperboy unhooked the basket of undelivered papers from his handlebars and threw it on the ground.

"Done!" he said, "hop on."

And so Sarah met Kareem, a boy far beyond his age in demeanor, intelligence and confidence. A boy who seemed to be at her side whenever she needed him, always reliable, always with a ready solution — until the day when the photo would surface and leave her completely broken open.

But on that summer morning, he was the knight, the warrior, transporting her upon his golden chariot as she careened through town on the handlebars. Her hair kept whipping his face, causing him to jerk to the side every few yards, which resulted in her panicked scream and then frenzied laughter by them both.

Amir, Kareem's father, watched with confusion as his older brother, sitting in a broken lawn chair behind the cash register inside their gas station, pointed to Kareem. The boy was peddling vigorously past them, the newspaper basket having been replaced by a young girl in cut-off jeans with her hair, a mess of brown locks, flying wildly behind her.

CHAPTER 5

Sarah pulled herself to her feet, unaware of the pink smudge on
the carpet where the blood was mixing into its fibers. Her hair fell
in wet strands in front of her face, and her body shook violently as
the salty air blew the drapes inward and burned her lungs. She
moved with the automatic movement that the brain provides
when conscious thought is blocked, picking up the pieces of her
clothing while the two men, the hollow sound of their bodies
beneath her feet, tumbled across the floor. Then she was walking
past the bed, one foot in front of the other.

She wanted only to move, to feel her body propelled forward
and have her legs carry her away. Her feet pressed down on the
carpet, which turned into the wood of the porch and then the
sand, tiny grains sliding inside her shoes; the friction against her
heels rubbed her skin red.

She walked, not feeling the heat of the sun as it burned her
face. The sand turned to asphalt as muffled sounds swirled
around her. She continued in a haze, staring downward at the
place in the road where her next step would be, until the reflection
of the sun off a metallic surface made its way into her irises and
sparked a neuron that carried a message to her sleeping brain, like
a firefighter searching the thick smoke of a burning home, looking
for life.

That glint of metal became two steel rails at her feet pointing
out toward the road. It was the end of the tracks of the Long
Island Railroad. She was just staring at the gray pebbles beneath

the tracks and down at the rails themselves, at the fact that they just stopped. No more tracks.

The end.

And just like that, she needed to go home. She wanted to be around people who understood her, to be tucked inside the mountains, away from the naked flat sand, to open her eyes in the morning and see the ceiling of her bedroom, to smell the detergent on the sheets.

She saw the train halt to a stop, a few passengers come out of the open doors and then she was there on the platform, standing with others, moving into the train, then sitting on the plastic upholstery as the car jolted forward and the low dunes with sprouts of beach grass were passing by the window.

"Tickets, please." The conductor moved closer to her, the clicking of his ticket puncher growing near.

And suddenly she was aware of her uniform. She had left her bag at the hotel.

"Stupid!" She thought of her uncle. He was as worthless as ice in the wintertime, and her parents who had dropped her in a foreign place with so few resources. Those same parents who she was running to then, wishing to be engulfed in their arms, to be protected from the world that was spinning out of control.

Silently, she berated herself, the ignorant girl she saw herself to be. She had thought she was on her way to something. Independence? Adulthood? At least to a down payment on her own car. The tips that people left in the hotel rooms were accumulating—but she'd left her stash behind, in her bag—wherever that was.

"Ticket?" The conductor did not seem to register the unusual circumstance of seeing a young girl in a maid uniform with no other possessions.

Sarah reached into her apron and pulled out some crumpled up singles, "Penn Station," she said quietly.

With the ticket tucked into the slot at the top of her seat, she stood up and took off her apron, counted out the tips, twenty-six dollars, and stuffed it into her bra, mistakenly thinking the lack of apron made her outfit look more like a dress. Then she settled back into her seat and watched the dunes turn to trees.

When Kareem had dropped her at the Atlantic Palace Hotel a

few weeks before, she had had such hope.

"I'm Sarah Petit." She spoke to the older woman at the hotel desk. "Andreas told me to ask for him."

"How old are you, honey?"

"I'm eighteen." It seemed like that was the age people had wanted her to be. She didn't see any harm in it. She thought of Uncle Mike's car, of Kareem's bicycle and she suddenly felt sure that a car of her own was the answer to all of her problems. She needed a mode of transportation, one that was solely her own, a means of escape when escape was necessary. But without an income, that would never happen.

"Okay—well, we don't see Andreas around here much before noon," the woman answered. "Are you a waitress or a maid?"

There was an aura of innocence about Sarah that prompted the older woman to say, "Waitresses make three times what maids do. You're a waitress, aren't you?"

"Well, I—"

"Okay." The woman pushed her toward the answer. "Don't worry, these Greeks think you need experience, but all you need are two arms and two legs, and even that is debatable." She laughed.

"I'm Maureen. My guy manages the restaurant. Go around back and tell him I sent you."

"Your guy?"

"I'm kind of old for a *boyfriend*, but if that makes you more comfortable—"

"Oh."

Sarah hesitated.

"Go ahead, sweetie. It's okay."

"I uh—well ya know, Andreas. He uh, told me—"

"Forget about Andreas. I'll talk to him." Then she added. "Listen – in a few weeks all the college kids are going to go back to school and leave us high and dry for the Labor Day weekend. You have the upper hand here. Do you understand what I'm telling you?"

Sarah nodded and wondered why the woman assumed that *she* would not be going back to college.

"The back door," Maureen waved her hand past Sarah, "and pull those shorts down a bit, honey."

The back door was propped open by a plastic pail. Sarah walked past it into the dim light of a hallway with restrooms on either side and she walked toward the sound of clinking silverware and voices. The hallway opened into a large dining area where the bright sunlight from the window created silhouettes sitting at one of the tables. As Sarah walked closer, the people noticed her. An older man with dark hair that was combed straight back stood up and met her eyes as his face emerged from the shadow. Sarah introduced herself and said that Maureen had told her to come in through the back door.

"So you're here for a waitress job?" It was George Theodore who spoke. "You have experience?"

"Yes."

"Where?"

She hadn't expected that, but she quickly created a restaurant. "Oscar's luncheonette." Nothing too fancy.

"Where's that? Never heard of it."

Sarah explained where she was from and that she had come to the end of Long Island to make some money for a car. She'd heard about it from her uncle who worked at the Yacht club as a bellhop.

"What's your uncle's name? Hm. Nope, don't know him. How old are you? Eighteen? Good. Where're you living? Oh Geez." George Theodore sat down slowly.

Ruth Middleground. That lunatic. He was grateful for Stanley's help, though. Without a doubt, the kid had saved his life. But much of that time he'd spent with Stanley back then, was pretty murky. His earliest memory of that day after they'd left Hicksville was like the illusive shadowy images of a dream upon waking – unsure of which side is reality. There was that blur of blue sky and wispy yellowness blowing up and down and someone screaming nearby, loud and long. He'd thought about sitting up, looking around. But he hadn't moved. The pain in his head had kept him glued to the sofa pillow, so he'd closed his eyes again.

Hours later, he'd woken up once more, the room a bit dimmer and his focus a little stronger. The screaming had become a mild screech and then he saw the seagulls confined to the other side of square glass panes in a giant French door, open wide with yellow curtains billowing inward on a cold breeze, up and down, inches from his face where he'd lain.

George Theodore, the restaurant manager, looked up at Sarah. "Okay, well if my girlfriend sent you back here, you must be a great waitress." He winked at the redheaded woman sitting next to him and they laughed.

"This is Jeannette. She'll show you around and tell you what you need." Then he looked at Jeannette, a young woman Sarah guessed to be in her late twenties, though she was actually a few years older and said, "Why don't you let her follow you today – see if she can take a few tables and then –" He turned back to Sarah, "We'll take it from there."

"Come on." Jeannette stood up. "Let's go meet the chef. Make sure you call him that or he gets really pissed."

She pushed the swinging doors into the kitchen and a wall of heat met them as they entered a rectangular room with a long metal counter that housed several square openings with hot water, steam rising from each. To the left was a cabinet with extra cook aprons, cook pants and tee shirts—collectively known as *whites*. A small countertop next to it had an adding machine and an ashtray filled with cigarette butts. Two older women, their faces drawn with lines of experience, stood together talking, one sucking on a cigarette.

"Hand me the monkeys," she said, her hand outstretched toward Jeannette, and Jeannette handed her a stack of small bowls.

"This girl is shadowing me today. What's your name again, honey?" She turned to Sarah who then introduced herself to the other women. When the introductions were finished, the older women realized that they were looking at themselves from the past—an uneducated young girl, not a college one—here for the summer to make a few bucks.

To the right of them stood a long row of deep sinks, filled with encrusted pots and pans. Sarah focused in on a young man bending over the sink, seemingly deep in concentration. His body swayed with the movement of the steel wool in his hand, his forearm moving up and down where beads of sweat became long drips sliding slowly down his golden skin and disappearing into the sink. But Jeannette did not mention his name and instead guided Sarah to the right of him where a pair of dark eyes from behind the steam table watched her with amusement.

"This is Big Gus."

The man nodded — an indifferent greeting, but his smirk told her he had seen where her eyes were. Naughty girl.

And Alexandros, the young man washing the pots had also felt her gaze, but lacking the words in English to protect himself, he stayed within the sink, glancing sideways only when he was sure she would not see.

"Over there is Little Gus," Jeannette continued and a man much larger than Big Gus nodded toward the women.

"Little?"

"Well, he was a skinny little guy when he started here. Came over from Greece when he was just a kid, a few years ago."

Jeannette continued. She pointed to another young man, this one in a grease-laden apron, squinting intently at Sarah from the other side of the steam table.

"That's Eagle."

"Eagle?"

"Believe it or not his name is Gus too, but he has an eagle tattoo, so —"

Eagle rolled up his sleeve and flexed the bird, which sat atop a brightly colored American flag. "Eh? You like?"

"Yeah, yeah. Stay away from her, *Romeo*." Jeannette picked up a pickle from the monkey dishes that were then laid out in front of the steam table and she threw it at Eagle.

"Ah, you like the pickles." He laughed and shook his head wildly, "God bless America!"

"Just ignore him," Jeannette advised. "Okay, here comes Lou. He's the chef."

A large round man in whites approached them.

"Chef, this is Sarah. Sarah, Chef."

They talked for a few seconds, and then Chef turned to the cooks behind the steam table. He barked at them in a language Sarah had never heard before, his voice punching the air with authority, just long enough to show Sarah the degree of his importance in that kitchen – but the cooks just looked at each other and continued with what they had been doing.

Both Sarah and Jeannette turned at the sound of someone loudly clearing his throat from behind them. There stood an older man, no more than four feet high, within the metal jungle of a large dishwashing machine, a smile stretched from ear to ear, his white apron coming to his ankles.

"Oh," said Jeannette. "This is Zeus."

Sarah looked down at the small man and envisioned a few moments in time, some forty years before, two parents cooing over an infant, naming their newborn son with such expectation.

Zeus smiled at Sarah and extended his hand.

"Nice to meet you," he said taking her soft hand in his.

"*Oh*," thought Sarah, "*he's very polite*," and she responded.

"It's nice to meet you too." Then she pulled her hand away and wiped it on the back of her shorts.

Jeannette went to a cabinet and grabbed a black apron, which she gave to Sarah.

"Pull those shorts down. Oh, never mind. Come with me."

A black skirt was found for Sarah. It was too large but she pulled it around her waist with the apron strings. As the women prepared for the lunch customers, a few more younger waitresses came to work — the college girls. They knew they were supposed to be there earlier but somehow the time just got away from them.

"Hey, Sarah." It was Debbie from the boarding house. "I didn't know you worked here."

It was a relief to be known, even if the acquaintance had been made only hours before.

"She's just following today. We'll see what happens." Jeannette said.

Following was not quite the word Sarah would have used. As the lunch patrons dwindled toward the end of the afternoon, the college girls disappeared, presumably to the beach, leaving Sarah with the three older women to pick up the stray tables. Jeannette sat down at the table near the window with George and the other waitresses. They began counting the dollar bills that had been taken from their aprons. Sarah was greasy from salad dressing that had fallen down the front of her apron as she juggled plates and rushed to keep pace with Jeannette. She was salty from the alternating steamy perspiration of the kitchen and its drying in the air-conditioning of the dining room as she ran back and forth retrieving whatever item Jeannette had needed. And she was exhausted from resetting all the waitresses' dirty tables, polishing their silverware and wiping their chairs.

She headed toward Jeannette to see what her cut of the tips would be just as a middle-aged man wearing a dark blue suit came through the kitchen door and walked into the dining room causing the two older waitresses to jump up as he made his way to their table and sat beside Jeannette.

"Do you want a cup of coffee, Minos?" one asked with deference, her head averted as if she were bowing to a king.

The man said something but was looking at Sarah and smiling. His accent was so thick, the words that followed were completely incomprehensible to Sarah, though he continued looking at her waiting for an answer, and she looked at Jeannette for assistance.

Jeannette's eyes turned to ice. "This is Sarah. She's new. See you tomorrow, Sarah."

"She should come back for the dinner crowd," George piped in.

"No, I don't think so." Jeannette put her arm around the man with the suit and gave him a little kiss on his cheek like a bird pecking a worm in the dirt and Sarah understood. But the man was still looking at Sarah.

Jeannette continued, "She needs to follow for a few more days. She's not ready," then to Sarah she said, "I'll walk you out."

Jeannette led her into the kitchen. Only Zeus was there to witness the threat, for he was the only English-speaker as he stood behind the dishwasher spraying dishes with the help of the young Greek Sarah had seen washing pots that morning. Zeus might have heard what was said, but he stared at the water spraying from the hose as if he were searching for gold nuggets in it. It was Alexandros, who watched and read the horror in the young girl's face as the older one held her shoulders tightly and spit words at her.

"That man is Minos, the owner. He's mine, okay?" The words hissed from Jeannette's mouth. "If I see you near him, I'll take a knife and cut your throat! Got it?"

Sarah just stared, her mouth agape and didn't notice the young Greek coming from behind the dishwasher or notice as he brought the clean dishes to the pile near the steam table. His eyes stabbed Jeannette's, and she coughed nervously.

"Okay?" She smiled and led Sarah toward the back of the kitchen, the eyes of the young man boring into her back as he followed. The three approached the kitchen exit, and Jeannette pushed it open to find most of the cooks sitting in the shade on upturned milk crates, smoking and talking. They greeted Alexandros in their language and began to talk as he brushed by the women and joined them. But he was still looking at Jeannette and speaking to the others, and then Jeannette felt the others' eyes on her as she pushed Sarah out the door and sang, "Okay, honey? See you tomorrow?" smiling as the door snapped shut and Sarah was left behind, in the circle of cooks. And suddenly there was Andreas walking toward her from the side of the hotel, his shirt slung over his shoulder, the skin on his chest glistening with sweat.

"Hey! Where were you? I was looking for you."

Sarah realized she had not been breathing for the last few seconds and exhaled loudly.

She wanted to tell him how Jeannette had threatened her because some old man in a suit that she wouldn't get near for all the money in the world, had looked at her. And how hard she had worked but no one mentioned anything about pay for training. But she *did* need *some* money. And how was she supposed to get it? She'd worked. She'd thought that was all she needed to do. A person works and then the person is paid. Her father punched a clock at the mill and a paycheck was born from it. She had seen the cash left on the restaurant tables. She'd done what everyone had told her to do, so where was hers? What was she doing wrong? She wanted someone to answer those questions that swam like drunken fish knocking against the inside of her head, but to Andreas she simply said.

"Maureen, in the hotel, told me to go to the restaurant. I was here at ten o' clock like you said."

"Yeah. She told me." He looked closely at Sarah and his head nodded a bit. "Nice skirt." He was making fun of her makeshift uniform.

"Oh, damn. It's not mine. I gotta give it back." She looked at the closed door but did not move.

"Obviously." He looked at the back of her where the skirt had come loose under the apron strings.

"Take it off."

She turned toward the others self-consciously and saw the men watching.

Eagle said, "Yeah. Take it off." He smiled and stood up.

"I um, it's okay. I'll—" But Andreas' hand was untying the apron strings and the cooks began talking loudly in their language and laughing as the apron dropped to the asphalt.

"No, Andreas. Really, I uh—I'll take it home." But the waist was large enough for him to stick his hand in and lock his finger into the belt loop of her cut off shorts underneath.

"It's filthy. Take it off." And as his other hand began to pull the skirt down, Alexandros was at Andreas' side like an arrow to its target, grabbing his hand and saying something in their language.

Andreas, his face white, pulled his hand from the skirt and turned to leave. "Okay, wear it home."

Alexandros was watching him.

"See you around." Andreas tried to maintain his air of confidence but the waver in his voice betrayed him. And Sarah looked at the young man at her side, his eyes on her as he nodded his head and she obeyed by pulling the skirt around her waist, retying the apron that he had picked up off the ground. Then she walked away from him. Should she have thanked him? Did he understand any English?

It only took her twenty minutes to walk back to the boarding house, even with her stopping to tell the driver in the black car that she did not need a ride. So that is how she decided she would get to work the next day.

It was after her shower, when she was walking across the street to get some money from Uncle Mike, having stopped half way when she noticed his car was gone, that she saw Kareem again.

"Hey, how'd your job go?" He was walking toward her.

"No bike?" she asked and then sighed.

"You need it?"

"Not really. What I need is money." And as she met his eyes, she felt her body relax for the first time since she'd been in East End and from her mouth flowed a steady stream as she told him her reason for being there, about the loss of Oscar, her trip with her parents, her horrifying first day at the restaurant. She stood in the middle of the street, hungry and defeated, talking to Kareem, who remained silent while she spoke, looking at her with the somber face of an old man.

"Come on," he said when she had finished, "let's go to my father's gas station. He has sandwiches there. I'm hungry too."

It did not occur to Sarah to wonder why this boy, who was obviously much younger than she, should be there at that moment and not with kids his own age. She was happy to have someone who seemed to have answers. So, they walked the short distance to the gas station. But when they got there and Kareem talked to his father in a language she did not understand, she looked more closely at the boy.

"Oh, are you Greek?" She smiled as she quickly tried to recall how she had portrayed the people in the restaurant. Had she insulted him?

"Turkish," he said. And the old man behind Kareem's father, his eyes on Sarah, spit on the floor.

Amir cleared his throat loudly, narrowed his eyes at his older brother sitting in the lawn chair behind the register, and said in his language, "this is a hungry child. Didn't you hear what Kareem said? We don't turn our backs on hungry people. Remember your own past, brother."

But to Sarah he said, "It's nice to meet you. Take a sandwich and a drink. My son's friends do not pay here." But the old man behind him made a throaty growl like that of a dog watching a suspicious stranger. Kareem went to him and kissed his forehead and said a few words, which seemed to soften him, though he never took his eyes off of Sarah.

Sarah was happy to be clear of the gas station as she and Kareem sat in the dunes and she ate without realizing that Kareem had eaten nothing.

*   *   *   *

By the time the train pulled into Penn Station, it was evening. It would be another three hours before Sarah boarded the bus to Albany. She spent a dollar fifty on a slice of pizza and a soda and then waited, saving the rest of her money for the bus from Albany to Malone where it would be midday by the time she arrived and she would be able to go to the mill and see her father. He'd be able to drive her home, back to Owl's Head.

Finally, she boarded and sat looking out at the city. The bus jolted forward under the streetlights and toward the bridge but Sarah did not feel the relief she'd thought she would. The city lights blurred and gradually turned to small specks as she sped toward the outstretched arms of the mountains. And she wondered if she was doing the right thing.

After she transferred in Albany she tried to sleep on that next bus, but she was beginning to feel foolish. What would she say to her parents? Why hadn't she just gone back to the boarding house? She could have gotten her stuff together. Maybe Uncle Mike would have driven her back. She should have called home first.

When the bus pulled into the Malone depot, it was mid morning, almost twenty-four hours since the incident. She walked to the mill and found the foreman in the office. He looked at her, then quickly at the secretary and Sarah read the concern on their faces. In her rush to be home, she had forgotten what she must have looked like.

"Sarah? Uh, hi." The foreman's voice was uncharacteristically quiet.

The secretary came from behind her desk. "Everything okay?" She was looking at Sarah's uniform. "I heard you were downstate living the good life."

Sarah nodded but before she could answer, the foreman asked, "Is your dad okay?"

"Huh?" Sarah looked at him. His question made no sense. "I just wanted to talk to him for a sec. Can you get him?"

"He's not here, honey," the secretary answered. "He called in sick. Haven't you been home?"

"Oh—no, I uh, well, I took the bus. I just got in." The secretary knew that it would not have stopped at a town as small as Owl's Head and started to understand as the foreman nodded to the two and disappeared back into the mill.

"Do you want to wait around? I can drive you home in a few minutes. Or call your mom?" She pointed to the phone on the desk.

"Um, no, it's okay. I have to go to Woolworths for something. I'll call from there."

The *something* she needed from Woolworths was her friend Karen Marie. She had a cashier job there and Sarah would be able to sleep in her car until she got off from work.

Karen Marie's first reaction was elation.

"Sarah! You're back!" But immediately her tone changed, "Jesus, what happened to you? You look like crap."

And tears filled Sarah's eyes.

   *   *   *   *

Karen Marie steered the car onto Church Street.

"Pull in the driveway," Sarah said.

"No. It's okay. My car leaks oil. Your dad will kill me.

Sarah didn't disagree.

"Come in for five minutes."

Sarah wasn't sure what to expect but her plan was to tell her parents of the incident and evoke sympathy before they had a chance to be irritated at her being there without forethought or at least having called for their advice or worse, blaming her for it all. She could hear her mother's voice, "Well if you didn't dress like a little whore . . . "

The house was unusually quiet. It was Karen Marie who heard them first. She stopped dead in her tracks and grabbed Sarah's arm.

"Oh my God, are they —"

But Sarah heard the groans a split second after her friend and turned toward Karen Marie mouthing the *oh-my-god* words. They tiptoed backwards toward the front door but didn't make it out before the breathless voice assaulted their ears from further in the house.

"Ron! Oh Ron, yes, yes, yes —"

The girls were running down the driveway toward the street, Karen Marie overcome with laughter, Sarah embarrassed and a bit surprised at the thought that her parents had that kind of intimate relationship at such an old age.

Within the car, the girls — once they could catch their breath — decided that they should wait it out. After all, how long could two old people do it?

"Wait ten minutes," Karen Marie tried to finish but started laughing again. "Yuk!"

"Stop it." Sarah lightly punched her friend in the arm and

Karen Marie feigned pain, pushing herself against the door, hardly able to breath from her uncontrollable laughter. And the two almost did not see Aunt Jackie's car pull into the driveway.

"Oh no." Sarah's hand was on the inside door handle when she saw her aunt emerge from the car, and then Sarah had the car door open and one foot in the road, ready to rescue her aunt from the embarrassment they had experienced, when she saw her mother emerge from the passenger door and she stood frozen.

"Holy shit." It was Karen Marie's voice.

Sarah was paralyzed. She should do something. In that split second before she sat back down onto the passenger's seat of the car, thoughts were racing through her mind. Save her mother from the horror, save her father from the guilt, save the family from destruction, and where was Earnest? But she sank down into the seat, stared at the dashboard and whispered, "drive, hurry, go."

Karen Marie turned the key, "I'm so sorry, Sarah." The car was moving.

Sarah thought about Kareem. She wished she had gone to the gas station instead

CHAPTER 6

Alexandros only knew a few words in English. He'd only been at East End for a few weeks, not nearly enough time to form an opinion about anything, but he knew he did not like the American women. Their voices screeched like mountain owls and the sound hit his ears like a blow to the head. They were loud and angry and they laughed at him when he tried to ask them for coffee.

The summer before, when Cousin Roula had visited Exohorio, their village high in the remote mountains of northern Greece, she had listened to his complaints of boredom and the impending military service.

As a young boy growing up in the arms of the mountains, Alexandros had been as free as his father's goats, running wild with the other boys, all day up in the brush where a stray stick from an olive tree doubled as a sword in a knight's battle or a gun in a shootout between cowboys. But those same mountain peaks had begun to feel like the bars of a cage as he yearned to unfurl his wings to their full length.

It was well known in the village that Cousin Roula's husband, Minos, had a restaurant in New York as they were reminded of it at every turn in Roula's conversations and with the lavish gifts she brought back for her family each time she returned: the refrigerator for yiayia, the hunting knives for Alexandros and his brothers, towels softer than the fleece of a baby lamb—too good for them to use so they sat in his mother's collection—a dowry for his young sisters. And Aunt Roula reminded Alexandros again of her husband's affluence when she suggested he go to America to work with Minos. It was an enticing offer to an eighteen year old, herding the goats in the mountains, waiting to be called to duty, two years in the service of the Greek military, not a pleasant thought.

New York—yes, it was very enticing—a city that had many Greeks; it would be easy for him. At least that's what Cousin Roula had said. There were many who spoke his language and he would feel at home. More importantly though, he'd be in *New York!* It was a place where poor shepherds were transformed into rich men. He'd seen it for himself with his cousin's husband—the man Alexandros' father had said was least likely to succeed in any location of the world with a brain the size of a pea and his backward ways. But there he was in America—Cousin Minos— wearing his starched suit and driving his sports car.

He'd been the one to get Alexandros at the airport. And he'd taken him to an apartment across the bridge from Manhattan, where Alexandros had spent a month until the immigration lawyer said that the papers were set, stating that he, a young shepherd from atop the peaks of a tiny village, was an expert restaurant worker, very specialized in an undefined expertise, and therefore approved for a twelve month visa.

When Cousin Minos had told him that the restaurant was outside of Manhattan, Alexandros had assumed he meant within walking distance, or at least a simple train ride, but East End— that speck of sand he'd been brought to—was smaller than their own village. His desire to be part of a larger world had landed him in a microcosm of his former one.

And those other Greeks—the cooks—they could speak English and some of them even had cars, yet they chose to stay *there!* It was all so baffling, especially Cousin Roula's husband, Minos, and the affection he showed for that sorceress, the one with the flowing red hair. She must have bewitched him. Why else would he want her?

"Why do you bother with her, Minos?" Alexandros asked him one day, as they stood in the restaurant kitchen, "She has a heart as black as night."

"You don't know what you're talking about, Alexandros. Anyway, I'm not interested in her heart, eh?" He elbowed the young man and gave him a sideway glance, showing his crooked smile as he pulled a crumpled pack of cigarettes from his jacket pocket and put it to his mouth. He slid a cigarette out by biting it gently with his front teeth and then he extended the pack to Alexandros.

Alexandros grabbed a cigarette and accepted a light.

He looked in the eyes of the older man and he didn't know what to say, so he laughed and replied, "I know what you mean."

"Get yourself a woman, my boy. They're all over the place and they're easy." He smacked him hard on the back, "It'll relieve some of this work stress – eh?"

Easy. Yes, Alexandros was aware of the colossal difference between the women in America and those on the other side of the Atlantic, or so he thought. He had been pleasantly surprised by that *difference* when he'd stayed near the city waiting for his papers. The landlady of the apartment where he rented a bedroom had been the first to introduce him to the American ways and later the girls at the club down the street—all of them Greek, but not at all like the girls from his village, so he wasn't sure what to make of it. There was no playing with flirtation or complex plans for a simple kiss in the dark behind the mulberry tree. Minos was right. It was certainly easy, but in East End—those girls, none spoke Greek. All he could do was watch and it had become clear to him for the first time in his life, that his eyes could learn more than his ears ever had.

The women at the restaurant angered him, especially that redhead. Her deceit. He hadn't paid much attention until the new girl had come. That one looked too young to be working among so many strangers and those legs—completely exposed all the way up her thigh. Where was her father? How could he allow her out of the house unescorted, half naked?

The cooks insisted the American girls were *putonas*—all of them loose and fast and easy. But that new one, the one they called Sarah, there was only fear in her eyes every time he saw her. He convinced himself it was a sense of protection he felt for her. She was vulnerable, like a baby bird, and he was needed to protect her from the predators. But a baby bird does not elicit the electricity that pulsed between them in that first moment she'd walked into the kitchen. He'd felt her fill the room. She was a wild fire that singed his skin and sucked the oxygen from his lungs. No — a baby bird does not do that.

Then the night before, he'd seen that redhead; he'd seen what she'd done. He'd been watching Sarah, not realizing he was holding his breath as she struggled to get the tray to her shoulder, poised to rush over to help her. But she was strong and she had that disc balancing on her shoulder with ease, until that redhead came in the kitchen. But the truth was of no concern to Minos, as Zeus had told him.

"Did you see that!?" Alexandros grabbed Zeus as Sarah's tray crashed to the floor, sending George Theodore running into the kitchen, the dining room music wafting in and mixing with the clanking chaos as the doors swung back and forth with the force that George had pushed them.

"We don't have time for that, boy," Zeus answered, "keep washing or we'll be buried alive here."

"She pushed the tray. The redhead, she pushed it!"

"It's not our concern."

"Alexandros! Get a broom." George yelled, "Come on; get this mess out of here, fast."

And then in English, he looked at Sarah and said, "Go home. Come tomorrow for your pay. Go. Use the back door."

Sarah could not answer; the tears were creating streaks down the grease and sweat of her face. She grabbed her purse from the waitress shelf, and turned toward the back door as George barked orders at cooks and waitresses, maintaining the steady flow of dining that was occurring among the vacationers out in the restaurant.

Sarah stepped out into the sticky night air and there was Alexandros holding a broom and a dustpan, returning from discarding the broken dishes into the dumpster. Her sobs had overtaken her and she barely heard the broom and dustpan fall to the ground as she buried her face in his chest, closing out the world, and his arms came around her, his one hand smoothing out her hair, his fingers lost in the tangled strands.

"I know," he said softly in his language, "I saw her. It wasn't you. I know." His face rested in her hair and he closed his eyes for a moment.

The murmur of his voice sedated her; the tears subsided.

Alexandros tried English, "I sorry for you. You good girl."

She looked up and smiled, her eyes red.

"Thank you, Alexandros." And she was gone from his arms, but her scent remained and he was left breathless. Turning toward the retreating shadow in the dark, he took a step toward her, just as the back door opened, an empty box flying past him and the cacophony of sounds emerging.

"Geez, Alexandros. What are you doing out here?" Eagle asked.

Alexandros picked up the broom and dustpan, then with one more quick glance behind him, he turned and disappeared into the kitchen.

Sarah walked from the dark beach area into the lights of Main Street toward the boarding house. George's words replayed in her head. *Go home.*

She thought of Owl's Head, of Oscar. And at that moment, she was walking past the drug store and she saw the edge of the phone booth. She went in, closed the door and sat on the small stool, staring at the dial. It was too early to admit defeat. She needed to prove to her parents, prove to herself that she was capable. She was someone.

Her finger went up toward the little holes in the round dial and then abruptly her whole hand fell to her lap. Her hand fought against her heart. Up again it went and down again. She exhaled loudly and put her head in her hands.

"Are you going to be done in there soon?" She hadn't seen that person waiting outside the booth.

She nodded and raised her hand to the phone again finally putting her finger in the hole and dialing. Then she listened to the operator, she put the coins in and she waited. A woman's voice answered the phone.

"Hi mom it's me."

"Sarah, I was just running downstairs to put a load of laundry in. Here, talk to Earnest."

"Wait mom, I—" But there was a muffled sound and then Earnest was on the phone. "Hey Sarah! Are you having fun down there?"

"Not really, buddy. I miss you."

"Then you should come home." And before she could respond

he began telling her about the squirrel that had come from the attic into the upstairs hallway and how dad had chased it around with a broom and about the sleepover being planned for Labor Day weekend.

"Me and mom are going to stay at Aunt Jackie's house and we're going to the drive-in. I'm going to sit in the front seat with the speaker and I can turn it up if I want and mom said I can get cotton candy, a big one; mom said–"

"Is that mom, I hear?"

But Earnest continued to talk until mid-sentence his voice was replaced by his mother's.

"Sarah – I'm kind of busy. Call later when Earnest is in bed."

"Okay." But she knew she wouldn't.

She sat in the telephone booth staring at the receiver that she'd dropped to her lap—the buzz of the dial tone filled the small space. She heard George's voice again. Go *home*.

She gingerly placed the phone onto its cradle, opened the booth door and walked out onto the street. She thought of the gas station and then walked slowly through the dark, back to the Middleground Boarding House.

*   *   *   *

Only Jeannette and George were in the dim dining room when Sarah returned the next day. She retrieved her money from George, forty dollars for two days pay.

"You're just not cut out for it, kid." He had softened quite a bit since the night before. Jeannette was watching her closely, but Sarah knew there was no point in pursuing it.

"Okay." Sarah's voice was a whisper. She stuffed the cash into the pocket of her jeans and walked through the kitchen door.

Alexandros and Minos were there, smoking and conversing in their language. Alexandros' eyes darted from Sarah to Minos and then he spoke in rapid fire to the older man. Minos smacked him on the back, said something Sarah did not understand and then turned to her and said in English, "My cousin here, tells me you're a good worker," but she still could not understand his thick accent and was only able to deciphered the word "worker," so she assumed he was verifying George's decision to fire her. Sarah felt

Alexandros' eyes on her from where he stood near the dishwasher.

"I'm sorry," she said and turned to leave, but Alexandros flew to Eagle's side and said something in Greek which prompted Eagle to say, "You understand, there? He's giving you a job in the hotel. You got it?"

"Oh."

Minos scratched his head. "That's what I said."

Just then Jeannette pushed through the door and slid her arm around the boss just as he was saying to Sarah, "Go see Maureen." Jeannette created the distraction she had hoped for as she slid her hand into his back pocket.

"See ya." Jeannette smiled at Sarah.

Waitresses make three times that of maids. Sarah remembered Maureen's words. She didn't want to be a maid, but she'd worked a full week as a waitress and had only forty dollars in her pocket to show for it. The night before last had been her first time with her own station and her own tables. It was remarkably easy considering she had only to worry about her own customers, a mere four tables, and not the whole dining room as the others had used her for their own personal servant during the days of her so called training. Sure, they'd thrown her a few dollars here and there, but Jeannette, her actual *trainer*, had given her nothing, though Sarah had seen the money left on tables. At the end of the night the waitresses pulled wads from their apron pockets and gave the busboy his cut, while she had worked as hard, if not harder.

"Tomorrow, you take your own station," George had said to her but had been looking at Jeannette, "We are going to need her up to snuff for Labor Day weekend," and he added, "she's a good worker Jeannette. You did a good job," giving her the compliment as a parent would give a toy to a spoiled child at the checkout counter, averting a tantrum.

Jeannette said nothing. And the next afternoon Sarah began her own shift.

Ah, that first tip! She held the hypnotic ten-dollar bill in the air, pulled taut between her two hands and she could smell the freedom emanating from it.

She'd get a car, drive to Owl's Head to show off her success, then down to South Carolina to see Oscar. She'd already been to the East End Library and found the place where he was training. The librarian had shown her several large almanacs and one consisted of different maps. It would be an easy drive; it was just a straight line down. They could buy a house with a big tree in the backyard where Sarah would sit and write poetry in her spiral notebook, her head resting on the pillow of a giant hammock—the kind that was suspended on a metal frame, like in the J.C. Penney's catalogue. Oscar would sit near her feet playing the guitar. He'd have to take some lessons and learn how to play but he'd write songs about her that famous people would sing and the songs would become number one on the charts. Mr. Durea would stop by her parents' house and say to her mother and father sitting on the porch sipping lemonade, "Well, look how well those two did for themselves!" and they'd all give a proud "Uhuh," as if they'd known all along it was inevitable.

It was all there in Alexander Hamilton's eyes, her future, her success, in that first ten-dollar bill until the next table left her nothing. She lifted up the empty plates, searching for some dollar bills or loose change—anything—and then she bent down low and scanned the floor under the table.

"Sometimes they think it's included in the bill." It was Debbie from the boarding house.

Sarah said nothing. The disappointment on her face spoke for her.

"Trust me," Debbie said, "You're gonna make money. It'll all work out by the end of the shift. Don't waste time feeling bad about the ones who stiff you. Just keep going."

And she was right. The end-of-the-night-haul was almost a hundred dollars. A full month's rent in one day's work. Unbelievable! She thought of her father at the mill, Karen Marie at Woolworths. She hadn't the experience yet to know that those tips were a temporary windfall – strictly seasonal – and would be ending shortly. But would be ending for her on the next night when Jeannette's plan would be quietly set into motion.

That night though, as the shift ended, she stuffed a wad of money into her bag and pulled her dirty apron off. Preoccupied with her dreams and expectations, she hadn't noticed Andreas lurking in the parking lot as she walked out into the cool late night air, and when Debbie walked away from him and came to her to ask if she wanted to join her at Main Street Bar, Sarah was thrilled to be getting such an invitation.

"Come on, I'll drive you home afterwards if you need it, but I doubt you will."

The innuendo flew past Sarah as she accepted the offer, ever so grateful to be finding her niche, finally.

The bar was packed with the smell of sweating bodies, mixed with the camouflage of cologne. And with each drink the patrons, almost all of them having just gotten off from work as the restaurants closed, barely noticed the stink of each other. A thick cloud of cigarette smoke added to the screen and the floor vibrated with the thump of the jukebox music. Sarah squeezed through the wall of people, keeping sight of Debbie as she led her toward the bar.

"Jack!"

The bartender, an older man of about fifty, glanced at them and then walked to the end of the bar and retrieved something from an ice bucket in the bar sink. He came back toward them and was handing Debbie two bottles that Sarah couldn't quite see over the head of the person in front of her. Debbie's hands were raised up toward Jack as Sarah began to rifle through her bag feeling for the wad of bills she'd tucked into a side pocket. Her hand was deep in her bag but her eyes were watching the bartender, and she saw him wink at Debbie and give her a thumb's up. Sarah hadn't expected to get drinks so fast. She felt the roll of dollar bills in her fingers and was able to pull a few from the wad to give them to Debbie but Debbie was still looking back at the bartender.

"Thanks, Jack." She smiled.

Debbie turned and handed Sarah a bottle of beer, the droplets of condensation running off the bottle and down her wrist.

"Oh — beer." Sarah took the bottle. Carbonation made her eyes water; she really didn't like beer, though most of the kids in Owl's Head seemed to prefer it. But her parents had always noticed when beer was missing from the store so she and her friends would drink whatever vodka they could steal from Oscar's father and then mix it with juice. It was easy to steal the vodka. Oscar would carefully replace what he'd poured out, by adding water to the vodka bottle. But in Owl's Head, it was the back of the cemetery — not openly in a bar — where they would take turns drinking from that one washed-out jam jar, which sometimes was not quite washed out and might have a bit of sweet preserve clinging to the edge. The alcohol taste was almost camouflaged by enough sweetness from the juice, until they began to feel the lightness in their heads and then the taste did not matter at all.

Sarah looked at the beer bottle.

"Thanks," she said and took a sip, a crumpled dollar peeking between her fingers and the bottle.

"Put your money away," Debbie yelled over the music, "I promise, you won't need it. Look — there they are."

"Who?"

Debbie didn't answer. She made her way through the crowd again, stopping every few steps to talk to someone. Sarah sipped at the beer and tried to keep her face from betraying her.

"Buy you a drink?" Andreas was suddenly next to her with a man that appeared a bit older than all of them. Debbie called the older man by his name, Bakus. And then she attached herself to his lips for a long sloppy kiss, while Andreas looked at Sarah waiting for her answer, "What're you drinking?"

"I have one, thanks." She raised her beer bottle to show him, though he'd have to have been blind not to see it.

"You said that drink tasted funny," Debbie said breathlessly as she pulled her lips from Bakus.

Sarah did not answer, but thought, "*I never said that,*" as she looked at Debbie in confusion.

Debbie pushed her away from the men and leaned in close to her. "He's just trying to pick you up."

"Pick me up?"

"You know. Sleep with you. Have some fun."

Sarah thought, "*what!? Are you nuts?*" but said, "What about Emily's roommate? She told me that — "

"What's that got to do with anything? You're on the pill, right?"

"Pill? What? Birth control, you mean?" Sarah swallowed hard. "Oh sure." But her thoughts were racing. "*Is this normal? How would I know?*"

"So what's the problem?"

"Nothing. Um, really — I don't like him. I have a boyfriend."

"Yeah, I do too. No one wants you to marry Andreas. He likes you. Just sleep with him and he'll buy all your drinks. He'll take you around. They have money. I went to the city with Bakus. He lives there. We had a wild weekend. He bought me this bracelet." She extended her arm for Sarah to get a better look. "Bakus is married to somebody back in Greece."

"He's Greek?"

"They're all Greek. You think Minos is in love with Jeannette?" She laughed hard. "That girl makes a boatload of money! George has his orders from Minos. And the guy's wife even comes into the restaurant with her kids sometimes! She probably knows. She doesn't care. That's how those people are. Greeks are different. They're not like regular people."

Sarah was shocked. *"She doesn't care!? That can't be true."* But she did not trust her judgment. This girl, Debbie, knew things.

The two men moved closer and Sarah looked at Andreas and said, "I'll have another beer." Then she tilted her head back and took several long gulps and handed him her empty bottle.

Someone put more money in the jukebox and Debbie turned to Sarah.

"Oh my God! I love this song—*One way out*—we have to be high for this song. Come on!"

Debbie pulled her through the crowd to the bathroom hallway, pushing through the line of girls waiting to use the restroom and continuing on toward the back exit where she ducked into a tiny room. A damp mop in a pail of grey water emitted a moldy smell. Debbie pulled a makeup compact from her purse, quickly opened it and flattened the mirror portion in her palm.

"Here, hold this." She handed it to Sarah, "make sure it stays flat."

Then she took a small glass vile from her bag and poured its white powder onto the surface of the mirror.

"From Bakus," she said as she took her college ID card and cut the powder into two neat white lines. "You're shaking too much. Hold your hand steady."

Debbie rolled up a dollar bill, stuck it in one nostril and sniffed the powder up into her nose. She handed her new friend the rolled up bill. "Go ahead," she nodded. A fine white dust clung to the rim of her nostril.

Sarah's head had begun to swim from the beer. She looked at the white powdery line on the makeup mirror. "*Cocaine,*" she thought, "*Weed is one thing, but coke? That can make you an addict, living on the streets, homeless, turning tricks, a pariah of society.*" Her heart pounded in her ears. She thought of the drug films in health class. She stared at the mirror.

"*I don't want to do coke.*"

Then she took the rolled up dollar from Debbie, put it to her nostril and inhaled the powder, sucking it up hard into her nose until it made her cough, and the frenzy of music suddenly came under the door, loud and wild. After a few more snorts, she was back in the bar, dancing at Debbie's side in a crowd of other moving bodies. Sweet aromas circled her as she moved wildly with the beat of the music, her hair bouncing off her shoulders as her body fought for space. Andreas handed her a cold bottle moving up and down with the music as he fit himself between her arms. Bakus watched from a few feet away, leaning against the wall near the bar, his body conspicuously motionless among the chaotic movement of the others — a faint smile on his lips.

*   *   *   *

Sarah was surprised to see the light on the dunes peek through the front windows as Jack came from behind the bar and unplugged the jukebox, sending the music into a whining spin downward until it cut off mid lyric. He grabbed the twenty-dollar bill Bakus was extending to him before Bakus disappeared out the back exit with Debbie. Then he tactfully pushed the other two toward the front exit, a full hour after closing time, thankful that his brother worked in the sheriff's department. That's when Sarah realized she and Andreas were the last to leave the bar. As Jack closed the door between them, Sarah heard the click, click, click of the deadbolts as he locked them out.

The smell of salt and damp sand laid an early morning heaviness in the air, but Sarah's limbs continued to pulse with an electric current, her eyes wide with anticipation. The world was hers — there to serve her. As Jack disappeared from behind the glass of the front door, Sarah saw her own reflection with the sunrise behind her. The red light shone shimmering around her head like a distorted halo, and Andreas came closer pressing his body into hers, kissing her neck as she watched their reflections meld together. His lips felt so soft; every nerve in her body had awakened.

"Let's go to the hotel," Andreas said. He pulled a ring of keys from his pocket, "I have all the keys — whatever room you want."

Sarah turned, closed her eyes and kissed him. Moments later, she found herself in one of the hotel rooms, standing face to face with Andreas, their lips still pressed into one. Yes — it felt right — her first time — with this Greek god.

Andreas reached into his pocket and took out a small plastic bag, the kind his father put sandwiches in when he used to make the brown-bag lunches for school. The plastic was crunched into a small crinkled ball. He pulled two small round pills from it and pushed it back into his pocket.

"Here, take one," he said as he held the little white orbs between his thumb and fingers, inches from Sarah's face.

"What is it?" Sarah looked at the pills.

"It's nothing. It'll just relax you."

"Oh — I don't know," she said slowly.

"Look." Andreas put one on his tongue and closed his mouth, swallowed and reopened his mouth to show Sarah that it was gone. "I'm taking one."

"Here." He put the second pill on the tip of his tongue and pushed it into Sarah's mouth as he kissed her.

Sarah felt it move to the back of her throat and she swallowed instinctively, feeling its dry film as it made its way to her empty stomach. She accepted it as another gift from East End. There was so much to learn.

But before the Quaalude could take hold, before it had a chance to wrestle the speeding of her heart to a slow thump, one small splinter of reality somehow wedged its way between her and Andreas as she remembered Debbie's words: *You're on the pill, right?* Andreas was fumbling with her bra clasp when she whispered, "I don't want to get pregnant," and he froze.

"Debbie said you were on the pill." It was louder than he had intended. He sighed and looked into her eyes, kissed her gently and crooned, "there's other stuff you can do that won't get you pregnant," and he pushed her head down.

Now, if his pants had not been hanging open, her lip would never have gotten caught on his zipper, causing a screeching halt like a record player's needle scratching across a spinning vinyl, permanently destroying its music.

"Ouch! What are you doing? Stop it." She brought her hand up to protect her lip where she'd felt it pull. Her tongue licked the spot briefly and she tasted metal as she looked at a wet smear of blood on her fingers.

"Sorry," he said, making a mental note to give her the Quaalude sooner, next time. "Look, I gotta work in a few hours. I'll see you later."

He walked her to the door and had her in the hallway before she understood that he was kicking her out—the door closing with him on the other side, and the sound of the shower turning on.

Worse than that, she suddenly realized that she had no idea where her bag was—her first night's tips gone!

"Andreas!" She banged on the door but there was no response.

"Andreas!" Still nothing. Silence, except for a few early morning calls from seagulls, loud enough to penetrate the walls and the muffled sound of the waves hitting the shore, or was that the shower water?

She looked down the hallway in both directions and it suddenly felt strange to be standing there alone, so she made her way out into the blinding sun and walked along Main Street. She passed by the drug store phone booth without a glance and she thought of the sandwiches in Kareem's gas station as she cut through the park to avoid being seen. She was on the path around the lake and could see the boarding house ahead, just as a pressing weight pulled down on her legs and she slowed to a relaxed stroll. She noticed suddenly the leafy branches of the brush as she walked along, having to stop to examine them more closely, the intricacies of light green veins within them.

As she came off the path, into the yard behind Mrs. Middleground's trailer, she spun around to look more closely at the lake. The surface sparkled in the sun like a thousand diamonds floating in unison. She held her hands up and spun around once, twice, her eyes closed, the chirp of the morning sparrows mesmerizing her, the damp air washing through her disheveled hair, until she bumped against Mrs. Middleground's picnic table and came to rest in the mud next to it.

She picked herself up and slowly approached the boarding house door, watching her feet as they pressed into each step and then she tiptoed down the hallway toward her room, the sun spraying a stream of dust particles across her path as she passed the kitchen window.

"Morning." Mack's voice startled her. His eyes went from her disheveled hair to her muddy feet and rested on her watery eyes. "How're ya doin'?"

"Fine." She smiled and continued down the hall.

"Ol' Lady Middleground's looking for you. Wondering when you're gonna start cleaning—getting a bit dirty—'specially the bathrooms."

"Okay." She continued to her room. Emily was not home yet. She looked at the clock. 5:30. Mrs. Middleground was looking for her? So early?

"Are you sure you're okay?" Mack stuck his head out of the kitchen and called down the hallway.

"Yes—positive," she sang.

After taking a lengthy shower and walking across the yard to work out a cleaning schedule with Mrs. Middleground, who she suddenly felt great affection for, she laid on her bed to get a few hours of sleep, just a few. But the pillow sucked her head down deep and a sweet steady humming sound like a far off motor kept her in the far corners of her hazy dreams, until she felt the weight of someone sitting on her bed. Then she felt her body being shaken and the words getting through, pulling her from the sweet escape of sleep.

"Are you working? It's late. You need a ride?" It was Debbie wearing her waitress uniform, her hair tightly pulled in a braid, her eyes without any hint of fatigue.

"I can't wait for you. I don't wanna be late again. Sorry."

"Oh no!" Sarah sat up. "Just give me a second." She put her hand to her head. "I have no idea where my bag is. It has my uniform skirt." She exhaled hard, "and all my tips!"

"Jeannette didn't give it to you?"

"Huh?"

"You left it in the bar. Jack gave it to Jeannette. She said she was going to give it to you. You didn't see her?"

Sarah said nothing, her mouth open, shaking her head from side to side slowly.

"I gotta go," Debbie said, "I'll tell George something—I don't know. Let me think." She paused. "I'll find Andreas or Bakus and tell one of them to smooth it out for you, but hurry up." She stood up, "I'll get you a skirt. But I want it back, okay?"

She didn't wait for an answer. She disappeared as Sarah jumped from the bed and began to sift through her clothes looking for a clean blouse. Debbie returned with the skirt. "Hurry. I'll see you there." And she disappeared down the hallway.

"Wait," Sarah called after her. "Do you have an apron?"

"Nope. Sorry." And just before the door slammed behind her, Debbie called out again, "Hurry up!"

Hurry? How?

Her uncle's car was still not across the street. As she walked—or rather *trotted*—down Main Street, she considered her options. None looked good. She needed that job. She needed her bag.

When Sarah made her way into the restaurant dining room, Jeannette was talking to George and Minos. "I told you about her, didn't I?" she said. The three looked at Sarah as she approached, breathlessly.

"I'm sorry, I—"

"Here's your bag. You left it last night," Jeannette thrust it at her and added, "completely irresponsible," to no one in particular and then walked away leaving her with George and Minos.

"This cannot happen again," George said. Minos reached out and stroked her face gently, saying a few words in English that she did not understand, then he shook his head and walked into the kitchen as George continued, "Tips were taken off tables last night. You understand—you do not touch money on anyone else's table. Got it?" George was thinking of the Labor Day weekend. He needed all the hands he could get.

Sarah gasped. The outrage produced by his words boiled into a raging fever, reddening her skin as her heart banged against her ribs.

"What are you saying?"

"I'm saying to get to work." His tone silenced her.

Sarah pushed the kitchen door open and passed into the heat.

Jeannette was holding her apron.

"I washed your apron for you." It seemed odd but there was no time to question her motive and it would be hours later, on her walk alone in the dark, that Sarah would discover her purse empty and the tips from the night before gone.

Minos was talking to the cooks behind the steam table when he looked over at Sarah, her face aglow with the pink hue of anger. She was pulling a tie from her hair which began falling in thick amber strands around her face, down onto her shoulders. He watched as she raised both arms, gathering the mane into her hands, her breasts pushing up through her blouse. Was that the hardness of a nipple he saw?

Both Sarah and Jeannette felt his eyes like lasers searing through Sarah's clothes. But neither of them noticed Alexandros' gaze. Sarah, the fire raging from George's accusation, turned to Jeannette and stared hard for a few seconds, then quickly she turned back to Minos and walked around the steam table with a big smile, her eyes never leaving him.

"Oh it's so hot in here," she said gently, her hand on her neck, falling to the top buttons of her blouse.

"Yeah! It's a kitchen. Whattaya think?" Eagle's voice was heavy with sarcasm. "Go to your side of the steam table." He shooed her with his hand.

"Be nice to this one. She's a good girl," Minos said to the cooks in English, which Jeannette heard, but Sarah still unable to decipher through his accent thought he was speaking Greek— though his smile and his eyes as they studied her from top to bottom conveyed his message more clearly.

Alexandros turned his back on them.

The lunch rush began and Sarah did not get any tables until late in the afternoon as the sun began to make its way to the west. Her customers sat for a long time, demanding her attention, so there was no time for her to eat anything other than the few broken french fries she'd grabbed from their plates as she stacked them on the tray. And then the dinner rush began to fill the dining room. The normal frenzy between the dining room and the kitchen went on without incident, until Minos sat at the bar, earlier than usual. Jeannette found a few seconds to stop and greet him but he seemed to be preoccupied with his thoughts, and dismissed her with his inattention. If Minos was not going to accommodate her plan for Sarah's demise, then she would have to use George. Each time she passed him by, she murmured a complaint about Sarah, whisking past at a speed that ensured he would not be able to question her but she saw the irritation pulling at the muscles in his jaw as he watched attentively. And then, Sarah happened to drop the frozen daiquiri down the front of the pregnant patron, just as Jeannette walked by her. But it was the full tray of dinners—eight of them stacked high—at the height of the dinner rush that finally sent George into a tirade as he rushed into the kitchen and Jeannette was there to help. She calmly divvied out Sarah's tables among the other waitresses as they watched Sarah melt into tears, moving toward the waitress station where the purses were kept. And Jeannette saw the young Greek watching her, but he could do nothing and then he was summoned to clean up the mess of broken dishes and food like the lowlife servant he was. Minos' attention would be hers again and she would maintain her status. They had all seen it—all of them, the cooks and the waitresses—and they knew that she was the woman who led the man, and they'd better respect her.

But she never did quite understand that her status hung by the thin threads of Minos' pant zipper and that the young newcomer, Alexandros, would be her eventual demise for she had clearly declared war on the wrong girl.

Alexandros would later avenge Sarah—though neither would realize it—by slowly unleashing all of his anger on Jeannette at his inability to be the person he actually was, trapped within the shell that kept him separate from the English speakers. He was a prisoner and he felt it deeply but there seemed no release in sight. So, he'd refuse Jeannette the clean plates she needed, bump into her mistakenly when she held heavy trays of food, put his cigarettes out in her coffee and provide a constant barrage of irritants until Jeannette would mistakenly think that she was going to rid herself of Alexandros.

One afternoon during the lull between shifts, she sought out Minos to have a *little talk* in the back room. But Minos' thick accent and the chasm between cultures would work against her.

"Minos, we need to have a talk."

"You crazy? This restaurant. We no can have *dog* here."

"It's important, Minos."

"I say no, Jeannette! No in restaurant. Never!"

"It doesn't matter where people have a talk, Minos! Come on. We can have a talk anywhere. You and me, in the backroom. We need to have a talk. It's very important."

"No is important. We no need dog! No dog!"

"Just a short one, Minos. Please!"

"No short one, no tall one, no dog! What's your problem? You being crazy! First time you say this."

"What's *my* problem? I just wanna talk. Normal people have talks. We've done this before. What's wrong with *you?*"

"I say no dog! That's it! You no like? You leave!"

And she would. She'd take her apron off, throw it in his face and walk out the back door, Minos shaking his head, "crazy Americans. Love the dogs," the cooks enjoying the show—none interested in telling him his error—least of all Alexandros who would immediately go off to look for Sarah in the hotel.

But that scene would not play out for another few weeks and Sarah had no window into the future. So as she stood in the kitchen watching Jeannette with her hand around Minos while Alexandros and Eagle watched from behind the steam table, Sarah accepted defeat. She ended her short stint as a waitress and walking across the parking lot to talk to Maureen about her new position as a maid.

CHAPTER 7

Dina was in the cooking house, elbow-deep in dough and cheese when she heard her name echoing up the mountainside. Like the other homes in the village, her cooking house was built in the corner of the yard, a few meters from her front door so the smoke from the cooking fires would not disturb the house. Yet it was close enough that she needed only to walk a few steps to enter it in the cool morning air.

"Dinaaaaaa! Whoaaaaa, Dina! Yoohoo Dina!" She put the mixing bowl aside. "Whoa Dina! Come to the window!"

Instead she ran out the door, still wiping her hands on her skirt as she made her way past the woodpile and down to the rocky platform near the well, waving to her elderly aunt below.

"What is it?"

"The Americano telephoned the post office in the village. He's going to call again tomorrow at two. He says it's very important but everything is okay."

Dina's husband, the Americano, George Theodore, rarely telephoned her. This was a very strange and troubling occurrence.

"Hmm," thought Dina, "*Why now . . . why for me? His Greek is so terrible. Why not get my brother, Minos, to make the call?*" She swallowed hard and yelled down to her aunt. "Did he mention our son? Andreas?"

"No—just it's important and be there at two. But not to worry. Everything is okay."

"Thank you, Aunt. I'll bring some tyropita down as soon as it's done."

"No, no don't bother yourself. I don't want it." But the old woman knew her niece would bring it anyway and she looked forward to the visit.

The village of Exohorio was well protected at that height with its rugged, almost impassible roads, which gave Aunt Toula, as well as the ninety other inhabitants of the village, a sense of security, but that same isolation also kept visitors from them. Traveling on the steep dirt road, pocked with holes and weather-created debris, was rare. The closeness of neighbors and family—though most of the neighbors actually were family—was the glue that kept the community thriving, even when they were blanketed in the winter months with snow. They knew the land like a honeybee knows nectar, their lives sure and predictable—which some had believed was the reason Dina returned fifteen years before, though the truth had eventually spread to every ear.

It was a joyous event when Dina had come back with the little one, Andreas. They'd missed her and at first it seemed an ordinary circumstance, for many women raised their children alone while their husbands were far away making a living. But Dina's mother had confided in Aunt Toula—after all they were like sisters—so Toula had known the actual story and had only told a few others, in confidence, of course. And when the Americano did not visit—no packages or letters brought up the mountain from the village postmaster, the few who had not heard began to understand.

And then, without warning, the Americano had come with the policeman in the black car, with papers from the American government. Oh it was a terrible mark in the history of their village! That poor little boy cried for his mama as they held him down in the back seat of the car. Andreas surely did not remember his father. He just wanted his mama, his grandma and grandpa—all the people he'd come to know in that five years he'd spent on the mountain and he couldn't understand why none of them rushed to help him, how they let that stranger drive away with him. Poor Dina. She'd lain on the rocks outside the church, the place where her son had been ripped from her arms and cried louder than her little boy—her agony echoing all the way down the mountain. There was nothing anyone could do—and of course, one does not intervene between a husband and his wife. But Dina's father never recovered, losing that boy, his namesake.

"Grandpa! Grandpa! Save me. Mama help me!" It was a scene none of the villagers would ever forget and so when Dina finally came out of her fog, after the death of her father—most people believed it was Yianni whose insistence on having her help with his goats, had kept her alive. And when Yianni had moved into the tiny three-room house with her—no marriage vows exchanged—everyone ignored the obvious, content to see poor Dina emerge from the dead and to begin living life again.

Dina went back into the cooking house. "*I know what this is about,*" she thought, "*that letter from Alexandros. But I wonder why George is not calling his mother, instead of me. Hmm. Well, he knows I would have been the one most likely to read it to her. And George's Greek is so bad, he sounds like he's gargling. Maria would never be able to understand him. Yes, that's it. It's about Alexandros' letter. Alexandros had undoubtedly solicited the help of George, thinking the older man would be able to influence his father.*" Dina smiled to herself. "*Poor Alexandros—he has no idea how despised George is, in this village. He should have gotten Minos to call.*"

Dina put her energy into rolling out the dough, but a mixture of thoughts kept creeping into her head. She decided to make a small pie for Alexandros' mother, Maria, and stop by her house on her way down to Aunt Toula.

But the visit was brief. No, Maria did not have any further messages from her son. She was still contemplating how to handle his request to be released from their promise. Alexandros' father would not discuss it.

"Ridiculous!" he'd said the month before, after Dina had read them the letter that had come from the postmaster with a small paper folded into it, an American flag pressed into its corner—the paper that the post office would exchange for drachmas.

"He doesn't know what he's doing. A few pretty faces over there and he forgets his place. He expects me to go against my honor? To take back the promise I made to Sauteris? He will marry Sauteris' daughter! That's it. No more discussion. Get a paper and pencil—you, Dina come and sit here. Write this—"

But Dina and Maria had convinced him to wait. Calm down and then think of some words that would give his son comfort in that far off place, for they suspected that was all that he needed. He would do his duty when the time came and become the husband he was meant to be.

"Okay. Okay." Alexandros' father began to settle a bit, realizing he would be unable to write the letter himself and he did not want to argue with the only person he trusted to write it for him and still to keep silent about that shameful breach of tradition.

The people of Exohorio were not a bad lot, but gossip was as common as goat droppings on those mountains. And if word got out that Alexandros was not going to fulfill his obligation, the family would be deemed unreliable which was the worst label possible for a man with three young daughters of his own to marry off.

The next day, Dina descended the mountain on the back of Yiannis' tractor. She had forgotten about Alexandros and was focused on Andreas, having tossed and turned all night, knowing full well that George would not call her to the telephone for anything trivial. It was midday when they reached the post office and convinced the postmaster not to close for the siesta. He agreed and joined them as they sat in the café across the street and sipped coffee. They chatted with each other and occasional passersby, but Dina held her hands tightly in her lap and felt a weight pressing against her, making it more and more difficult to breathe with each passing moment.

When the post office telephone rang, they and all the people in the plaza heard it. They moved with a small curious group into the post office.

Dina heard the familiar voice of her brother, Minos, coming through the telephone.

"Dina, I'm here with George. I need to tell you something."

"Minos, what's going on? Just tell me. Is Andreas okay? Is he there? Let me talk to him."

"Listen, Dina he's okay. But uh, he's in a facility."

"What? Minos—what are you talking about? A facility? You mean a school—a hospital? Facility? What are you saying?

"Well, it's a facility to uh, well, help people."

"Oh, a school. He's going to plumbing school. He mentioned that when we talked last time. Let me talk to him. Why are you—"

"No, Dina, not a school. It's more like a hospital, but not really."

"What the hell are you saying? Give George the phone."

"Dina, shut up and listen to me for a second."

"Give-George-the-phone!" The swallows in the eaves outside the post office window scattered into the air above, some of them hitting the window in their frenzied rush to escape.

"Uh, hello? Dina?"

"George, where is our son?"

"Dina, he has a little substance abuse problem and he's resting comfortably in a rehabilitation center. It's very —"

"Give Minos back the phone."

Minos' voice was small, "Sister?"

"I cannot understand that man's Greek. I don't know what he is saying. Tell me straight Minos. Stop lying to me for once."

"Dina, he is taking drugs. He attacked a girl. We put him in a place so they could help him to stop. It's better this way so he doesn't end up in jail."

"Oh my God! Virgin Mother Mary! He's in a crazy hospital."

The tears began to flow — the weakness in the dam having been breached — the post office room flooding. Her words continued between sobs, "Oh America!" *sob*, "so much better," *sob, sob*, "a boy — his father," *sob* "you two stole him," *sob*, "you took him," *sob*, "from his home," *sob, sob, sob*, "my baby," *sob*, "I'll kill you," *sob, sob*, "both, of you."

Her grip on the receiver was like a cobra's on it's prey as Yianni tried to pry it from her, "I'll cut your manhood," *sob, sob*, and there were simultaneous cringes by the men lining the post office, as the small room had slowly filled with curious onlookers and she continued spitting madly into the receiver, "I'll feed it to the goats —"

But Yianni had the phone. The tailor's wife, one of the villagers in the crowd that had gathered at the entrance to the building when the yelling began, came up the steps and pulled Dina to her bosom. Dina continued her rant, though it was muffled by the front of the other woman's bodice.

"Sh. Sh. There, there, it's okay, now." The tailor's wife patted her head as though she were a child.

Yianni was saying something to the postmaster who took the

phone and wrote the words: TWA Flight 021 from Athens to Rome to New York. And then the telephone call ended.

Once they were out of town and on the path back up to the house, Yianni stopped the tractor.

"Dina, it's not a crazy hospital. It's a nice place. Minos told me it's like a fancy hotel. After all, it's America and —"

"Oh, America! America! Stop it, please. I was there. I saw America. It's dirty and lonely."

"Andreas is asking for you, Dina. It seems he will not stay in the drug-helping-place unless you come over. And Dina, he needs help. Minos explained it to me." Yianni held her head with one hand on each side of her face and he looked into her wet red eyes, "Do you understand?"

"Of course, I understand."

"Minos has a plane ticket waiting for you in Athens. You need to be there in two days. And listen to me; look at me. Bring the boy back. We can heal him here. Go get him. He'll come. He'll remember his home."

"Yes," she whispered, "my little boy. He doesn't need the American-drug-fixing. He needs his mama." She wiped her eyes with her sleeve, "But Yianni, what if he doesn't want to come back? How will I convince him?"

"He'll come, Dina. That's what he wants, you'll see. Now let's get up this mountain so you can pack, find your passport, you need to be on a bus for Athens tomorrow morning. We'll go in the morning and find Stavros' cousin. He can drive you to Piomegalos, to the bus depot."

The bus to Athens did not come up the mountain to their village or to the lower village where the post office was or to the valley far below that. Piomegalos, forty kilometers away, was the nearest city. It had the bus depot where Dina would be able to board the bus she needed.

*　　　　*　　　　*　　　　*

Darn, that tractor! The morning sun was blinding as it came over the opposite mountain. Dina shielded her eyes with her hand.

"Go faster, Yianni! I'm going to miss the bus."

"It's going as fast as it will go — you don't want to plunge off the side, do you? Then you'll miss the bus for sure." He turned back briefly and smiled at her.

Stavros' cousin was not in the plaza with the other men when they'd finally crawled into the lower village. Someone said he had driven Stavros to the city for a farm tool or was it a machine part? It wasn't clear but earlier that morning, they'd seen the two men take off in the old sedan—the only car in the village.

"Ack, stupid!" Dina hit the tractor seat hard. "We should have talked to him yesterday. If I hadn't been blubbering like a child. Virgin Mary! Stupid me."

"Take it easy, Dina."

Yianni climbed back onto the tractor seat. "We'll go down into the valley and find a taxi."

It was late in the afternoon, Dina and Yianni sat in the valley at the corner café in a small village. The taxi driver would be back in a few minutes—so said the café owner over an hour before when the couple had climbed down from the tractor and inquired about a ride to Piomegalos. When the taxi finally pulled up to the curb, they all knew that the bus to Athens would be long gone. Yianni bargained with the man. He would give him two live goats and six thousand drachmas to drive through the night to the Athens Airport. His word was good. The men shook on it. Yianni kissed Dina on the cheek and she was gone. The long voyage to America—to rescue her son—had begun.

CHAPTER 8

Sarah climbed out of the greyhound bus in New York City and made her way to Penn Station. She looked at the schedule board and saw that the next train out to East End would be in twenty minutes. She leaned up against one of the giant metal pillars and watched the people pass. A few of the passersby looked her up and down before continuing on their way and Sarah self-consciously pulled at the pants Karen Marie had lent her, knowing they were at least one size too big and much too short. In fact, she realized, as she shifted the bag with her dirty uniform from one hand to the other, she probably looked ridiculous but it was better than the maid uniform, she thought.

The hotel maid job had given Sarah a bit of respite from the world after the chaos of the restaurant. It was quiet and simple. For the first few days she worked beside Teresa, a young girl her own age who had come from a country somewhere in Central America, one that Sarah would not have been able to identify on a map. In her broken English, Teresa often spoke of the family she missed, her child she'd left behind and her mother to whom she sent her pay every month in a village that sounded much like Owl's Head. At the end of each workday, Teresa split the tips that had been collected from the pink envelope on the nightstand in the rooms that people had checked out of, and she handed half to Sarah.

On Sarah's first day with Teresa, Andreas had appeared some time before their noon break and had stood in front of their supply cart.

"What are you doing? The only reason to be here is as a guest in a room." He gave a little wink and smiled at Teresa, who looked at him as if he were part of the wall and pushed the vacuum into a guest room.

"I got fired." Sarah said, " didn't you know?"

"Why didn't you tell me? I can fix that." He came close to her. "I can make it right for you. Give me a few days and you'll be back there with the best station, making the most money." And before she could respond he added, "What time do you get off? We'll go somewhere and party."

"I'm not sure. It's my first day."

Teresa appeared again.

Andreas took Sarah's hand and pulled her away from the cart, then quietly said, close to her ear, "I'll take care of you. I don't know what time this *Mexican* finishes, but I'll be back to get you at three."

Three o'clock came and went and Andreas did not appear again until the day of the incident.

In the meantime, Sarah settled into the routine. For some reason that she did not question, Kareem seemed to deliver his papers earlier than usual and was at his father's gas station when she walked by each morning at six. He joined her for the walk to the hotel and she spent the time telling him about the bizarre items left in the rooms and about the unusual guests like the man who sunbathed completely naked on the patio outside his suite when she came to clean the room. His old wrinkled body lay on the lawn chair while his young wife sat further on the beach in a bikini.

"I doubt that's his wife," Kareem said and they laughed.

He told her stories of what he'd seen in the wee hours of the morning as he rode his bike around the town—windows illuminated in the dawn, shades pulled up—a virtual soap opera being played out before his eyes as he threw newspapers on lawns and porches.

Sarah looked forward to his company on those early morning walks. He was easy to be with, easy to talk to—like Oscar.

In the evenings, Sarah found herself returning to the boarding house when many of the kids were leaving for restaurant jobs.

Debbie would always talk about coming back to get her to hang out after work but she never did. Most evenings, Sarah usually sat by the lake, eating a sandwich at Mrs. Middleground's picnic table behind the trailer. Her unlikely companions were Mack and a few other fishermen as they watched the sunset and talked about the places they'd been.

Sitting there with her hair pulled back tightly in a ponytail high up on her head so that it split and fell forward like the leaves of a coconut tree, Sarah looked younger than her seventeen years. Mack watched her as he relayed his stories. She held her head between her two hands with her elbows resting on the picnic table and again he began to miss his own daughter. From time to time, for the briefest of moments he could have little Belle back, in Sarah's eyes—and he saw her then watching him as he talked at that table behind Mrs. Middleground's trailer. It sent a surge of longing and regret straight to his heart, as though an arrow were lodged deep inside his breastbone. He could see Belle's little head, soft brown ringlets poking out in all directions from the pony tail she'd worn all day and stray hairs falling over her brow into her eyes as she lay belly down on the floor, her head held between her hands as Sarah was doing at that moment. Belle loved to hear his stories back then.

"*She's a teenager by now,*" he thought, but he couldn't picture her that way. She would always be the little girl on the floor, kicking her legs in the air, back and forth as she listened intently — those same stories filling her with the look of fascination that he saw in Sarah's eyes. And for a few brief moments Belle was there, close by, until he reluctantly slid back into the present and it was Sarah sitting across the table again.

Sarah would wait until the sun was completely down and then she'd go into the boarding house to clean the common areas—it was easier then. The fishermen retired to their rooms and the other boarders were at work. Later, as some of the kids returned from their jobs, she'd sit in the kitchen and make small talk with them before they all disappeared into their own worlds. The routine was comforting and reassuring as any routine is when one wishes to hide from the pain of forward movement.

But then there was the day of the incident.

The morning before, during one of their early walks to the

hotel, Kareem had said, "After you finish, come by the gas station. I want to show you something."

Sarah was intrigued but Kareem would not tell her more.

"I think you'll like it."

Later that day, the sun was just beginning to sit on the roofs of the beach houses when Sarah walked with Kareem into the tall grass at the back of the park. The ground became a soft sponge beneath their feet as water seeped into the side of Sarah's sneakers. Kareem was leading her away from the path that cut around the lake. It was a direction she'd never gone before.

"Where are we going?"

"You'll see."

He pulled the tall grass aside, and stepped onto a rock as the ground gave way to muddy water. From one stone to another, Sarah held his hand and Kareem helped her through as the grass grew taller and the ground wetter. And then they were at the side of a brook, as they continued stepping from one stone to another until the moving water widened. And they were standing at the side of something bigger than a brook, but barely able to claim its title.

A river.

The sky had begun to glow pink, and Kareem pulled a wooden canoe out from under the camouflage of the reeds, and he got in.

"It's going to get dark soon," Sarah said, "Are you sure?"

"Trust me."

She sat up front and he guided her through the tunnel of the wheat-colored stalks. The paddle pressed down into the water's mirrored blur of pink and brown. Insects skied on the glassy surface ahead. Kareem pulled the paddle from the surface of the river at the back of the canoe and then lifted it into the air, sending drops of water overhead as he brought it to the other side.

Drip. Drip. Drip. And then a light splash as the paddle reentered the water and the smooth movement of the canoe cut further into the glass ahead. Then he pulled the paddle out of the water and rested it on his knees.

"Listen."

There was only silence except for the lap of the water against the wooden sides of the canoe.

He heard Sarah sigh softly and then she twisted around to face him.

"This is beautiful, Kareem," and as if on cue, the smallest sliver of a full moon shone its light on the horizon behind the reeds while the western sky remained a pink hue.

"Really, this is great."

Kareem smiled as she turned forward again, and he put the paddle back into the water. The reeds grew further apart as Kareem steered the canoe from the little river into the lake and Sarah realized they were heading straight across it toward the light of Mrs. Middleground's trailer.

But Kareem took his time paddling, waiting for the full sphere of the moon to show itself above the horizon, his plan complete after having consulted the lunar calendar on the drug store wall and offering Allah all that he could in exchange for a cloud-free evening.

When they reached the shore, the bullfrogs were in full symphony and the night sky had emerged. Kareem jumped from the canoe into the knee-deep water and pulled the front of it to the bank. He reached toward Sarah to help her get out, and as he felt her hand in his, it just seemed a natural progression of movement to pull her forward and put his lips on hers, to kiss her deeply as he'd seen it done.

But he hadn't considered the law of physics. So his movement, as he pulled her hand forward and her feet remained planted inside the canoe, caused the canoe to push backwards into the water and Sarah to trip over the side of it. As she went down into the water, she grabbed at Kareem with a scream that turned to a laugh. They hit the muddy bottom together. And though it was not the impulse he felt at that disastrous ending to his carefully executed canoe ride, Kareem laughed with her.

The next morning as he walked with her to work, he said, "I have another surprise for you later."

"What—you're going to drown me in the ocean?" she laughed.

"No, really. This one is better. I'll meet you at the hotel."

But he arrived after the incident and Sarah was gone. Teresa would tell him nothing; only that if he found her he should tell her that Teresa got her bag and would put it in the hotel office for her. But he didn't find her. She was not at the boarding house or with her uncle, nor did she pass by the gas station the next morning, though he waited until noon, his uncle admonishing him for giving his heart to a non-Muslim, a girl with her legs naked all the time, allowing his heart to be impure, a disgrace to their ancestors!

But his father said nothing.

CHAPTER 9

Sarah sat in the train, watching the trees give way to flat farmland as she sped away from the city on the familiar road back to East End. She unfolded the note Oscar had left with Karen Marie. Karen Marie had been the only one he'd told about enlisting when he showed up at her door after fleeing Sarah's house. A crumpled magazine page in his hand and those nearly illegible few words scrawled in the corner of a shampoo ad would be his only communication with Sarah until he saw her again in East End.

It was the first time Karen Marie had ever seen him without his protective tough-guy shell, his eyes red, his face streaked with the wetness of heavy tears. And he'd handed her the note, the crumpled words, a pointless message to Sarah, which Sarah was opening and reading again as she sat there on the train to East End. *Sarah, I love you, but we will never be together again.* It didn't mean anything. Why take the trouble to even write it, or better yet, why leave Owl's Head in the first place? All he'd needed to do was wait. Just wait it out, like the other times. What could have caused him to leave so fast without talking to her, or anyone else? There were so many unanswered questions.

Karen Marie tried to get Sarah to stay in Owl's Head, at least for the night.

"Wait Sarah, I'll drive you down." She'd hoped her friend would possibly talk to one of her parents, but she would not. So she lent her a pair of jeans and a tank top, the bus fare back and gave her the note from Oscar. Then she watched Sarah disappear into the greyhound bus.

Sarah had no plan. She still wanted to *go home*, to have her family, to play Lincoln Logs with Earnest, to sit behind the register of the general store and know the world around her. But none of that existed anymore, so she was returning to East End. She thought of her father and closed her eyes, squeezing the lids into nothing and shaking her head, hoping to erase that moment with Karen Marie when they'd heard the woman call out his name. She fought the nausea that followed—knowing her father was not who she thought he was. Her parents were merely a man and a woman, not at all the perfect unit she had come to see them as. And the incident in East End suddenly seemed like nothing as she replayed it in her head.

She'd just finished cleaning her last room earlier than she'd expected. For some reason, her work chart had fewer rooms than usual on it. And there was Andreas, coincidentally appearing as she pushed the vacuum out into the hall and he pushed her gently back into the room, closing the door with a swift tap of his foot.

"No Andreas." His arms were around her, his head coming to her neck.

"I'm sweaty and dirty," she said.

He agreed. "Yeah, you are a little salty." His pupils were large black dimes embedded in their sea-blue irises. "I could rub you around a margarita glass." His lips covered hers and her heart hammered against her chest.

He whispered into her ear, "let's take a shower together."

"Together? Naked? Oh God, no."

She pulled away from him.

"Here," He put his hand into his pocket, "We'll do a few lines first."

"Oh, um," Sarah took another step back. She wasn't sure what to say. "Um—okay, after the shower. I'll take one first." She was standing next to the bathroom door, her hand moving toward the knob.

"What's wrong with me?" she thought. She didn't want to be there with Andreas but she had no idea how to proceed, what to say, how to free herself.

Andreas moved to the bed and was sitting on the side of it, holding a vial of white powder. He looked at her and smiled his

Adonis smile.

"Don't be so shy," he said.

He shook the hair from his eyes and put his head down to study the powder that he was spilling onto the night table. Sarah watched him rolling a dollar bill as she opened the bathroom door.

"The human body is—" He coughed and the word *"beautiful"* squeezed out as he tried to talk between snorts. "Come on, over here." He coughed again, his wet eyes gazing at her as he motioned with his head, "come on."

"You know what, Andreas? I think it's a better idea if I go back to Middleground's. I'll go back to the boarding house." She paused. "Yeah. That's a much better idea. I'll wash up, make myself beautiful for you and we can hang out tonight."

He patted the bed next to him. "You look beautiful to me right now. We're here. Look at this room. No one's going to bother us. Come on." His voice was smooth and low as though he were enticing a child to come forward and take the candy.

"Take a hit. This will make you more beautiful than any shower." He got up from the bed, extending his arm. And he was about to walk toward the bathroom door when he spied something under the dresser.

"I'll just take a second," Sarah said, "I'm too dirty."

Sarah pulled the door shut and quickly turned the lock. She went to the shower and turned the faucet on so the water splashed down onto the bottom of the porcelain tub. She stood there staring at the flow of water, watching the steam collect around the edges.

"Think, Sarah." She whispered to herself. "What's the big deal? It's just a shower."

And what about that other time she'd been with Andreas? It might even have been the same hotel room. It had felt so different—so much better, so real and right. Nothing had changed, had it? But she felt different this time. This girl standing there at that moment, trapped within the slowly-rising steam, her feet planted firmly on the ground without the drug-induced wings of euphoria, this girl was Sarah—a rose pedal blown into Andreas' finely woven web. She listened to his movements on the other side of the door and then there was music, low and almost undetectable through the gush of water hitting the tiled walls.

"Okay," she thought in her seventeen-year-old logic, *"I have to take a shower. The water's been running too long. What will he think?"*

As she undressed, she listened carefully to the muffled footsteps mixing with the beat of the music. Was he dancing? She shook her head slowly and reached for one of the neatly folded towels that she'd put there only moments before, and she placed it on the toilet seat to have it close by; then she stepped into the stream of hot shower water.

Her eyes were closed but she could still see a bright flash of light. Instinctively, she opened them wide and saw Andreas with a camera in his hand, a key ring dangling from one finger, and then another flash as he pulled the shower curtain completely open.

"Stop!" she screamed for the shame of his seeing her naked — entirely exposed — and then the thought of the drug store attendant who would develop the film and then all the Greeks that she had worked with as Andreas passed it around — Alexandros' face came to her mind for a split second, then the boarding house kids and she could see poster-sized pinups of her soapy body on telephone poles for the vacationers to gawk at, and Kareem's family, Uncle Mike, his friends.

She was out of the shower, grabbing for the camera, screaming at him, "Stop it!" as the camera continued to flash, until her fist came down hard on his arm and the camera rolled to the floor and she lunged to get it, realizing he was no longer interested in the camera as she felt his hands on her slippery body.

And at that same moment, Alexandros was leaving the kitchen by the back door, repeating to himself the English words Eagle had taught him.

"Jeannette is gone. You come back to work." Over and over he whispered to himself. Again and again, *Jeannette is gone. You come back to work.* Until he found Teresa outside of the room where Sarah had left her cart, her face as white as the sheets in her hand and then he heard the screams over the music coming from the other side of the door and saw the ring of keys Teresa had extended to him.

Sarah sat on the train, remembering it all, even that moment when the door opened and she saw Teresa's look of horror. But then the events meshed together only coming clear again when she had ascended the wooden steps of the train platform in East End — looking for *home*. She remembered putting her clothes back on, and the sound of fists hitting bone, the blur of the two bodies rolling into pieces of furniture, the grunts behind the power of the punches and then the guests on the beach, their eyes on her as she made her way over the side of the porch, climbing into the sand.

She shook her head and looked out the train window. It was an awful memory but suddenly there was that new heartache and Andreas' camera seemed ridiculous. Her father — how could he? She was wondering what had happened when her mother went into the house with Aunt Jackie. It was such a betrayal to the family. Everything that had been known before was a lie. She trusted nothing. No one.

"*I'm alone,*" she thought. She wished Earnest were older, more of a peer and she thought of Kareem.

As she came off the East End platform, hours later, and her feet sunk into the soft sand around the station, there was a feeling, unidentifiable — barely noticeable — a feeling of being back in a place that was hers. She headed to the gas station.

Amir was there alone. "Well, here she is!" He greeted her. "Kareem thought you disappeared into the air." He would not tell her of his son's agony, waiting that morning until noon and then riding between the boarding house and the hotel, back and forth, over and over.

Sarah was disappointed. "I thought he'd be here."

"No, he went home. Are you hungry?" He was holding out a sandwich and Sarah realized the empty feeling she had, a deep hollowness — a great hunger.

"Thanks." She tore chunks of the sandwich with her teeth and felt it fill her as she thought about the hotel. She needed to go back there, but her fear froze her. Would she bump into Andreas? Was her job gone? And the camera, the photos, Alexandros. She was paralyzed with indecision. It was too late in the evening to find Debbie. She'd be at work already. Sarah thought of the yacht club and her uncle. She needed him to step up and help her. It would be a long walk.

"I wonder if I could borrow Kareem's bike."

She was mostly thinking out loud as she talked quietly to herself but Amir heard her and gave her directions to their house.

She was surprised to find that it was not as close to the boarding house as she had assumed based on the fact that Kareem seemed to be so often passing by.

But more surprising was the woman who answered the door, who Kareem called mom. Her ordinary attire, her blond hair in giant curlers and her heavily made-up face did not seem to harmonize with what Sarah believed herself to have known about Kareem. His name was that of his great grandfather, a devout Muslim from the mountains somewhere in Turkey. Kareem had told Sarah many stories about his family and those stories had led her to expect a Muslim mother who was covered from head to toe in cloth like the picture in her history book. But this woman, holding the front door open, was more modern than her own mother.

Those tales that Kareem had told about his great grandfather, the man he had been named for, a shepherd who had been murdered because of his courage, had created characters in Sarah's mind that went with such words as *shepherd, murder, Muslim* and Kareem's mother, as she lit a cigarette and introduced herself, was not one of them—not even close. This woman, Sarah thought, seemed very much to deviate from her expectations, as did Kareem's great-grandfather.

According to the tale that she had heard more times than she could count, Kareem's great-grandfather had arranged an escape from a labor camp for two of his neighbors. After that escape, however, when the entire Christian family suddenly disappeared and Great-grandfather Kareem was seen in their vacant home, the other Christian neighbors believed it was he who had seen to their demise. They waited for their chance and a few weeks later, when the Greek army came to liberate their people, the hand of power turned. A few days after that, Great-grandfather Kareem was found dead in his sheepfold, badly beaten, the culprits unknown. They had scratched a cross into the wooden door—their signature. And later, there were a few Christian men on the mountainside who paid for Great-grandfather Kareem's death with their own lives as the saga continued.

Kareem had often repeated the story to Sarah, highlighting his great-grandfather's courage, especially in light of the fact that he had risked his life for a woman. But Kareem had no idea—nor did the other family members who retold the story—that the young boy in the tale was George Theodore's father, Dimi. It was Andreas' grandfather. He had escaped Death in that labor camp, and then again on the mountain cliffs above the sea, though Death had followed him to America, waiting patiently to claim his prize. Kareem was an American boy living barely a mile from Dimi's grandson, Andreas. And they were both no more than a link in a chain that stretched across continents and generations—a chain unbroken.

Sarah would hear Kareem tell that story more than once; sometimes a slightly different version, each producing a more heroic character that Kareem saw as himself and hoped Sarah would eventually see in him. It was usually in the dunes that it was told as they shared a meal, one he provided from the gas station, though it was just occurring to Sarah that it was she who was usually eating and he who was watching with his hungry eyes as he told his tales.

Sarah stood at Kareem's front door and absorbed the reality of his life. She was surprised to see how ordinary it was but she wasn't surprised by his joy as he saw her and pushed past his mother, "Where were you?" For she felt it herself at seeing him— that feeling of home, like when Earnest would greet her at the door, the sweet comfort of being with someone who cares for you in a place you belong.

Nor would there be any surprise at her Uncle Mike's indifference to her situation once Kareem peddled breathlessly up the hill and toward the bay, Sarah perched behind him on the seat. Uncle Mike remained consistently detached from her and as time slipped by, he would not waver in his indifference.

"Who's this little kid I keep seeing you with?"

Kareem was appalled. Little kid? The worst insult to a burgeoning adolescent and he was certainly prepared to go beat the crap out of anyone who was bothering Sarah, which was more than he could say for that skinny loser in a monkey suit. And those words were about to spew forth when Sarah said, "Wait here a second," and pushed her uncle out of earshot.

"Uncle Mike, I'm scared. I need your help." What she really wanted was to talk to him about what she'd seen in Owl's Head. It was his brother, after all. He might be able to help her understand, or at least to share the pain and provide some comfort. But instead she said, "This guy's name is Andreas."

"First tell me what happened, exactly."

"He bothers me when I'm at work." She thought for a second. How could she explain being in the hotel room, in the shower! "I just need someone to go back there with me to get my bag. I left it there—and to see if I still have a job. And maybe just show your face so that guy knows I have someone here to help me."

"How big is the guy?"

Sarah sighed.

"Okay, okay. But I don't see what the big deal is. Just go there and tell him to stop bothering you. Tell the boss. Why wouldn't you have a job, anyway?"

*   *   *   *

On the way back down the hill, the last bit of daylight disappeared into darkness. Kareem barely had to peddle as he let the momentum move them along and Sarah, having decided to sit on the bar that went from the seat to the handlebars, was enclosed within his arms. She was able to look at him and talk to him—a circumstance for Kareem that made the whole trip worth the humiliation from Sarah's uncle. Kareem turned the bicycle toward the beach.

"Hey, where are you going? I, I—uh—can't go, I don't want to go there. Not yet, Kareem. Wait." He was headed toward the restaurant.

"It's okay. I'll take care of it. Stay here and wait."

He pulled the bike up onto the curb and let it lean against a telephone pole after Sarah had gotten off. He left her there as he disappeared into the hotel lobby and reappeared moments later holding her bag out and beaming with pride.

Sarah's relief was visible as she rushed to him and hugged him so tightly, that she lifted his feet from the ground, which deflated his *warrior-saving-the-maiden* image he momentarily had of himself.

"How?" She had grabbed the bag and again her arms were around his neck, "you're too much!"

The lightness in his head threatened to topple him as she

planted a loud wet kiss on his cheek.

"Kareem!" she said. This kid was always there — so reliable. It was unbelievable. "How'd you get it? How'd you know it was here?"

As he explained it to her, she realized for the first time that she had stood him up that afternoon.

"Oh no, Kareem - I'm so sorry. I had this thing, well - it uh was like this fight with Andreas and ya know, he really, um — he made me so mad. I forgot about everything."

Neither of them saw the red glow of the embers at the side of the dumpster near the back of the restaurant.

Eagle had gone out the kitchen door for a cigarette a few moments before they'd arrive on the bicycle. He had been leaning up against the back door when Alexandros had come out dragging a large plastic barrel of trash. Eagle helped him lift it to the dumpster's edge and the contents spilled out noisily. They turned to go back to the kitchen, but stopped so Alexandros could pull a cigarette from the pack Eagle was extending to him. Alexandros had just put the match to the end of the cigarette when the bike jumped the curb and came to a halt near the pole.

"I'd give anything to be that little Turk right now," Alexandros said to his friend as Sarah emerged from between Kareem's arms.

Eagle laughed. "I'd rather be the bicycle bar." But the look on Alexandros' face stopped him. "Listen Alexandros — these girls are good to have some fun with, but none of them are serious. They make bad wives. Americans all get divorced. Look at George. His third wife — well she's not even his wife; he's still married to Minos' sister but Maureen stays with him — and look at his son. Andreas is a waste of a human. He can barely speak Greek and he lived there for five years! He's as dumb as this rock." Eagle kicked a stone hard. "He's a coward too. His father kept him out of the military. American boys are supposed to go to the army — same as us. Did you know that? And he's a criminal. That kid belongs in jail and if your little American girl ever figures out what to do, he *will* be. I'm telling you. Listen to me, man. Don't get serious with an American girl. Forget about this one."

Alexandros did not answer. His eyes were glued to the figure waiting under the streetlight. He thought to go to her, to see if she'd been injured. Then he looked at his purple knuckles and smiled at the thought of Andreas' swollen face.

Eagle continued, "Have some fun, but don't be so serious. I'm telling you—I know. We'll find someone to help you get your papers. Save up your money so you can pay her and after your divorce you can go get a girl from your village. The American girls are for fun, but for serious, you have your own kind. I'm telling you—listen to me. I've seen a lot. These women are no good. They're not like Greek women."

Alexandros was barely listening. He had his own thoughts and he turned to Eagle and said, "How do you say, *'are you okay?'* in English?" But at that moment, Kareem came out of the hotel lobby door and Sarah wrapped her arms around him.

"You see? Like I told you. Look at her. She's got his thing pushing up against her. I know what I'm talking about."

Alexandros repeated, "How do you say *'are you okay?'*"

Alexandros walked toward the two as they mounted the bike together. He whistled to get their attention and then yelled, "you okay?" which caused them to turn in his direction.

"Oh. It's Alexandros." Sarah had a flash of memory and saw him charging into the hotel room and then she felt the shame. She was grateful for the evening sky to shield her reddened face and her humiliation.

"I'm—I'm okay. Yes. I just want to explain." But not in front of Kareem who was not quite sure what had happened. "I wasn't with Andreas. You see, he well, he—um—wanted me to, uh. I had my clothes, I was taking a shower." But only Kareem understood her. Alexandros stood there, his face showing the struggle to decipher her words, his eyes deep with concern. And then George was running toward them breathlessly, Eagle having disappeared into the restaurant at the same moment Alexandros had decided to approach Sarah.

"Ah, my favorite waitress—Sarah!" he proclaimed.

"What?" Sarah was baffled.

"I heard about your little scuffle with Andreas. Terrible boy. He's decided to take a little trip so he will not bother you. It was nothing, right? Just kids doing stupid things. When are you coming back to work?"

"Work?"

"Yes, come work." Alexandros parroted the words but also

knew the meaning.

And George gave her no time to think, "We need you. It's Labor Day weekend. Whatta ya say? Help me out a bit. Guaranteed a hundred a night."

"Are you saying in the restaurant?"

He nodded.

And Alexandros nodded, "the restaurant."

But the thought of everyone knowing — Alexandros must have told them. George seemed to know and where was that camera?

"Don't I have my maid job anymore?"

"Of course! Yes." George's voice was a little louder than was comfortable for Sarah and she quietly answered, "I'd rather work in the hotel," and then, as if the words had just made it to her brain, "Andreas is gone?"

"Yes. Yes. Gone." George said it quickly. "No need to think of him."

Then he said something to Alexandros in Greek and Alexandros walked back to the restaurant.

"Okay, so Minos, he uh understands of course, that you needed to take one day off to, uh let's say, recuperate and he told me — " George was reaching around to his back pocket, "he told me to be sure you were compensated for your lost wages." His wallet was in his hand.

"He did?" This was not at all what she had expected.

"Oh yes! He feels terrible that you had to miss a day of work. Uh, no need to discuss it with him — we can't be bothering the boss with such trivia. He told me to give you this." George was pulling twenty-dollar bills from his wallet. The perspiration that had collected on his forehead was shining in the glow of the streetlight.

"Yes. Yes. Here you go." He was watching her carefully as he handed her a wad of twenties and he misread the innocent questioning of her eyes, "And this." He pulled out two more twenties and pushed them into her hand. "Alright, then. You go home and rest. Come to work tomorrow." With a nervous laugh he shooed her with his hand and then turned to walk away but instead of walking back to the restaurant, he disappeared into the hotel lobby entrance.

"Whoa — how much is it?" Kareem asked.

Sarah was still staring ahead at the door where George had gone. It all seemed so bizarre but it was also a relief. She looked down at the wad and began to count.

"Twenty, forty, sixty, eighty, a hundred, twenty, forty—holy shit! What just happened?" Sarah looked at Kareem.

"Yeah. What *did* happen? What did Andreas do to you? I think you just got paid off. What did he do—tell me."

Sarah left out the part about the shower as she told Kareem that Andreas had attacked her in the hotel.

"You gotta go to the police!" Kareem was picturing Andreas on his girl. "Let's go now. There's a little station by the harbor. Come on, I'll take you—"

Sarah had been thinking of the camera.

"No!" She said it louder than she had wanted, but Kareem was still bent on revenge. "No! It's not your business, Kareem." She looked at him hard. "This is my problem."

Kareem became silent. He got back on the bike and waved his hand over the seat, indicating that she should sit there. Then he peddled her back to the boarding house without a word.

Mrs. Middleground must have been sitting by the window because she called to Sarah from the trailer door before Sarah's feet touched the ground.

When Sarah met her at the screen door, Mrs. Middleground looked at her through glazed eyes and said, "Your father called—twice—hours ago. He wants you to call him back immediately. It sounded important to me, but he didn't want to leave a message." She continued. "I told him I'd tell you. Now, what do you suppose it is?"

"I don't know," Sarah said abruptly and turned to leave.

"Where're you going? You can use my phone."

"No thanks." Sarah swallowed hard and walked away.

She called her father from the drug store phone booth the next day after Uncle Mike found her in the boarding house.

"Your father called me," he said, "Listen, I don't want him down here again. What did you do? You told him about that guy, didn't you?" He didn't wait for an answer. "Call him. Do it today, or he's going to drive down here. I'm watching out for you, aren't I? Call him!"

*   *   *   *

"Hi dad. Yeah, I'm really sorry about that. I should have gone to the house. I know – that was selfish, you being sick and all. How are you feeling now? That's good. Well, there was this concert in Plattsburg, so like, I um, I went with Karen Marie. There was no time for me to come, well – I had to get back to my job. How're mom and Earnest? Oh really? A trip without you? Oh – uhuh, Aunt Jackie. Yeah, I know how it is. Well, sorry I didn't stop back at the house. Oh, I have to put more money in the phone, um sorry, no more change. Talk to you soon. Okay. Yep, me too.

CHAPTER 10

"How you say? We eat. You and me? Go to beach, uh we—uh have a, a—for table, for eat? You know?"

But Sarah didn't know. She had no idea what Alexandros was trying to say as he stood in the hallway outside the guest rooms holding a box in both hands. All she could think of was the incident. Was he talking about that?

It was Teresa who presented Alexandros with a bed sheet from her cart when she realized what his struggle was about and she said, "This, you want?" Somehow, those two people who spoke no common language understood the situation that Sarah did not.

"He wants to eat on the beach with you." Teresa released a sigh, frustrated by Sarah's ignorance.

"Oh," said Sarah, turning back to Alexandros, "picnic."

"Pick-Nick?"

"Yes, you want a picnic."

Alexandros had no idea why she was saying that name nor did he care, for the light that lit in her eyes and the smile that pierced his heart led them to the edge of the receding tide where he put the sheet down and laid his feast at her side as she sat.

Earlier that afternoon, Eagle had seen Alexandros packing the picnic lunch in the restaurant kitchen, and had intervened as Big Gus gave him some tips about the English language so that he could talk to the young American girl.

"I-want-to-touch-your-ass." Big Gus said it slowly, enunciating each word and then in Greek, "go ahead, repeat it. It's very nice.

111

She'll like it a lot."

"Come here." Eagle took Alexandros by the shoulders and turned him around, "Don't listen to that moron. Take this box. Here—put the spanakopita like this." He packed it in, added a dish of olives and a loaf of hot bread from the warmer and called to one of the waitresses.

"Go get me two beers from the bar. Tell George it's for the kitchen."

So there sat Alexandros next to Sarah, the spanakopita sticking in his throat like sawdust as his hands trembled under the beer bottle that he was bringing to his mouth and gulping deeply until half was gone. He looked at Sarah and smiled. He looked out at the waves. He wanted to say to her, "*Your beauty blinds me and paralyzes my every move. These rolling waves are like the rhythm of my heart whenever I see you, and I long to bury my face in your amber hair, to kiss your body until it aches and to make love to you like no man ever has.*" But instead he said, "The water is good."

"Yes, it is." She was watching him, and thinking of the incident. "Alexandros—about Andreas and uh, well we um."

"Bad guy. Is gone."

Maybe there was no need to explain, though even if there were, there seemed not to be a way to do it.

"Alexandros, where's the camera?"

He repeated the word and shook his head slowly.

"Camera?"

"You know." She put her hands in front of her face and mimed the action of taking a photo. "Click—a camera."

It was almost the same word in Greek. "Yes, camera. I know, I know. No camera. You have camera?"

"Okay," she thought, "he doesn't know—just leave it alone."

Her fear became amusement as she watched his uncomfortable fidgeting while he pulled the label from the sweating beer bottle and glanced sideways at her. The breeze whipped her hair into her eyes. She took one hand and pulled it back to the side of her neck and held it there.

"You like the sea?"

"Yes, I see." Alexandros said with confidence.

Her smile widened with his response and she touched his arm, sending a wave of electricity through him.

"Alexandros, see." She put her two fingers to her eyes and then to his. "I see you." And before he could figure out why she was saying the obvious she said again the word *see*, or so he thought.

"Sea." She pointed exaggeratedly at the water, "sea." And then back again at him, "See—I see you." Until it dawned on him.

"Yes! I get it. See. It has two meanings." And so he found a road into her world. "You give me English, no?"

Sarah, laughed hard, so hard she couldn't catch her breath.

"Yes, I give you English. Sure, why not?" She liked the idea as much as the look on his face when she saw him watching her.

There was so much Alexandros wanted to say.

"I prefer the mountains. I was born high up among the gods, where you could look down into the valley and feel the pulse of the world below you." But he just took the beer cap and drew an upside down V in the sand. Then he put the cap on the top and pointed to it. "My house—very beautiful."

Sarah smiled.

"Mountains," she said and then continued the lines of his drawing, up and down, up and down until there were several zigzags in the sand. Then she put an olive at the bottom of the mountain and said, "My house—it's in the mountains too! Very beautiful." But the sigh that escaped her was one filled with sorrow.

Alexandros watched her. Were those tears? He also missed his mountain village. He thought he understood. He reached out and brushed her cheek with his hand, feeling the wetness with his thumb and she let him pull her closer until she sat with her head lying on his chest, the rapid rhythm of his heart pounding against her ear. She tilted her head up to look at him and his lips were there, just brushing her eyelid, his breath warm and sweet. And as she stretched up to meet his lips, just as she felt the gentlest touch of them on hers, a cold wave washed over their legs, jolting them like a live wire and they scrambled to save the sheet as the olive dish rolled back down the sand into the sea.

*   *   *   *

The next day as Sarah walked past the back of the restaurant with Kareem, her heart jumped as she saw Alexandros by the dumpster smoking and talking to Eagle. He wasn't usually there that early in the morning. She waited for him to make eye contact so she could wave or call to him and Kareem didn't notice how her eyes were focused on something behind him as he spoke to her, or the disappointment in her face as they parted at the lobby of the hotel. But Alexandros was there the next morning and the one after that, though he never seemed to be looking in her direction—something that would have been a natural reflex for any person seeing two others passing by so closely. So, on the very next morning, Sarah called to him, "morning Alexandros!" and he looked up, nodded his head and smiled. And that time, Kareem noticed the light appear in her eyes, and he felt a rage that surprised him.

Teresa was perplexed at Sarah's questions that morning.

"I was thinking to go down to the kitchen for some coffee. I'm kind of tired—could use a little something, like maybe coffee. Is that okay? You know, like to go get coffee down there?"

"I think is too early for a break."

"Oh, not a break. Just like, well—are we allowed in the kitchen?"

"I guess. But we have coffee in the break room."

"Ugh! That Mr. Coffee sucks. The urn coffee they have in the kitchen is like, you know, so much better."

"I like the Mr. Coffee."

"I think the milk is bad." Sarah tried a different direction, "I smelled something in the fridge."

"Huh?"

"The break room fridge. It smells kind of funky. I think we need milk—maybe I could get some from the kitchen."

"Now?"

"Well—not now, but in a little while?"

"Sarah—you want to go see Alexandros? Is okay. I'm no your boss. Do what you want. But I thinking we need the sugar packets for the guest room coffee stations. We running out of them soon." Teresa smiled at her and pushed her cart down the hall.

Eagle was at the back of the restaurant and he held the door open for her.

"He's at the steam table, helping the chef with pie dough."

"What? Oh, no—ah, Teresa sent me for sugar packets. We ran

out."

Eagle followed her in and called out in Greek to no one in particular that she could see, until Alexandros peeked his head around the corner with a smile that sent her heart banging against her ribs.

"Sugar packets," she said, surprised at her sudden inability to produce sentences.

Alexandros looked at Eagle for translation. "She wants sugar packets for the hotel rooms—that's what she's saying anyway."

Alexandros nodded his head for her to come toward him. His hands were thick with dough and he held them up like a surgeon who'd just scrubbed for surgery.

"Sugar," he said, "here." He tilted his head to indicate the shelf by his knees.

She bent to retrieve a large canister but in anticipating her movement Alexandros had mistakenly moved in her way.

"Sorry." He swept his body quickly to the side but she was there against him—a momentary touch, her soft cheek brushing his arm, igniting a spark that sizzled over his skin setting his body on fire. She looked up at him; his eyes penetrated hers, paralyzing her.

"That's salt." Big Gus awakened her and Sarah looked down at the salt canister. "What're you doing in the kitchen?"

He was soaked in sweat as he loaded pans of food into the steam table. His shirt stuck to his skin and the front of his apron was drenched. Beads of perspiration rolled down his forehead into his eyes and dripped from his nose. "Get me a *teesha*."

"A what?"

"A teesha, a teesha—you deaf?"

Sarah just stared at him as she continued to hold the salt canister and then Alexandros was speaking Greek to him, as it dawned on her what he wanted. She ran around to the cabinet and grabbed a tee shirt and tried to pass it to him through the steam.

"Here."

"What I do with this?"

"A tee shirt."

"Yeah, a teesha—over there." One of the older women walked in, "Never mind. You—Vicky give me teesha"

The older woman handed Big Gus several tissues from the box next to the cabinet and he honked loudly into them and shook his head. Then, he turned to Alexandros and spoke in Greek.

"What do you want with this one? She thinks I want a shirt to blow my nose."

"Don't bother her."

But Sarah was too overcome with embarrassment and was grateful to have Vicky lead her to the back storeroom for the sugar packets, and grateful that the back door was a step away. But before she had pulled it open, Eagle came toward her.

"You know Alexandros wants to drive you home. You're working too hard and then walking home. That's no good. He wants to drive you. I tell him you say okay?"

"Okay," she said and she was out the door, walking across the parking lot—her heart soaring up into the cloudless blue sky, her whole body as light as a flower petal caught in a breeze, floating back and forth on its return to earth.

So she didn't see George and his son at the far end of the parking lot, Andreas in a headlock, his own father pinning him to the asphalt as they disappeared behind the car.

CHAPTER 11

Oscar waffled between relief and regret during those long weeks of basic training. On his first day, he'd stood in line and watched the grimaces of his soon-to-be battle buddies, as the razor buzzed each row across their scalps and the thick balls of hair fell to their shoulders and around the base of the barber chair. With each buzz on his own head, Oscar felt his former self fade away and when he stood with the others, naked and bald, he was able to forget Owl's Head and transform into the machine that was expected. The physical training was grueling. They were up before dawn every morning. The drills were non-stop until every muscle cried at the smallest of movements, and along with that physical pain, the sergeant fed them daily doses of psychological abuse. But for Oscar, the boot camp training was a deep cave into which he descended, escaping from his thoughts. Those endless hours of abuse and fatigue kept him from the memory of that night on the porch with Mr. Petit.

But slowly as he became accustomed to the routine and the end of boot camp came into sight, Sarah kept sneaking through those walls of protection until she was all he thought about. He should have stayed in Owl's Head one more day—to explain. Or better yet, he should have run past her father and back up the stairs. She deserved to know the truth. But the shock of it had knocked him senseless and he was already in fatigues, a gun over his head, trudging up the incline in the pouring rain before those thoughts came to him.

So with graduation from boot camp looming in the near future, he thought about the leave he would take for that one trip — just for her. She needed to know. But he pushed himself further, through the mud, past the others until the pain in his limbs took over and he could forget — for a little while.

In the meantime, Sarah found her way across the front seat of the blue Impala Alexandros had borrowed from Eagle, sitting a bit closer to him each time he drove her home. Kareem only took a few days to figure out why Sarah no longer walked by the gas station in the evenings after work. She had avoided telling him when he asked, not quite sure of the reason, except that she sensed it would cause him pain. And though she longed for that moment each day when she would slide in and take her place next to Alexandros, she also did not want to hurt Kareem.

For that first ride home, she'd waited breathlessly for the workday to end and when he pulled onto the dirt of the boarding house and up under the elm, she thought the pounding of her heart would knock her unconscious.

"Thanks for the ride." She closed her eyes, bringing her lips to his, but he had brought his head up higher, his lips going to her forehead, hers kissing the air below his chin.

Message received. Her disappointment was great.

"See you tomorrow," Alexandros said quietly, and his eyes dove into hers, but neither of them moved.

"Okay." It was a whisper as she unglued herself from the seat and pushed herself backwards slowly toward the car door, "tomorrow."

He inhaled hard as Sarah reached for the handle, their eyes remaining locked.

"Tomorrow," he whispered, and then she was out of the car while he gripped the steering wheel tightly and watched her and she watched him through the windshield. Then her hand was on the knob of the front door and she turned her back to him and went in. But she continued watching him from the sitting room window as he sat without moving, looking straight ahead, through the wild tree branches that grew over the top of the boarding house and hung in front of the sitting room window. After a few seconds, he slowly backed the car off the dirt and was gone and Sarah stood at the window looking through the lace curtains at nothing.

"*What was that about?*" she wondered, "*a kiss on the forehead. What am I doing wrong?*" She heard Debbie's voice in her head. "*Greeks are different.*"

Each morning Kareem, loaded down with his schoolbooks, continued to walk with Sarah on her way to the hotel. He knew he had lost her in the evenings but he looked forward to those mornings and was grateful that the secondary school was a short distance from the hotel and that Alexandros would not be at the restaurant yet. But the joy those walks had once brought him, disappeared and were replaced by thoughts of revenge and plans for Alexandros' murder. He fantasized about his father's gun under the counter at the gas station. He was the warrior saving his woman from the clutches of the evil villain.

And Sarah thought of the money she'd saved as the autumn air bit her on those morning walks.

"I should buy a car," she said.

"You have that kind of money?" Kareem knew a car would put an end to that coveted time alone.

"A used car," she answered, "I have a couple hundred saved. You know anyone selling one?"

He shook his head, "I'll ask around." But he didn't.

*   *   *   *

As autumn progressed toward darker days, the Atlantic Palace Hotel was boarded up. Teresa moved back to Queens to help her sister clean houses and Sarah joined Vicky and Lenore in the restaurant to serve the locals who came in mostly on the weekends.

Sarah stopped in the drug store a few times and sat in the phone booth but she couldn't bring herself to dial. She thought about Karen Marie, but still her arms stayed at her side, her hands in her lap as she stared at the numbers within the round dial as if she hoped to find answers to her questions there. She felt adrift like a seagull bobbing on the ocean waves, moving up and down but not floating in any particular direction. She longed to pick up the telephone receiver and have comfort surge through the line and fill her. No one had come down looking for her. No one had even tried to call. She didn't know that Mrs. Middleground had somehow misplaced the little index cards with the messages she'd written for Sarah from the calls that came intermittently. Sometimes they came during her soap opera, sometimes after her evening tea. And sometimes she'd walk out her front door with an index card in her hand and stop to pull a weed from the dirt or to check inside a parked car, or to tighten the top of a garbage can cover or to shoo a squirrel away from her window sill and by the time she'd get to the other side of the yard, her hand would be empty. So she'd go back across her footsteps to look for the index card and find herself back at her door, completely forgetting why she had left in the first place.

Sarah bought a space heater at the drug store, a box of pencils and a small pencil sharpener and she moved into the single room at the end of the hallway. The house was almost empty except for a few of the fishermen, so one of her companions that fall was Mack when they happened to meet in the hallway and exchange a few meaningless words. He always seemed eager to start up a conversation, though Sarah didn't have much to say to him. Mrs. Middleground was another of Sarah's companions when she needed vacuum bags or cleaning supplies and would have to sit, drink tea and listen to her slurred stories of the past. And of course, Kareem was still there each morning.

Sarah also found the used car she'd been looking for. It was Eagle's blue Impala — though he had not known he wanted to sell it until Alexandros had convinced him to buy a new one, an old candy-apple-red Duster.

With the newfound freedom of the car, Sarah ventured further away from East End, shopping in Southampton and on a rare weekend night when they both could get away from the restaurant, she'd go with Alexandros to a disco further up the island. He'd dance with her, though he really didn't want to. It seemed like there were specific steps that he couldn't quite get, rocking and bumping and spinning, not like the dancing he'd learned in the village. But they moved around the dance floor, laughing and having fun. There'd be a slow dance or two and they'd cling to each other, a chance for a kiss or an intimate touch. But Alexandros would always pull away and Sarah was left baffled but content to keep trying.

Minos saw the budding romance and thought he could use them to investigate an idea he had. He approached Alexandros with the proposal.

"There is a business up the island a bit. I was wondering if you'd like to check it out for me." He was talking to Alexandros in the kitchen of the restaurant.

Alexandros looked at his cousin with interest but said nothing.

"They call it *The Melting Pot* and it's a place with just wine and cheese. It's very successful. I was there with—someone. The waiter brings us a cutting board with an apple and a block of cheese and a bottle of wine. Uncomplicated. At some of the other tables, I saw pots of melted cheese and cubes of bread, but I don't think that part will really catch on. Melted cheese. Strange, right? But I was thinking to copy it and make something like that here, in the hotel. Maybe we can use part of the office and build something out from that."

"Wine and cheese? Are you sure?" asked Alexandros.

"Yes, I know. But the Americans seem to like that sort of thing. That place is busy every night of the week. Maybe I could get my sister's goat cheese—import it. I think the Americans would like that—fresh mountain goat cheese. Maybe yogurt. Those things we grew up on, they pay a lot of money for over here."

He reached around to his back pocket and took out his wallet. "Take that American girl. See what she thinks. Get her reaction. You know what I mean?"

Minos handed a fifty-dollar bill to Alexandros.

"Sure. Why not." Alexandros was glad to find another excuse to be with Sarah.

He drove Eagle's car to the boarding house and found Sarah at the picnic table by the lake, the sun getting low over Mrs. Middlegound's trailer, a sharp chill in the air. She didn't hear him approach and was startled when he said her name.

"Sorry. I scare you."

"No, it's okay."

"You have work?"

He was looking at the spiral notebook lying flat on the table. "Is too dark out here, no?"

Sarah suppressed the instinct to snap the book shut as she'd done when the others had seen her there. She felt safe with the knowledge that Alexandros would not be able to read anything in it. But she did not count on his own love of poetry or his eye for understanding the placement of words on the pages and the small breaks for stanzas.

"Poim-a," he said. She also didn't realize that the words were so similar in both languages.

She turned quickly and closed the book.

"Poim-a, I like it," Alexandros said. "I have poim-a book. Is very beautiful."

"You like poetry?" It was such a surprise.

"I like poim-a-tree." Alexandros tried the English, but it tumbled against his tongue and knocked into his teeth. He checked Sarah's face. Yes, she understood. He knew it from her smile and the excitement in her voice as she accepted his hand and his help up from the picnic table.

"You like poetry." She said it again, as though she needed to hear it once more to understand it.

"Yes."

For a moment they were clearly speaking a language they both understood. The chasm between them was briefly hidden. Both had known from the beginning that the depths of difference between their worlds—the places into which they'd been born, in which they'd taken their first steps, spoken their first words, felt their first moments of rebellion—were as wide and impassable as a canyon. But it seemed that this mutual interest in poetry was one small step across the unstable bridge that swung wildly between those two worlds.

"*Poetry*." Sarah cocked her head to the side as she looked more closely at the young man who stood in front of her and she thought, "*I would never have expected that from one of those tough guys in the kitchen*."

"I have poim-a-tree book. Is very good."

"I'd love to see it. Is it here in East End?"

"Yes. Book is in my room."

His room. Sarah had never thought about his life outside of the restaurant kitchen. He just always seemed to be there.

"Your room. Do you share it?" Maybe it was more private than the boarding house.

"Share it?" Alexandros did not understand.

"Do you have a roommate?" Sarah pressed on, "another person? Who lives with you?"

"Oh, my room is in house of Minos—my cousin."

"Oh," her disappointment was obvious.

"But I bring you here poim-a-tree book. I read you."

"Okay."

Alexandros remembered the fifty-dollar bill in his wallet.

"Tomorrow, we go nice place for wine and apples and cheese." It was a question.

"Yes, that sounds good and you bring your poetry book," she answered, but she thought, "I'll bring my notebook." She wanted to hear her poems aloud, to breathe life into the words and hear them as they needed to be heard, rather than timidly whispering them to herself and watching them fall from the pages in dull thuds. They needed oxygen and space; they needed life. They were her words pulled from the depths of her soul, deeper than any vital organs—though much more vital. Alexandros would not be able to judge the words, simply because he would not understand them, but he might feel the rhythm, the movement, the emotion. The thought of presenting her poetry to Alexandros thrilled her—but also frightened her. She would expose herself and he would see her—completely. But how much would he grasp? Without a common language, with her fear of being open and unprotected, her thirst to be understood would likely go unquenched.

*　　　　*　　　　*　　　　*

The Tiffany-style lamps hung low over the tables in *The Melting Pot*. As Alexandros slid into the booth next to Sarah, he noticed how the dim glow against her face made her irresistibly desirable.

Genius—the décor, the decadent atmosphere.

Though he'd been sent there with a clear goal in mind, he quickly lost his focus. He was trying to examine and mentally record for Minos, the sultry music, the warmth of the dimly lit corner that he and Sarah were sitting in—each table was somehow in its own private space behind carefully constructed walls. There were only booths with long cushioned benches, no stand-alone tables. And the delicious sense that they were the only ones in the café, opened the door of possibilities. Alexandros slipped comfortably into a deep sense of freedom that seemed to grow as each moment vanished into unmeasured time, the shackles of the outside world removed and Minos forgotten.

Sarah pushed herself closer and he felt her hand on his thigh. The warmth of it took away his guard as his self-control slowly spilled out into the warm air. They were completely alone. A candle sat at the middle of the table, deep within a fragile holder. It flickered and wildly licked the edges of the glass.

"This is nice," Sarah said as her hand burned a hole into Alexandros' thigh.

"Mmmm." He grabbed her hand and pulled it to his lips, kissing each finger slowly.

"Not yet," he thought, "soon, but not yet — after the letter. I need the letter."

But to her he said, "You like it?"

"Oh," she feigned interest in the surroundings and looked around. There was only that small corner to observe, "Yes. Beautiful."

Alexandros sighed. He was a mere mortal, a young man alone in a world he barely understood, barely able to battle the forces around him.

"What good is tradition," he thought, "loyalty, a family name?" His reasoning was askew. He felt intoxicated without having yet taken a sip of wine. There was only that one small fragment of the universe, only he and Sarah, and he was melting slowly like chocolate in the sun, a sweet sticky mess.

He shook his head as he looked at her.

"What?" She questioned.

But he didn't answer. He pulled her to his side and devoured her. His tongue pushed through her lips; his fingers were lost in the strands of her hair. And her hand moved slowly over his jeans, a moan escaping from deep inside him. They only pulled apart because they heard a discreet brush against the wooden booth as the server came to them several minutes later.

Flushed and breathless, they managed to order a bottle of wine. A cutting board with slices of cheese and an apple was brought to the table with the wine. As the server opened the bottle and poured some into each wine glass, Sarah reached over, took the knife and was about to slice into the apple, but she changed her mind and put the knife back on the cutting board and took the whole red apple in her hands. She brought it to her mouth and bit into it, leaving her lips wet with juice as she brought the apple to Alexandros' mouth. He took it between his teeth and bit it hard, the meaty flesh mashing against his tongue. The server disappeared and the two sipped their wine slowly and talked quietly and then not at all.

When Alexandros was finally able to pull away from Sarah to pay the check, he dug into his wallet to find Minos' fifty-dollar bill. One bottle of wine and a few slices of cheese and apple – the bill was exorbitant, but he didn't notice.

Sarah slid from the booth and Alexandros helped her with her coat, stopping to kiss her once more, pressing her into his body and thinking about the dark corners along the road where they might be able to park the car. Sarah, breathless with anticipation, felt him against her.

As he turned, she followed closely behind him while they made their way through the maze of walls out into the cool night. But as they entered the world again, Alexandros remembered the letter and Sarah felt the barrier come between them as she sat on the passenger side of the blue Impala. It took a while for her to cool down. She went over the events of the evening, each small movement and tried to figure out which it was that seemed to drive the wedge between them.

Sarah thought of the poetry book Alexandros had taken from the passenger seat and thrown onto the back seat at the beginning of the evening when she'd opened the car door at the boarding house.

"Alexandros, come back to my room. Read your poetry book."

It was late when they pulled under the elm outside the boarding house entrance. He didn't trust himself in her bedroom but he didn't want to leave her, and there was the poetry.

It was an act of intimacy – much more so than making love. Sex was a primal act, removing clothing, uncovering the body to its natural state, all merely a means to propagate a necessary release – nature's urgent push. Whereas the written verse, the pieces of himself that needed to be carefully hidden – would reveal so much more, leaving him completely open and vulnerable. To share that love, to lie completely naked and unprotected without defense — that was risky. Yet he yearned to share it with Sarah as much as he longed for her body against his. If he were to reveal himself fully, would she still want him? She would never understand the words as he recited them. It seemed safe enough.

He turned on the light inside the car and stretched his hand to the back seat. He found the book, held it up to the light and handed it to Sarah.

"Come in the house." Sarah's fingers lingered over his hand as she took the book from him.

He shook his head. "In the car," he answered her, "your book."

He reached back again and grabbed her spiral notebook. He opened the worn cracked cover. The top part had been pulled from the spirals and was hanging off.

"Oh no," Alexandros said.

"It's okay. You didn't do that. It was ripped already."

He gingerly turned page after page, running his fingers over each and smoothing them flat with his palm, as carefully as if they were made from a delicate web. He stopped at one page.

"Here, you read." He handed her the book, still holding it gently, passing it to her slowly, both hands supporting it from underneath.

Sarah looked at the tattered page, "You, first." It was almost a whisper, "please." She'd lost her courage. She picked up his poetry book from her lap and looked at its Greek lettering on the cover.

The only parts of the book that she understood were the page numbers. Page twenty-one was dog-eared and bent back with so much use, the spine of the book so permanently creased from so much bending, that the book opened there automatically when Sarah placed it flat on her lap.

"Here," she pointed and looked up at him. It made no difference to her from which page he would read; they all looked the same. She knew she would not be able to understand.

"Ithaca," he said and nodded his approval as if she, herself, and not gravity, had chosen that poem. He smoothed out the page and nodded again, acknowledging page twenty-one was Sarah's favorite, as it was his.

He began to read and it was true; she understood none of the words, but the yearning in his voice captured her and pulled her into his world as she sighed softly. Leaning back against the window she listened to his voice fill the car.

As you set out for Ithaca hope the voyage is a long one, full of adventure, full of discovery. Laistrygonians and Cyclops, angry Poseidon – don't be afraid of them; you'll never find things like that on your way as long as you keep your thoughts raised high, as long as a rare excitement stirs your spirit and your body. Laistrygonians and Cyclops, wild Poseidon – you won't encounter them unless you bring them along inside your soul, unless your soul sets them up in front of you.

Alexandros heard the poet's voice reaching out, through the ages, and though he'd read those words more times than he could count, it was as if he were reading them for the first time. They were as familiar as the fingers on his hand but it was in the car with Sarah, at that moment as he read, that the meaning found its real home. Suddenly there was an answer to his uncertainty – an answer to the letter his father had yet to send him.

Alexandros had been a brooding adolescent when the schoolmaster had given the older students that book of poems as a gift. There were only four of them in his grade – all boys, but he was the one Mr. Thaskalos had chided to stop waiting for life to happen. *It's a journey and you're on it. Don't wait for a destination; look around you Alexandros. This is life.* But at fifteen, he'd thought he knew more. He needed to go somewhere, do something, but what? His restlessness had blinded him. With the other boys, he'd made fun of the poetry book. What were they to do with it? It was of no use to them when hunting or herding. But the village boredom that inevitably creeps into the young inhabitants of the mountains, led him to the book one snowy afternoon and as Alexandros read it, he was surprised to be moved by mere words. He memorized certain poems – *Ithaca* was the first, appealing to a young boy because it spoke of Odysseus, hero of the Trojan War. He traced over those same words again and again until he found himself reciting them inside his head while herding the goats or cutting wood. But it was in this place, with this American girl, where the message of the poet became as clear as a mountain spring pouring from the stones.

There he was on an island in America, a jetty of sand sticking into the Atlantic Ocean, six thousand miles from home, and he'd found it—*the spirit that stirred him*—Sarah. The wall between them—the letter, his Laistrygonians and Cyclops and Poseidon—it was he who set that monster between them. Suddenly, the letter lost its power. Mr. Thaskalos' words were in his head: *Look around you, Alexandros. This is your life.* Yes, this was his life. She was his life and he was hungry with a desire to live it. He put the book down and looked at her.

But just behind Sarah's head, outside the car window, the distorted face of a strange creature was pressed against the glass. Alexandros gasped and sprang forward to grab Sarah and save her from that awful creature. Sarah saw his reaction and turned to see Mrs. Middleground pushed up against the glass so close to her own face, a loud short scream came from her throat and smacked the window. Mrs. Middleground jumped back a few steps, causing her to trip over the roots of the elm and her face disappeared from the window as her body hit the dirt.

Alexandros was out of the car and standing next to Mrs. Middleground before Sarah could even open the passenger side. He extended his hand to her and helped her off the ground.

"I saw the light on in the car," she was saying as she examined her knee, "I thought I would come and turn it off for you, young man. That can really wear down your battery, you know."

Sarah shook her head.

Alexandros asked, "you okay?"

"Oh yes, I'm fine." She was brushing off her thin nightgown, "but you shouldn't park here if you're going to stay in the car." Her voice took on an accusing tone. "That's just not right, you know."

"Mrs. Middleground, we weren't—we were reading poetry."

"Poetry? Hmm. That's a new one."

Sarah didn't see the point in defending herself against the woman and Alexandros barely understood what she was implying. Their night out was finished. The three of them separated under the elm and went their own ways.

But the next morning, when Minos saw Sarah, he asked her how she liked *The Melting Pot*. She tilted her head as if contemplating, and there was a distant look in her eyes as she reminisced momentarily, and then she could think only of one word.

"Fantastic."

Minos smiled but shook his head in wonder, "cheese and apples. Interesting."

*   *   *   *

As the holidays approached, Uncle Mike made an effort to find Sarah. He found her, one evening after work, in the community kitchen at the boarding house.

"I'm driving up north for the holidays. Wanna drive together?"

"No, thanks."

"It's a long ride. Don't you want the company?"

"I'm not going."

"Why not? What's up with you? Your father said you haven't called home. How come you don't answer his calls?"

"What calls? I didn't get any calls."

"He says he keeps calling. The old lady takes a message."

"She doesn't tell me. I don't know what her problem is. I'll call him tomorrow."

"Well—ya know, I told him I was looking out for you. You sure you don't want to go up for the holidays? It gets pretty dead here until after the new year."

"I'm positive. I have some stuff to do here."

Mike didn't pursue it. He was wrapped up in his own world, anxious to see his brother, hoping to convince him to sell the store and front him the money he'd need for the luncheonette on the harbor. He had thought he would be able to talk to Sarah on the way up there. Maybe she had some money saved.

"We should go out for a drink or something before I leave," Mike said.

"Yeah. We should."

The sarcasm was not at all subtle.

"Hey, ya know, the summer was hectic. I was gonna come around. You were never here, either. You don't have to have an attitude." He turned to leave the kitchen, "I thought you might be interested in a way to better yourself, but if you're not, that's fine."

"Better than this?" Sarah swept her hand around the tiny

kitchen and laughed. "So what? How?"

Mike stopped in the kitchen doorway and looked at his niece, "Take a ride with me. I'll show you."

They drove to the harbor and parked next to the marina.

"See that shack over there?"

"Yeah."

"I'm gonna buy it and make it a little luncheonette. And make a killing in the summers. I'm getting too old for this other crap. Time for a change. Look at it; it'll work. I'll open up before dawn, catch the fishermen going out on the boats and the partiers leaving the bars to go home."

"That's actually a good idea."

"Yeah. Thought you'd be able to help me convince your dear ol' dad to sell the store, give me a little cash — get me started."

"Oh."

He needed something from her. For a few minutes, as they'd driven in the dark toward the harbor, she'd felt like they were together — part of a family, like he was there to share something and maybe be willing to lighten her load a little. She'd almost brought it up. There were just a few seconds when he'd asked her how she was doing at the hotel — or the restaurant. He wasn't quite sure where she worked. She'd started to feel a little lighter at the thought of his knowing what she'd seen in Owl's Head. She'd given him the superficial okay to his question and then had begun to form the words in her mouth, to say: *Uncle Mike, my father was with another woman — he's cheating, and I think my mother caught them. I should have done more.* Somehow she saw her own actions as part of this terrible assault on the family. She wanted to hand this all to her uncle so that she wouldn't have to drag it behind her anymore. They could carry it together and it would be more manageable. But they'd reached the harbor before she could say anything and then his motives were made clear. But instead of feeling deflated, she felt herself rise with something. What was it? A feeling she couldn't quite identify. She looked at him and nodded her head.

"It's a great idea. And you know what? I was thinking as we were driving. I *will* come up north. But I'd rather have my own car."

The lie felt good, much better than sharing her pain. It was satisfying in a way she'd never felt. She couldn't quite identify it. Control?

Uncle Mike smiled, "Great. And ya know—you can be part of this. You have any money saved?"

"Oh sure. I have a lot." Oh, yes, it was a sweet syrupy feeling. "I'd love to be part of it."

"Really? How much have you got?"

"How much do you need?"

"Well—let's see. The property is ten thousand. I have five."

"You have five?" That was shocking. How had that nitwit saved five thousand dollars and she'd saved nothing?

"Wow, I had no idea parking cars was so lucrative."

"I did other stuff on the side."

"Like what?"

"Just stuff."

"Hmm. Well I've got three thousand. It's all yours. Just tell me what my cut is."

"Your cut?"

"Yeah. Ya know—like am I a partner?"

"Absolutely! You're a partner. Done!"

Uncle Mike wouldn't figure out Sarah's deceit until he got to Owl's Head and she wasn't there, nor did she show up later.

Ron liked the idea of selling the store, though he wasn't too sure about handing money over to Mikey, the little brother whose incompetence had followed him to adulthood and to whatever location he wandered. It was different when he was young. Then it was called mischief, later rambunctiousness. But when Mike had been expelled from high school after years of tormenting his teachers, it started looking more like criminal behavior.

Mike had admitted to the firecracker in the principal's bathroom. What else could he do? He'd been seen. He'd lit it and thrown it behind the toilet, expecting a little diversion from the monotony of his day. The Math teacher had gladly given him the pass to the boys' lavatory, never suspecting his motive, and poor Mr. Delisle was left permanently deaf in one ear after his injuries healed. He'd seen that Petit boy running from his private bathroom and through the back door of his office and when he went to investigate, the M80 blew the porcelain tank into chunks of shrapnel. Mr. Delisle didn't press charges even though he'd wanted to. But his wife convinced him otherwise. The boy had been so young when he lost his parents in the car accident and the older brother, Ron, was doing the best he could. And she begged him to remember their own friend, Anne Petit. She was doing what she could to help those kids. So Mr. Delisle had relented, but he had no doubts when he made the decision to sign the form expelling the boy.

Ron realized that Mike, as an adult far from Owl's Head, still dove into chaos with the same mindless instinct as a moth flying straight into a flame, so he naturally felt uneasy about handing over such a sum of money. Eventually, though, Mike would convince him and Ron would put the store up for sale hoping the proceeds might produce a solution to his younger brother's aimless wandering.

But there were no buyers; no one seemed to want it. Almost no one inquired about the for-sale sign tacked to the porch railing except for the purpose of conversing about the old days and how they'd all loved that store. There was one out-of-towner who had come to look at it for a possible bed and breakfast for the ski tourists, which got Ron thinking about the store in a different way, but then that person never came back and the ideas and conversations disappeared. The for-sale sign became detached with a gust of wind during a winter storm. It swung from the railing, it's words hanging down, swaying back and forth until the side that was attached to the porch worked its way loose and fell to the unkempt grass below the house. And the store was forgotten—for a while.

Mike would somehow get his money by the end of the following summer. He was seen in East End with Surfer Jim when he wasn't parking cars and he often seemed to be busy with that other *stuff* he'd mentioned. Years later, with his wife—a local girl—and their four children, he'd become one of the upstanding business owners living year round in East End—a dream he'd had since the day he'd set foot there.

But he spent that winter in Owl's Head waiting for the sale of the store while Sarah spent it almost exclusively with Alexandros downstate. They were together every day. Uncle Mike had said East End would be *dead until after the new year* but Sarah didn't see it that way. Yes—it's true. The tourists were gone, the restaurant often empty and mostly she worked on weekend evenings. But for her, East End was more alive than it had ever been.

She and Alexandros explored the cliffs in front of the lighthouse, and sometimes they would have the pleasant surprise of coming up over a boulder to see a group of harbor seals resting on the rocks ahead. And if they were very still they would have several minutes to watch them close-up before their intrusion was detected and the seals would jump from the rocks and disappear back into the sea. There were days to fish with homemade rods that they made from the long reeds they plucked from the lake. And when they had the first snow, Eagle took them to the beach and showed them, with some old skis and poles that were in the restaurant basement, how to ski on a flat surface, an activity neither of them had ever done. Then, when a Nor'easter blew up the coast and buried the little town in a white blanket of snow, cutting power for three days and causing the New Year's celebration at the town hall to be cancelled, they took the skis and drew lines in the snow from north to south and back again. Minos invited the restaurant workers to stay at his house because he had a generator, which kept the heat running. A few of the cooks took him up on it as did Vicky and Sarah, but Minos' wife warned them in English and in Greek to behave in front of the children.

"No bad words, and no hanky-panky-ing each other." She'd learned some of her English from American movies.

Eventually, as with every year before that one, the gray days began to lengthen and winter began to slowly melt away. But Sarah and Alexandros continued to spend all their non-working time together, though Sarah was confused by Alexandros' obvious desire for her and his clear attempt at denying it.

Alexandros tried to respect his family name and the unspoken rules of his village, but the longer he spent in America, the further away both seemed. He continued to read page twenty-one of his poetry book, searching for that certainty he'd had the night in the car with Sarah. If he could just get the letter, he would be able to satisfy those he loved on both sides of the Atlantic, which is what he wanted so dearly.

*   *   *   *

"Let's go here tomorrow." Alexandros was standing against the steam table in the kitchen and Sarah had just put a tray of dirty dishes down on the dishwasher ledge. He was pointing to a glossy-finished photo on a postcard he'd found in the dresser drawer in Minos' guest room. It was the Statue of Liberty against a backdrop of New York City. The closest Sarah had ever come to visiting the city had been when she'd driven past it with her parents on the way downstate.

"Good idea," Sarah answered. "I'd like to see that too."

The fact that it was a bitingly cold March day and that any boat sailing to Liberty Island would be doing so over turbulent water in the icy air of the New York Harbor did not occur to either of them. Like every new love, each moment alone was a celebration to which logic and reality were never invited. So the next day, a day they'd managed to get off from work together, they got in the car with an old ripped map that George gave them and Sarah drove west in the blue Impala. Her confidence had increased with her driving between East End and Southampton, but she made a mental note to look into taking a road test at some point. Alexandros unfurled the map onto the dashboard and studied it.

In New York City, Sarah pulled into the low narrow entrance of a parking garage. It seemed too dark and small to have a large vehicle, like a car, driven into it but Sarah was beckoned to continue forward by a man standing in a little booth, and by the car behind her that almost hit her bumper. The man handed her a ticket and told her to put it on the dashboard. She drove slowly, deeper into the cave-like garage, handing Alexandros the ticket, which he took and placed inside the glove compartment.

Sarah swallowed hard and pressed lightly on the gas pedal, leaning forward over the steering wheel as she looked for a space to park. She followed the arrow painted onto the blacktop as it curved around and around, one curve after another, down, down, deep into the earth. She realized she had been holding her breath and let it out in a long sigh as she saw the first empty space and pulled into it. She put the car into park, turned off the ignition and got out, looking sheepishly across the roof at Alexandros whose smile arched across his face. He looked as he did every other day since the day they'd met, yet she convinced herself that his smile was an attempt at a brave face, as was hers, as they stood in that deep underworld.

They were so far from the surface; it would be a long trek back to the street and there were so many cars coming around the corner—not much room to walk back up. And—well, she was responsible for him. After all, he barely spoke English so he wouldn't know how to get back to the street level.

She came around the car and hooked her arm into his, pulling him toward the direction where she thought she'd find daylight—into the line of slow moving cars. Her legs felt like thin cardboard.

"Where you go?" he asked.

She looked at his quizzical expression and answered as if he were a small child.

"The street, Alexandros."

He pointed to the wall behind her.

"We go here." Then he led her to the elevator that was a few feet away and pressed a button.

"Oh." Her face turned a light pink hue.

The metal doors parted and Alexandros looked at Sarah and then at the people in the elevator.

"Up?" he asked. They nodded and held the door open as Alexandros guided Sarah inside and Sarah smiled and looked at the elevator floor as all the other heads shot up to watch the numbers blink, on their way to the street level.

Sarah and Alexandros walked all day gaping at the sights—they were two mountain yokels with heads bent upwards, staring into the sky looking for the tops of the buildings. They walked for miles without feeling it, enthralled by the majesty of the skyscrapers and dumbfounded by the variety of people around them. They stopped outside the Empire State building to count the floors before going into the lobby and taking the elevator to the top. From the observation deck they stood side by side, looking out on the world as the sun bent over the buildings creating a mirage-like glow. Sarah squinted looking in the distance for the Statue of Liberty, not realizing she was facing the wrong direction. She knew only where she wanted to be without knowing how to get there.

"It's further south," the elevator attendant told her as they descended to the street. When they got to Time Square they gaped at the billboards, their frosty breath swirling between them as they talked and slowly the sky grew darker while the streets became more alive with the mosaic of colored lights and flashing images. They never quite figured out where the ferry to Liberty Island was, so they promised each other to do it again, soon—but they never would make it back there.

They had no idea that the landscape of their world was changing as slowly as drops of water from a leaky faucet, collecting drop by drop, working its way into a trickle that would soon become the destructive force of a flood. They simply made their way back to the parking garage wanting nothing more than to be together, no thoughts of how that could continue.

"I drive," Alexandros said.

"It's not like East End, you know. You have a license?"

"No."

"Oh. Well, uh-okay."

"Is okay, Sarah. I drive good."

Alexandros pulled the map from the back seat and turned the overhead light on. He opened the giant paper between them, the ripped parts flapped down onto Sarah's lap.

"We don't need the map," she told him, "I can read the signs and get to the tunnel."

Alexandros was remembering his first month in the U.S. and wanted to find his way to the place he had stayed with the Greek shops and restaurants.

What he really wanted was to walk with her in his own village. He wanted to show her how the sunlight pierced the rocks of the mountain, how the wild rosemary and oregano grew randomly along the path filling the air with their fragrance. He wanted to open the gate in the stone wall and welcome her into his yard with the enchanting scent of lemon and orange blossoms. He wanted to sit with her on the ridge above the well and show her the valley below—to walk with her along the river, its running waters mixing with the melody of the songbirds overhead. And when the snow begins to fall, to sit within the warmth of the little house, adding wood to the fire. He wanted to feed her warm bread from the oven and olives he collected from the trees and slices of soft cheese made from the milk of his father's goats. He wanted her to sip the red wine made from the grapes that hung on the vine in the summer months—so plump with sweetness that their weight would pull the vine low enough for her to reach up and grab a bunch as they sat at the table in the courtyard.

But he would settle for showing her Astoria, Queens instead. It was the place he had stayed while he was waiting for Minos to finish with his immigration papers—very unlike his own village but it could give Sarah a tiny glimpse of Greece, and he so wanted to share his world with her, to coax her across that bridge that remained between them.

Alexandros shook his head.

"No, Sarah. Different place we go. Is close but is no in the city."

*   *   *   *

They found their way to Astoria and Sarah began to taste the awkwardness of being a stranger in a foreign land. On the bustling streets she tried to make out the words on the signs but they were so different from English, she couldn't seem to crack the code behind the strange symbols, so she had to rely on Alexandros, who felt that heavy shift in reliance and quite liked it. Sarah watched him closely. He spoke in his language to different shop owners, smiling, sometimes laughing. She'd never seen him so talkative, and with such animation and confidence.

As they walked past a newspaper stand, one of the headlines caught Alexandros' eye but Sarah could only search the photo.

"Problem with Turkey," he said and he picked up the paper and handed the man standing there a few coins.

He talked with the vendor for a while. Alexandros' hands darted back and forth, accentuating whatever it was he was saying and the newspaper seller began spitting words at Alexandros at a volume that made Sarah cringe. Then the two men hugged each other as they continued talking, their noses almost touching, and then they parted and Alexandros was at Sarah's side again.

"My village," he tried to explain, "his sister marry my village."

"Oh."

"I know sister's husband."

It was an incredible thought that there in the outskirts of New York City, one of the biggest cities in the world, Alexandros had just met a friend from home—thousands of miles away.

"What a coincidence," Sarah thought, *"What are the chances?"*

But the chances were much better than she realized. Though Greece was a small country, its largest export was men. A random conversation in a city far from home could change a stranger into a friend.

Sarah and Alexandros walked a bit more until they came to a row of restaurants along the boulevard. As they turned a corner, Alexandros recognized the area, one door in particular, so he pushed it open and they went inside. The air was filled with cigarette smoke and bits of conversation floating among clinks of glassware and the clatter of silverware. After they were ushered to a table, Alexandros spoke to the waiter, making small talk before he ordered two drinks and looked at Sarah.

"We try ouzo. Is strong but is Greek."

The waiter said something to Alexandros in Greek and they laughed.

"He says too strong for woman." Alexandros nodded. "Is true. Too strong for woman and for man." He smiled. "But you try, okay?"

The waiter was a bald man who looked to be about fiftyish with a belly pushing against his starched white shirt, testing the strength of the two buttons midway from his belt. He disappeared for a few minutes and returned with a small round tray balancing so perfectly on the outstretched fingers of his right hand that it might have been an appendage that had grown from his fingertips. Two glasses with a clear liquid, sat on top of the tray's surface. The waiter placed each on the table and stepped back a few paces, curious to see the outcome of their first sip.

Alexandros and Sarah took their glasses, oblivious to their waiter who was saying something to another waiter as he passed. That caused the other waiter to slow his pace as he kept his eye on Sarah. Alexandros and Sarah brought their drinks gently against each other in a toast, as Sarah said, "Cheers," at the exact moment Alexandros said "gia mas — to our health." Neither understood the other's words but both felt the same sensation as the first sip entered their mouths. Sarah closed her eyes tightly as she received the full impact.

The air around her had been sweet and warm, the background chatter adding to the warmth but as that first sip passed between her lips, that warmth turned to a raging fire, the ouzo searing her tongue as it burned its way down her throat sending flames up into her nostrils and out into the restaurant air.

She felt sure she could feel each micro-movement of the liquid as it slid into the depths of her body. Was that the esophagus she felt? And then the stomach, the duodenum—was it already flowing into the intestines? She saw the diagram of the digestive system on the classroom wall—the biology class she'd failed last year—that same class probably having been in session earlier that day—and she thought of Mr. Reid and his droning voice. Now, if he would just add a glass of ouzo with that lesson, those kids might remember it a little better.

Alexandros was laughing as he poured water into her glass, changing the ouzo to a milky liquid and cutting its potency. He wiped away a tear that was rolling down her cheek.

"I'm on fire! What are you trying to do, poison me or something?"

They both laughed so hard, they didn't notice the onlookers grinning from afar.

After a few minutes, the waiter brought a plate and placed it between them. Alexandros named the unusual food as he lifted a forkful, reached across the table and brought it to Sarah's mouth. Sarah accepted the fork, pulling it between her lips, the mixture on her tongue, a warm melody of taste.

"Mm," she sighed and closed her eyes. Alexandros felt her satisfaction and his was equaled by her gaze, her eyes sleepily opening as the tip of her tongue moved across her bottom lip, leaving its wet trail.

The waiter continued to bring dishes of food and they barely noticed him as the savory flavors continued to pass between them.

Afterwards, it was time for bouzouki.

"You must hear it—is best music!" Alexandros was so excited to have this chance to share his village music with Sarah.

The club was only a few doors away. They made their way through the cold night air, but the ouzo protected them from its frosty bite. As they entered, Alexandros watched Sarah's face, the whine of the clarinet wafting toward her from the makeshift stage near the bar where the clarinet player stood. The bouzouki player sat on a bar stool next to him and strummed his instrument with his eyes closed as if his fingers were caressing a woman's body.

To Sarah it sounded like a long grating noise, somewhat like her high school band when the wind instruments were tuning up, but Alexandros kept looking at her in anticipation, watching for some kind of rapt expression to reflect what he thought sure she must be feeling, as was he. He eyed her carefully and noted the beginning of those odd facial movements he sometimes saw her make.

Oh no.

There it was again — that look, the one she'd always have in the restaurant kitchen when she had to serve the crabs. She hated their smell and she said so each time their aroma slid into her nostrils while she struggled to lift the tray to her shoulder. It was that same look, the crunched tip of her nose, the eyebrow line that pulled tightly together. Alexandros was watching her carefully.

Before she could turn to him with that expression, he grabbed her and pulled her onto the dance floor, breaking into a circle of dancers. A woman next to her, detached herself from the shoulder she'd been holding and reattached herself to Sarah's shoulder, as she and Alexandros seamlessly became part of the dance circle. Sarah watched his feet and did her best to follow. It didn't help her much that she was still feeling the effects of the ouzo. Step sideways, kick back, kick forward, oops — sorry about that! Giggle — try again — step sideways, kick — ouch.

She kicked the woman next to her as often as she kicked Alexandros but neither seemed to care. Everyone was laughing and drinking and dancing. The line of dancing bodies moved around the club but there were other dancers also. Men with men, women with women, some gyrating like belly dancers while groups of people encircled them, clapping and throwing money — dollar bills floating to the floor like autumn leaves. And then plates! One by one, waiters delivered armfuls of plates to people who then threw them onto the dance floor — shards of glass everywhere.

Afterwards, breathlessly they walked back to the car. Alexandros took the driver's seat and navigated through the streets under the elevated train tracks. A train came rumbling loudly overhead, its sparks flickered along the rails, moving quickly as its cars — one by one — blended into the buildings, the train vanishing into darkness as if it had never been there.

The Impala pulled out from under the trestle and onto Grand Highway. Sarah pointed to a sign. "That's the way upstate, where my family lives."

"Your family?"

"Yes."

"Your village?"

"Yeah."

"Under the mountain."

"That's right."

"We go there. Maybe next week. Is far?"

"It's too far. I can't go back."

"We go back. I drive you. Minos says okay."

"No, Alexandros. I um." She thought the darkness of the car hid her sadness but Alexandros understood her; he had learned to hear emotion when the words were unreachable.

"Come here." He put his arm out toward her and she slid next to him. "Tell me, please. I want to know," he said.

So she told him about what she and Karen Marie had seen and heard. He understood most of it and said nothing. After a few hours, they stopped for coffee at a diner close to an exit. Sarah looked around.

"This is where I stopped with my parents on the way down. I had no idea, then." She shook her head.

"Your friend. She's good. You call her tomorrow."

"Yeah, okay." But she knew she wouldn't. There were too many words Alexandros wouldn't understand; she couldn't explain what she barely understood herself. Instead she pulled a weathered photo from her bag.

"My best friends," she said.

Alexandros took it and looked closely. "Who's the other girl?"

Sarah laughed. "That's not a girl. He just has long hair. That's Oscar. He's in the army now."

A boy for a best friend—that was a new idea. He wasn't sure he understood. Was Sarah promised to someone, as was he?

"You love him?"

"I thought I did, until I met you." She smiled.

Alexandros said the phrase over and over again in his head: "*I thought I did, I thought I did.*" That was how he remembered it when he found Cousin Roula the next morning in her kitchen and asked her what it meant.

CHAPTER 12

Andreas sat on the passenger side of George's car with one foot on the dashboard and his knee pressed against the window, his hand examining the rip in his jeans, thinking about the day his father had wrestled him to the blacktop weeks before. He'd gone to the place in the city—they called it a half way house. Half way to what? He had stayed only a few days before his friend, Bakus, had come and picked him up. The weeks after that were a bit of a blur—until his father came and found him in Astoria. Now he sat silently as his father drove the car east.

"He could have taken me," George thought. He looked over at Andreas and then back through the windshield, *"that day in the parking lot. It would have been easy for him to get away—but it was nothing to wrestle him into the car. I'd thought it was a good sign. I'd thought he wanted help—it seemed that way. Maybe the city was too far. This time will be different."*

The Southampton place would be better. It was expensive, but that only meant it would work—it would be a place that would give him the son he dreamed of.

George spoke. "It'll be good Andreas. You'll get what you need there. It'll feel good to be clean. And I'll be nearby."

Andreas said nothing.

A few weeks before, after George had pulled Andreas from the hotel room, after the attack on Sarah—he'd realized how far his son had fallen. He knew something had changed, something in Andreas had come undone and he'd thought the halfway house in the city would be a good idea. What do you do when you see your child unraveling? It's easier to look at other families—easier to judge them and their children. But your own? First you look away—it's a reflex—like blinking your eye when a sharp object comes toward you. But after the days become months and then years, you're not dealing with a little boy anymore, and by then, the wall between you and him seems unbreakable.

Minos had recommended the halfway house in the city but George wondered now as he looked over at his son if that suggestion had been more of a means to hide the mistakes he'd made. After all, it was Minos who had convinced George to marry his sister, Minos who had brought him over to Greece for the wedding—Minos who seemed to want to distance Andreas from the hotel. But George had agreed without much forethought, so maybe he also found it painful to watch his mistakes unfold day after day.

"Listen," George said quietly, "I get it. I suck as a father. But I know what you're going through. It's hard to uh—well, the pain is um—" Andreas let his father struggle for a few more seconds.

"Yeah. You do suck," he said, "and if you know it, why did you take me from my mother?"

"You don't remember that place," George said. Andreas' words were a direct hit to an open wound. "You're my son. I couldn't leave you there. I wanted you to have a better life."

"Yeah? Good job. It's been great."

It was easy for Andreas to romanticize the life he hadn't known, the vague memory in the village and of a doting mother, Madonna herself, and other people, lots of them who he'd built into his own reality of the past—all of them loving him. A place of sun and trees with a house—a home!

He let his leg fall hard to the floor of the car and his thoughts spilled from his mouth. "You can drive me to Southampton, drive me to California for all I care. But I'm not staying. I want my mother. I want to see her."

He knew her voice. They'd spoken over the years on the telephone. But her face was faded. He wasn't sure anymore if he was remembering *her* or the photo of the wedding that he'd seen at Uncle Minos' house. He knew that she had come back to East End and tried to live there again. He didn't remember it, but he knew about it because George had told him a thousand times, as he told him then again in the car as they drove.

"Your mother abandoned you," he said. "She could have stayed here." George's voice grew louder. "We could have been a family. It's her! Not me." He was almost shouting now, "You were just a little kid. She left you here with me. If she wanted you, she'd be here right now." His voice cracked a bit. "Get it? We *were* together. I needed her too—she left." His voice became softer. "We both wanted her—we both needed her." He didn't trust himself to speak anymore. "End of story," he said quietly.

But the words cut hard into Andreas. He thought of Bakus. He'd call him and get him to come out.

They remained silent for the rest of the ride. When George pulled into the circular driveway of the Southampton Rehabilitation Center, there was an attendant waiting. He opened the car door and Andreas looked back at his father. Something in the boy's eyes, caused George to say, "I'll go get your mother. I'll bring her here myself. Stay here and you'll have her by your side in a few days. I promise. Okay?"

They both knew his promises meant nothing, but Andreas took it and held it.

"Okay," he answered.

*   *   *   *

Minos arranged with a friend in Athens to pay for a ticket to New York. Both he and George were together in the restaurant office when he called his sister. It didn't go quite as well as they'd planned but at least she was coming. So Minos arranged to have that friend in Athens meet her at the airport with her ticket. It was settled.

"Someone needs to pick her up at JFK, the day after tomorrow," Minos said to George. He had no desire to spend two hours in the car with his sister's wrath, driving back to East End. "I can't do it, George. You'll have to."

George was thinking the same and decided that having his son as a buffer would be good for Andreas as well as for Dina. And when he told his son the news, he was pleased at his reaction. Two days at the facility and he already looked happier, though still a little pale and glassy-eyed. Well—it was certainly costing him enough. He thought of his own struggle at trying to get sober. He had expected his son to suffer some kind of withdrawal, as he had. But perhaps, drugs were different than alcohol. It seemed to be easier.

"Well, some kids just need to get away from their environment," the manager told him as they walked from the outdoor pool into the game room, looking for Andreas who sat with his visitor—his good friend Bakus.

"I guess you're right."

George handed him the final check, much of his savings; he'd have to put off the plan for that little bait and tackle store. But everything else was finally falling into place. His son would get well. He would have the boy he had dreamed of. Maureen was patient and willing to help—she'd even suggested using the money they'd saved for the store, which meant she'd need to continue working for Minos in the hotel. George was lucky to have her; he knew that and everything else was falling into place. He'd have Maureen and he'd have his son. Dina would see the wisdom of living in America. She'd visit, have some time with Andreas, and return to Greece satisfied that George was a wonderful father. He was ready for the *happily-ever-after*.

*   *   *   *

Bakus pulled out the plastic card and cut the powder on the glass coffee table as he sat on the floor between it and the sofa.

"Did you lock the door?" Andreas asked him. "The other residents just walk in and out of your room like it's theirs or something. No respect, man."

"I checked it already. It's okay. So I'll drive you to the airport. Don't worry about it."

"Father? My ass. He can't even meet her with me." Andreas took the rolled up dollar bill from his friend and there was a knock on the door.

"Oh shit. Just help me take the table into the bathroom."

The two carried the coffee table and squeezed it between the toilet and the shower and pulled the bathroom door closed. Then Andreas went to the bedroom door, opened it a sliver and peeked into the hallway.

"Oh man, you gave me a heart attack." He pulled the young girl into the room.

Helen was one of the residents. She made no effort to hide her countenance as she crunched her eyebrows together and looked from Andreas to Bakus and back to Andreas again.

"Listen—I just saw something on T.V. in the rec room—about a plane crash—from Greece, I think. I'm just saying—'cause I know your mother's coming."

"No man, she's in the air already," Andreas answered.

"It happened last night."

"No way." Andreas stared at her for a second blinking wildly, the air in the room becoming warm—too warm. "What else, Helen? From where in Greece? Athens? Tell me."

Helen shook her head, "I'm not sure. I think—"

But Andreas didn't wait. He ran out of the room and down the hall to the common area.

Another resident, a young man around Andreas' age, lying on the couch in the rec room said, "No—it was Italy, from Rome, I think. Helen doesn't know her ass from her elbow."

"What airline?"

"TWA—but it was definitely Italy. I was thinking, when I heard it, I was thinking about—I backpacked through Italy a few years ago. I'm positive it was Italy. Don't worry, man. Your mother is okay."

But Andreas could not relax.

"Let's go now," he said to Bakus. "We can hang around the airport."

"The plane doesn't get in for another couple of hours," Bakus said.

"I don't care. Let's go. It'll take time to get there anyway. Come on."

The car radio repeated the report. "TWA flight zero-twenty-one, from Rome. A bomb. Muslim terrorists. Two hundred and forty-nine passengers dead."

Andreas' heart was racing. "It's the same flight number." He was holding the paper George had given him. *TWA Flight 021. 7:30 JFK.* "But she's coming from Athens."

"Don't worry, man. They use the same numbers for different

flights. It happens all the time. I mean, like how many numbers are there, right? They have to keep using the same ones. It'll be okay."

Bakus parked the car and they went into the terminal. It would be too early to get information on the flight's arrival time, but to their surprise, the arrival screen had that flight on it. TWA from Athens to Rome to New York and it was flashing red with a message to see an attendant at the TWA desk, but there were already teary-eyed people talking to the attendant and then being led to a room, and the door closed.

George was at the rehab center looking for his son. He'd heard the news and had rushed to be with Andreas but he was already gone. He walked back and forth in the little apartment like a caged animal and then went into the bathroom to throw some water on his face. But he couldn't open the door all the way because of the glass table and what was that white powder on it?

Oh no.

The attendant said Andreas had gone to pick his mother up at the airport. George raced to his car and got in behind the steering wheel. He turned the knob and clicked on the radio as he put the key into the ignition. He could barely hear the newscaster above his own yelling.

"We put her on that plane! We did this!"

He was thinking of his conversation with Minos, about their decision to make that call to Greece to convince her to come. Again, they had steered her life into the headwinds of a storm, but this time instead of a loveless marriage, instead of the loss of her son, they had taken her life. He pounded on the steering wheel again and again, the blast of the newscaster in the background. He had been driving west on the parkway, passing exit after exit before his rant, his repentance that he'd been emptying out into the car, subsided and he was left with the scratchy blast of the AM radio. The words of the newscaster hit him like punches and he winced as he began to listen.

"Muslim terrorists, Islamic extremists, believed to have been targeting . . . their motive still unclear."

Unclear.

George thought of his father, Dimi, and so much was still unclear. Those wild winds of discontent created as religions clashed, pulling the unsuspecting bystanders into their spinning vortex. Those were the winds that had yanked his father's family into their destructive path and landed his father, Dimi, alone in America. And now they had taken his son's mother. He knew Andreas would never recover from this blow. It was an illness without a remedy.

Is that who those terrorists were? Little boys trying to plug the bleeding of their own souls, used like pawns in a game with no end. George knew Andreas was already at a boiling point. If they had lived in a different part of the world, would this new pain claw at him in such a way that he would be able to take a gun, wear a guerrilla uniform, pledge allegiance to any deity in the name of avenging his mother, or for the chance to transfer his pain to another, hoping to lessen his own?

George realized his speed and eased the gas pedal up a bit, slowing the landscape that passed in the side windows. He continued on to his destination: JFK airport. But he would not find Andreas there nor would he find him in East End when he returned. He wouldn't see Andreas again until he arrived at the Southampton police precinct the next morning.

At the same time, Yianni was opening the gate to the goat shed high above Exohorio. The animals ran free, jumping over the stones and climbing higher to where the bushes hugged the stone wall.

"Come on. Out you go, you little devils."

He walked to the side of the goat shed to fill the dogs' water dish from the rain barrel that sat against the wall of cinderblocks.

"Yianniiii!" A woman's voice called up the mountainside. "Whoaaa Yianniii!"

"Yes, I hear you. I'm coming down."

As he approached the path to the house, he heard what sounded like the screeching of a cat, but he wasn't sure. And the sight of the taxi—the one he'd sent Dina to Athens in the day before, put him off guard. It was parked, almost touching the side of the house, completely blocking the dirt path.

"Hmm—he didn't waste any time coming to collect the goats," Yianni thought, "he'd risk his taxi on these roads to pick up animals?"

Yianni was wondering how the driver expected to transport goats in a taxi when suddenly the man came from the other side of the gate toward him.

"My friend," Yianni began, "I don't know how you'll get goats into a taxi, but—"

He heard commotion inside the house, and the long whining sound continued but it was not a cat; it was someone crying—Dina's mother, maybe.

The taxi driver was speaking to him as Yianni pushed through the gate and made his way to the house. "Sir, your wife—I tried; it just wasn't enough time. I didn't want to leave her there. I tried to help her get another flight."

As Yianni walked into the sitting room, he saw that it was *not* Dina's mother he had heard. Dina, herself, eyes red, sat crying into the shoulder of Maria as her mother sat on the other side of her, holding her hand.

"What happened?" Yianni asked.

"We didn't make it." Dina wiped the tears from her eyes with the back of her sleeve. "I tried to call Minos, but the number you gave me is wrong."

"That was for inside America, Dina."

She pointed to the taxi driver, "I know you tried to help, Cocho," she sniffled. After their long journey to and from Athens, Dina and the taxi driver had become friends.

Dina turned to Yianni, "Cocho talked to the lady at the airport. She said I needed ten thousand drachmas to change the ticket."

Cocho said, "The next flight wasn't until tomorrow morning. I didn't know what to do. I knew I couldn't leave her in Athens alone. So here she is—no charge."

"Nonsense. You did much more than was asked of you. Thank you, my friend."

It was decided that Cocho would take them back down the mountain in his taxi to make the call to Minos. He needed to know not to meet his sister at the airport—though everyone realized, by the time they would get to the post office to make the call, Minos would have been to the airport already and would be wondering why Dina wasn't on the plane. No doubt, he might be making his own phone call to them, before they had a chance to get down there.

Yianni could not console Dina, no matter what he said.

"You'll go a different time. Next week. Your brother will get another ticket. Don't worry."

"Oh no. You don't understand. My baby. He thinks I've left him again. He won't understand. He's a child."

"He's a man, Dina. He'll understand."

But Andreas did not understand as he emerged from that awful room at the airport where he'd been told about the crash. Hours had passed since they'd entered that door and joined the others, some with blank cold faces. One woman screamed and fell limp at his feet and he heard the rush of shoes across shiny tiles reaching for her, but he did not move. How could it be that his mother was dead? It was not penetrating, not getting in.

They were going to be a family! He could have talked her into staying this time. He could have helped her with the language. The picture was still bright, the one he'd created piece by piece since the moment he'd heard she was coming. He could see them together in an apartment in Astoria, in a Greek neighborhood, near a Greek market and a Greek church, so she could be with her own kind and be happy. He'd get a job and take care of her while she stayed home and cooked. He could smell the pastichio warming in the oven. He could see himself sitting at the kitchen table with her, reading the newspaper and laughing and eating pastichio.

"Hey ma, look at this!" That's what he'd say, "Hey ma." Like they did on television, and then they would laugh. And she would say, "Oh you." And she'd rustle his hair.

He hadn't realized he'd been crying until Bakus spoke.

"That's rough, man. I'm really sorry. Let's get out of here. There's nothing you can do."

They left the room and Andreas was just staring up at the arrivals board, the red flashing line: *See TWA representative for information*. And suddenly he noticed the bulbs flashing and a fat microphone was put in his face.

"Did you lose a loved one, sir?" The reporter asked.

"What?"

Bakus grabbed Andreas around the shoulder and pulled him through the crowd of reporters.

"Sir, did you have someone on the plane?" A few reporters were following them, "Sir? How do you feel about it being Muslims terrorist? Sir?"

They'd made it out the door into the darkness of night and were crossing the road to the parking garage when it suddenly hit Andreas.

Terrorists? Muslim?

"Like those fucking Turks at the gas station," he thought. He suddenly saw the dark eyes of those men at the gas pump, especially that older one.

"That one takes my money like he's doing me a favor"

"What?" Bakus asked.

"Nothing."

He pulled away from Bakus and said, "Yeah, let's get back to East End. Forget about Southampton. I'm done there."

The gritting of his teeth replaced his tears. *"Those Turks – Muslims – they killed my mother – and that kid, always hanging around the hotel looking for Sarah. He thinks he's some kind of Casanova or something; I'll wipe that motherfucker's face with the road."*

As they got in the car, Bakus pulled a small plastic bag from the glove compartment.

"Here man. Grab the rolling papers from the side pocket. Roll yourself one. It'll help you relax."

Andreas thought of the gas station again. "I don't want to relax. Got anymore coke?"

"Yeah. Better idea for staying awake to drive. Let's just stop off in Astoria, first. I got a friend there who can hook us up."

Hours later, they left the city behind in the early morning haze after midnight and on that last stretch of highway, they were alone; no cars had passed them for miles. Andreas held a magazine under Bakus' chin once more, as Bakus gripped the steering wheel with one hand and snorted white powder from the flat surface of the cover. The car weaved onto the grass median and then back again to the asphalt.

"Whoa, man!" Andreas screamed, "we're flying!" And they both laughed.

The sun was up when they drove into town and finally pulled into the gas station. Bakus expected to fill up his tank as Andreas had suggested. Kareem's father, Amir, walked around the front of the car to talk to the driver as Andreas pushed the handle inside the door, kicked it open and got out.

"Good morning, boys," Amir said with a smile that quickly

drooped into a straight line as he saw the young man coming around the car toward him, but he was unable to say anything more before the first blow sent him over the front of the car. He hit against the windshield, snapping off the wiper as he grabbed at it blindly trying to keep his footing before he rolled to the cement. As he lay there stunned, the white rubber half moon on the tip of Andreas' sneaker came toward his eyes as if it were happening with the slow flicker of an old motion picture rolling out of a projector, frame by frame—the halting blink of a strobe. Amir instinctively grabbed for the incoming foot but instead heard the snap of his bone as it tore free from the skin in his arm sending an electric jolt up to his shoulder blade. The last blow he felt was the crash against his temple just before the morning light of East End turned gray and he was sent floating above the Esso sign of his gas station, slowly passing the dunes until he sailed outward over the ocean.

Amir was a motionless particle trapped in the clouds. It confused him to watch the land recede into the background. If he were on his way to paradise, wouldn't the pain have subsided, the burning pressure of his arm and shoulder, the pounding spasms in his head? And should he be able to watch such a retreat, to linger in both worlds and long so desperately for his mortal life? He lay within the whiteness of the clouds for time unmeasured, until the mountains of Turkey were surrounding him and his broken body lay in a pasture. The cool wet grass soothed the burning in his limbs but he was pinned down like a paper doll. He thought to sit up and look around. It's what he wanted to do very much and he tried to send that thought to his extremities but nothing moved.

There, from the corner of his visual field came the faces of two shepherds. They looked with curiosity at him until one opened his eyes wide with recognition and said something to the other but Amir could not understand. Their words were like two stones hitting together underwater. The one who had recognized Amir extended his hand and Amir tried to lift his arm up to meet it but the arm was as heavy as an iron girder. So the old shepherd kneeled next to him and took Amir's hand, sliding his own into it and clasping it tightly and Amir suddenly knew it was the hand of his grandfather, the man who had helped his Christian neighbors escape the labor camp. He recognized him from the old crumpled photo his older brother kept in his wallet and he recognized him from his own son's face—the shepherd's namesake—his American son, Kareem. Those were the eyes of his son hovering over him, looking with concern from within the depths of his grandfather's gaze.

The other shepherd came around to Amir's other side to help lift him. His smile pulled to the side where a scar ran from his ear to his jaw. He looked at Amir as if they were old friends, but Amir could not have known him. It was Dimi—the grandfather that Andreas had never known, and he was trying to aid the other shepherd, to help Amir, to somehow repay a debt and to erase an injustice. There was no way for Amir to know that he had been beaten by the grandson of that man who was holding him gently, looking at him lovingly, a man who had survived to live a life, to come to America the way that Amir's father had done, to build a family, and to continue that link in the chain that connected them all—a chain unbroken.

Amir lay cemented to the wet pasture grass—the pain racking his body—staring up at them as his head rested in the sweet warmth. He watched the men calling to someone as they beckoned with their hands. The aroma of freshly baked bread wafted over him as he stared past them at the sea-blue sky and the small puffs of cotton-clouds gliding by. He closed his eyes for a moment, just to rest, just for a second and when he opened them, an old woman had joined the men. The three were talking like birds chirping, looking at each other and nodding. She stroked Amir's cheek and looked at the other two men. Their lips moved, sounds emerged, but he could not understand. They were conferring, discussing, analyzing and then they seemed to come to a decision. The old woman said something to Amir's grandfather. He nodded in agreement and then the three retreated leaving Amir to stare up into the sky. Amir waited. Surely there was more to this—some shining light to lift him from the pain, an all-knowing deity to guide him further, the choral songs of the departed. He waited for at least the shepherds to return but they did not. So, what had his life been about? Had it simply been an exercise in survival—no end reward, nor punishment? Simply days of random actions, countless faces. Was this his end, then?

He thought about what he had left behind, what he'd be remembered for and all he felt was regret. He lay there for hours, maybe days—centuries, until finally the light grew dim and his world dark.

CHAPTER 13

Cousin Roula, did not know the English language perfectly but she knew enough to explain to Alexandros what it meant when someone said: *I thought I did.* After leaving Sarah, he had said the phrase over and over again until he fell asleep with the words still sitting on his lips. It was the first thing he thought of when he came into the kitchen and saw his cousin making coffee. As Roula explained the words to Alexandros, Kareem was at the boarding house getting into Sarah's Impala, throwing his backpack at his feet on the car floor. Sarah had been driving him to town as they continued their routine, and on this day they had decided to go out for breakfast before Sarah headed to work and Kareem to school. After Sarah parked in a space outside of The Pancake House, she and Kareem went inside and found two seats at the counter, side by side on swiveling red stools. It was an order of blueberry pancakes they were just digging into, Sarah reaching across the counter to stab her fork into the stack on the plate, when they heard the police siren screaming past, and then the ambulance. The customers jumped up, Kareem and Sarah included, and ran to the windows to get a look, though they didn't yet know that the person the rescuers were rushing to help, was Kareem's father, lying beaten unconscious near the gas pumps.

Sarah learned of it from Vicky a short while later as she entered the back door of the kitchen just as George flew past her, knocking her into the door jam, running to his car in the parking lot.

He put the key in the ignition but did not turn it. His head dropped to the steering wheel and a flood of tears emptied into the car with great sobs that shook his shoulders violently.

He remembered the beginning.

When Andreas was born, he'd been filled with hope and grateful for a second chance. He'd tried to be like his own father, Dimi, but they were not at all alike. George could see his wife, Dina — Minos' sister — her pleading eyes. What would she have made of all this? Their marriage had always been a terrible mistake, but through it he'd gotten his son, and that — well, he couldn't regret that for even one second. Andreas was confused; he was lost, but it could all be turned around. George had done it. Andreas could too. George just had to keep him out of jail and get him away from East End — a new start. George thought of his own past and of his *second chance*. There'd been so many opportunities for a family and he'd blown them all. Thank God for Maureen, but if it hadn't been for Stanley Middleground, he'd never have found her.

After George's eviction from the Levitt house, he'd awoken on the sofa in that Southampton summer retreat — the Middleground summer home. That's where Stanley had taken him on that spring afternoon. George remembered the withdrawal from his drunken stupor, the frightening hallucinations that went on for hours — or days, it was impossible for him to know in his broken state. But always there was a soft voice nearby, a gentle touch. When he finally emerged as a sober man, he'd learned that it had been Stanley Middleground's girlfriend, Ruth, who had nursed him. And then it was Stanley who had introduced him to Minos — a diner owner in Southampton. George owed his life to those two kids, Ruth and Stanley, but how had he repaid them? By ruining theirs.

A knock on the car window caused George to look up and see Maureen. She opened the car door.

"Move over. I'm driving. Which police station was Andreas brought to?"

At the very moment she was pulling out onto Main Street to drive to the Southampton Police Station, Oscar — down in South Carolina — was packing his duffle bag on Parris Island. Four full days on leave — plenty of time to get to Owl's Head and see Sarah and then get back to the barracks.

Thirty hours later, as he emerged from the Greyhound bus in Malone and walked into Woolworth's to surprise Karen Marie, it was he who was shocked at the changes that had occurred in the few short months he'd been away. Not only was he surprised to know that Sarah had left, but he was reeling from the news of his mother's return. And when he went to see her, the reunion he'd longed for since the moment she'd disappeared, left him empty — *how could she embarrass him like that? It was so humiliating!* So, he tried not to think about it as he watched the scenery from the car window, fidgeting in his seat, vying for a comfortable position, until he accepted the unlikelihood of such an occurrence in Karen Marie's old car, and he settled into quiet contemplation.

Karen Marie drove toward New York City — knowing their time was running out.

"I have a phone number," she said. "We can just drive to the end of the island. I mean — she told me about it. Like, I know basically where the town is, and the place is called middle-something."

Oscar's head did not turn to look at her; he remained facing the window.

"We'll find her," he said.

*   *   *   *

Mrs. Middleground poured the boiling water over the tea bag that rested at the bottom of the teapot as Sarah took her place at the small fold-up table near the window. She hadn't been able to find Kareem. No one answered the door at his house. The yellow police tape had blocked her from the gas station so she'd returned to the boarding house looking for a reason to visit with Mrs. Middleground to see if she possibly knew anything, but the woman offered nothing.

"I don't know, dear. We'll find out soon enough."

Sarah put the vacuum bags on the floor near her feet and looked at the young fisherman in the frames hanging from the walls. She pretended not to notice the bottles of scotch on the counter.

"Is that your husband?" she asked, nodding her head at the

photo of the bare chested man holding the fish.

"Oh, dear. You don't recognize him? That's George Theodore." She smiled as if she were telling Sarah something as nonchalant as how lovely a morning it was.

"What!? You were married to George? No, wait a minute. Your name is Middleground. I don't get it. Why do you have all these pictures of George?" Her head spun back and forth looking more closely at the photos that she'd seen many times before without ever having looked at them and suddenly she saw the resemblance.

"Who's Stanley then?" She'd seen the mail addressed to *Mrs. Stanley Middleground.*

Ruth Middleground could not have been happier to have someone finally interested in her stories. She brought the teapot over to the table, poured some into Sarah's cup, a little more scotch into her own cup and began:

"Oh Stanley was my husband, God rest his soul—but George is my true love. Close your mouth, dear. Drink your tea. There's plenty more in the pot. You young ones—you don't know. I saw you out there with that Greek. You think you have things figured out? I was only seventeen, myself, back then. Oh boy—his mother gave him quite an earful—Stanley's mother, that is. She was a hard woman, raising those kids alone with her husband travelling all the time—and she knew a bad idea when she heard one; she told him not to get involved—but there was no stopping Stanley when he put his mind to something. And Mr. Theodore—well, George, that is—but back then he was Mr. Theodore to us. He had always been so kind. Stanley probably saw him as a father figure. He was only about seven or eight years older than we were— nothing now, but back then when we were teenagers and he was our teacher—it was an enormous age difference. Well, I sat next to George, wiping him down when he vomited on himself and all over that sofa. And he cried for his mama and carried on for days, sometimes screaming in terror—like he was fighting some terrible demon. But he finally came out of it. Stanley and I had to go back to school, so we left him there in that house—it was the Middleground's summer place—and Minos gave him a job in his diner—that was before he sold it and came out here. Minos never knew anything. He saw this clean hard-working guy who lived in this upscale house and he thought he was getting himself some nice rich Greek for a brother-in-law when he arranged for his sister to come over. Dina was her name. Humph—Dina. More like the Queen of Sheba. She knew about me and George but Stanley didn't—well, not for a long while anyway. And he almost didn't find out. But George—oh yes, George was so much more fun. And a wonderful lover, so gentle. He knew just where to touch me. Now, what's that look for? You think I was always this old and wrinkled. I was a beauty! You just wait and see what time does to those perky little breasts of yours. Here—have some more tea. Nope, I'm not answering any of those darn questions. You just hold your horses and listen. That's the trouble with you kids. Everyone wants to talk. Nobody's listening. Yep, I would drive out there on weekends and we would make love all night and then he'd have to go to work and I would sun myself on the beach—just waiting for him to come back. But then he had to move out here, to East End, before Memorial Day. Stanley's family always went out to the house on Memorial Day so he had to get out of there. I came out here a few times but it was hard for me to get the car—and then Stanley and I got engaged. Don't look at me that way—which one of those boys chasing you are you going to take, or are you going to leave them both crying in the sand? You're not so high and mighty yourself. Anyway, George was right, I had myself a nice Jewish wedding and stuck with Stanley—life is easier if you stick with your own kind. But I saw George once in a while and when I did, I can tell you, that flame burned hotter than any I ever lit in my life—do me a favor, sweetie; go get that bottle over there on the counter—well, even when that little girl came from Greece, Minos' sister that is—I tell you she must have been no more than thirteen or fourteen. George had disappeared for a couple of weeks and then brought her back, and he was drunk as a skunk when they had that welcoming party for her. That's when Minos bought him that nice house here in East End and before you know it, that one is all knocked up, her belly pushed out to here—flaunting it around town and there I was—sleeping with two men—running between our Hicksville house and the family summer place—and I couldn't even get one baby. Oh dear, oh dear. I hated that little girl. She couldn't even speak English the whole time she was here. And when I lost poor

Stanley in the Korean War, do you know what she did? Why, she spit at my feet, right there on Main Street after I'd come out here to get away from all that crying and carrying on—you know how funerals can be—she spit a big glob just like that— unladylike, those Greek women. Well that was it for me. I couldn't go back to Hicksville anyway. My mother-in-law didn't want me around; just between you, me and the lamp post, I think she blamed me for her son's death. It was after he came home on leave and George was standing there in our Hicksville kitchen, no shirt on and a look as guilty as a fox in a henhouse. And Stanley didn't even say a word. He turned around and left, right back down the driveway, George running after him, trying to explain. But what was he going to say? Stanley finally knew exactly what was going on. He went right across town and cried to his mama and then went back to fight without even a goodbye to me. Can you believe it—no goodbye for me? Right after that is when I had my son and I can tell you he looked a lot like that Andreas. I guess that's why I have a soft spot in my heart for that boy. Hand me a tissue, will you? Just give me a second. Hm. Well—I sold everything and came out here and bought this house—It wasn't a boarding house back then. Oh—it was a beautiful house and I bought George that boat he always wanted—even put my name on it so that bitch wife of his would know where she stood. She might've been married to him, but he was mine, and you know, he even spent most nights with me—oh we had a ball. Sometimes, he brought little Andreas with him and our sons would play together in the other room while we made love for hours. Those boys were like brothers—if you know what I mean—and they could've grown up together if she hadn't taken Andreas back to Greece with her for all those years. And then my Stevie—well he was taken from me—terrible accident. I never saw him go down to the lake. Oh, my heart, my heart. I didn't think I'd live through that. His tiny little body floating there. Oh my, my. Give me a second, just a few sips. Oh lord. But life does go on—I can attest to that. Well, I just thought George and I'd be together forever after that. He was such a comfort. But that Irish Mick came along and stole my man. Don't know what he sees in her. I can tell you they don't have the fun we had—I hear he's at those meetings down at the church every week, no matter what. She's really got her thumb on him.

But that boy of his—he still comes to see me. He's a sweetheart, that one. Doesn't like to drink too much but I think he does that other stuff—you young people do—you know. And oh, he's such a good boy, so respectful, a real charmer. You and he'd get along so fine. He is the only—now, what's the matter with you? Sit back down. I'm just getting started. I got lots more—where're you going?

The screen door slammed and Sarah was half way across the yard before she realized she'd forgotten to take the vacuum bags. Kareem was there, under the elm tree. Oh, poor Kareem! Sarah ran to him and put her arms around him, a comforting embrace for a little brother, and she didn't mention the puffiness in his eyes.

"I heard. How is he? What happened?"

Kareem did not answer. He pulled away and looked at her. "Can you give me and my mom a ride to the hospital? My uncle took the car. I guess he didn't think about it—that we'd want to go. But I really gotta see him. I got a bad feeling. I just need to be there. I don't know what happened—a robbery? I don't know. Why didn't he use his gun?"

"Uh, Kareem, I heard something. Well—I think it was Andreas. I'm not sure but, like a lot of people were talking about it and well, George took off—someone said he was going to the police station."

"Huh?" Kareem looked at her, his mouth agape, his head shaking slowly from side to side, "what are you talking about? Andreas?"

"That's what I heard. He attacked your father—I don't know why."

"No way. Andreas is in the city, in rehab. That's where he went after he fought with you. But maybe—you, Sarah—if you'd gone to the police, if you'd told them he attacked you, then—" He sighed loudly. "Why didn't you go? He would've been locked up."

"No, I don't think so Kareem."

"Yes! Why did he attack you? Maybe he was high or something. Maybe he was crazy on drugs—that happens, you know. I've heard about it. That's probably why he attacked my father. Definitely. You should've gone to the police, Sarah." His voice was loud enough to cause the curtains on the trailer to part and Mrs. Middleground's face appeared in the window.

"You can still go. It doesn't matter. You gotta tell them. He did the same thing to you — tell them Sarah!"

"Go home, Kareem. I'll pick you up in five minutes. Calm down and go."

Kareem and his mother were waiting at the end of the driveway when Sarah picked them up at their house. All three sat in the front seat of the blue Impala, Kareem sandwiched between the two women. He'd never had Sarah quite that close. His knee rested on hers — the outsides of their thighs were completely welded together and the heat of her shoulder pressed into him. Kareem wished the thirty-minute ride were longer, but he thought of his father and yearned to be with him. His guilt repelled his desire like opposing ends of a magnet.

His mother put her hand on his and he looked up at her. She smiled. The two women were alike, he thought. Sarah could convert to Islam. It was a small change to make for love. His head swiveled between them. Yes — they were very much alike, he thought.

Sarah sat next to Kareem in the waiting room. Kareem's uncle stood up and began to walk restlessly between the window and the chairs. He sat for a few minutes and then paced again, the muscles of his face pulled tightly together. Sarah wanted to comfort Kareem. As he put his head down into his hands, she spoke softly to him and rubbed his back gently until Kareem's uncle stood up abruptly and went to his sister-in-law and told her he would drive them home. He did not want that American girl there. It was all done in Turkish so Sarah had only the slightest idea that the plea from Kareem's mother was not her own as she was told to leave the waiting room. It was a family matter, and they'd rather deal with it as such — with family only. Kareem remained silent.

*   *   *   *

It was late and Sarah was tired when she returned to the boarding house and parked under the elm, so she didn't notice the red car on the street until Alexandros got out and called her name.

"Sarah. You okay?"

The sight of Alexandros warmed her. He came up into the yard.

"Sarah." He walked closer with outstretched arms and she instinctively slid into them as he enveloped her and brought his head down to her hair, encasing her like a capsule with his body. The fit was perfect.

"Sarah. You okay?"

She turned her head up to see him and her lips brushed his chin as they came to rest on his mouth. Without hesitation, with one smooth fluid movement, he felt her lips on his and devoured her hungrily until she pulled away with a breathless gasp for air.

After the interpretation of "*I thought I did*," Alexandros had analyzed Sarah's statement a hundred times in his head; "*I thought I did until I met you.*" And he'd tried to stay away. But he knew he was weak, not an honorable man at all, and he had admonished himself over and over again as he drove in the car to see her. The words of the poem—they fluttered about in his head knocking into each other like a flock of wild birds in a cage—*the voyage is a long one, don't be afraid—as long as a rare excitement stirs your spirit and your body.* And her reaction, just then, the expression on her face when she'd looked up and seen him there—it had erased any of his doubts, completely obliterating the last speck of self-control that might have been lingering.

"I'm fine now," Sarah smiled at him, "Come in the house."

Sarah closed her bedroom door behind them and said, "Make yourself comfortable," as she held her hand out toward the bed.

"Make what? What I make?"

"Just—that means, um—just sit down, Alexandros."

"No more English." Alexandros walked over to her slowly, "Now, I teach you Greek."

He held her head with one hand and put his other hand at the small of her back. Then, he brought his lips gently to her eyes, kissing each one, feeling the flutter of her lashes as soft as the wings on a butterfly and he whispered, "*mati.*" Then, slowly his lips brushed over her nose; "*miti,*" he whispered with another gentle kiss as though he were afraid to break the glass doll he held in his arms. And then he moved slowly to her mouth, "*stoma.*" And he kissed her hard, a deep groan escaping from his throat.

"Leimos," his lips swept hungrily down her neck, his arm holding her steady as she swayed on her feet. His other hand felt the smoothness of her shoulder as he slid it over her blouse and to the front buttons, unbuttoning one and then another, while his lips brushed over her collarbone. Sarah, eyes closed, took air into her lungs with quick short breaths, feeling his lips move against her skin. Her heart banged against her chest as her blouse fell to the floor. Alexandros stepped slowly toward the bed, guiding her backwards, momentarily fumbling with the clasps on her bra, until her head met the pillow and she disappeared into vapor, his hand cupping her breast, his fingers caressing her nipple.

* * * *

Mrs. Middleground had fallen asleep in her chair waiting for the red car to leave. But she was startled awake, not by the sun that had just begun to rise, but by the crash of glass and when she lifted her head she saw the Turk's son swinging a bat. Or was it a crowbar? It was some kind of heavy object, and then there was another crash into the windshield of the red car. She moved the lace curtain to get a better look just as he reached into a broken side-window and pulled something out. It looked like a spiral notebook and she watched him roll it up into a tight cylinder and push it down into his back pocket, as she reached for the telephone and began to dial.

CHAPTER 14

Maureen and George had been at the police station all night waiting to see Andreas. It wasn't their first time coming to a police station to find him but it was the first time bail was involved and the first time in such an official building. They were more accustomed to the tiny port police station down near the marina in East End. They wouldn't be able to smooth it over this time with a few cups of coffee or offers of dinner. It would take more than the superficial banter at the sergeant's desk. *Oh, boys will be boys – a bit of graffiti on the school wall – stolen shopping carts from IGA? Yeah, we were young once too.*

The officers in East End were men who came to the restaurant to eat with their wives, who stood in the surf watching their children play in the waves. They were at the high school graduation ceremony, flashing pictures of their own children on the same day that Andreas had received his diploma. They'd shaken George's hand, patted him on the back, congratulated him on a job well done – knowing that he was a father who attended the AA meetings at the Episcopal Church, a father who rescued his son from the clutches of a foreign land – Greece. Was that even a country? And he'd raised that boy alone.

But an assault was different – drug charges and an assault. George knew his son would be going to jail. He just needed to get him out on bail. Just for a few hours. That's all they needed.

"What about your brother?" He looked at Maureen and said what she had already been thinking.

"You're dead to me." That's what Maureen's brother, Michael Jr., had said to her at their mother's funeral last year, and it had been almost ten years since they'd spoken. She'd thought he would have softened after so many years, especially because the rest of the family had. Even her father had forgiven her for moving in with George, *living in sin* — as he had called it.

"With a married man! For God sake, Maureen — you'll not do such a thing and still call yourself an O'Donnell! Do you hear me? I won't stand for it."

Maureen's father, Michael O'Donnell, was as stubborn as moss on the trunk of an oak, but so was she. He'd come over from Ireland as a young man and worked the fishing boats until he'd had the money to build his motel near the marina. It was only ten rooms at first but as more people began to drive farther east looking for affordable vacation spots, he was able to increase its size, and the number of rooms in *Irish Gardens* multiplied as fast as the O'Donnell children. The motel had always meant to be nothing more than a means to make a living and to feed the family. Michael O'Donnell had no grand plans for becoming a rich man — though he considered himself so, as a business owner in America with his rooms to let — open all year round. His oldest child, Michael Jr., his only son, was supposed to take it over when he was old enough but the boy surprised everyone with an intellect that both he and his wife tried to claim, lobbing rationales back and forth like tennis balls — both trying to be the owner of such exquisite genes.

"Ah, that boy has my brains," Mr. O'Donnell would say as he pinned yet another of his son's grade reports to the wooden cabinet with a thumbtack.

"What brains are you talking about Michael O'Donnell?" His wife would counter. "I was just like that, you know. Smart with my numbers and letters. It's true! If only I could have gone to school, you'd see. I'd be *someone* instead of the chief cook and baby maker you've made me."

After all, it was the sixties and Mary O'Donnell was feeling the liberated spirit her daughters brought home, though neither parent had been quite ready for Maureen's nonsense with that Greek heathen working down at the ocean. How had they lost their focus and allowed their youngest to escape the O'Donnell net?

Maureen's four sisters, all one year apart in age, were always busy with their mother, either preparing for the season or cleaning up after it. Their brother, Michael Jr., was spared manual labor so he could keep up with his studies, and he'd soon enough pull far ahead of his sisters with acceptance to that fancy law school in a New York City university. Maureen's father was delegated to winter repairs and the constant maintenance needed for such a property. So by the time little Maureen came along, quite a surprise to her mother in her forties—a full six years after the last—there wasn't much for her to do except look busy and find ways to have some fun. And that was what she was doing the day she met George. She had been marching in the St. Patrick's Day parade, following the green line on the asphalt. It had been painted through the middle of town and continued toward the port until it stopped just short of the bay where the marchers would empty into the pub near the marina.

All over the island, there were parades in little towns from Manhattan to East End but it was the East End parade that drew hundreds to the sea. The parade-goers hoped to brush the dull gray days of winter aside and be reminded by the breeze that swept from the Atlantic into the northern bay, that they needed only to hang on a bit longer before summer would come to rescue them.

Maureen always marched in that parade as a member of one organization or another—depending on her age, but the year she left the O'Donnell fold to live a life of sin, she was a twenty-one-year-old in the ladies auxiliary of East End Fire Department. Stepping in synchronicity with the other ladies, she kept the rhythm of the march, her hips swaying to the beat of the clop—clop—clop of their black heels on the road. She smoothed out her black and white uniform, her head tilted to the side, looking for familiar faces in the crowd, but mostly looking forward, waiting for a glimpse of the pub, ready for the green beer and live country music.

That year, George was at the pub with another woman—Ruth Middleground. Ruth was sitting at the bar and George was part of a large group of tipsy square dancers, pounding the wooden floor as they stomped to the fiddler's beat, changing from one partner to the next, locking arms at the elbow, releasing and continuing on. George had his eye on Maureen from across the room as he did a lopsided *do-si-do* toward her and ended up at her elbow. The fiddler sawed his instrument wildly, sending the square dancers spinning in a different direction but George reached his hand into the crook of Maureen's arm and hooked it tightly, pulling her from the group.

If Ruth Middleground hadn't been sitting with her back to them, her head leaning on the bar, she might have seen the chemistry take hold, the pheromone-laced arrow as cupid struck George between the eyes. She could have pulled him away from that hypnotic moment and no one would have been the wiser. But she wasn't able to do that or anything else and by the time she realized George was slipping away, it was months later and he had already been staying at the Irish Gardens a few nights a week—for how else would Maureen have been able to spend the night with him and have it go unnoticed? In fact, the O'Donnell women thought he was no more than a guest. They knew who he was and that he was Ruth Middleground's beau, but married to a Greek girl who had left him and left East End. But they also knew enough about Ruth Middleground to suspect that George was hiding out from her, probably letting her blow off steam before he went back to his house where she might find him. A lover's quarrel with Ruth Middleground could end up badly, so his presence there at the motel didn't set off the alarm bells that it should have.

When Maureen moved into George's house a few months later, her family was up in arms. Her mother, her father, each of her sister's came to take her back and each left without her. Even Michael Jr. interrupted his work, at the request of his mother, and drove out to East End to bring little Maureen back home.

"I'm a grown woman, Michael!" she'd told her brother, the locked screen door between them.

When he put his fist through it and grabbed the inside door knob, George had him flat on his back, pinned to the porch, the door hanging from one hinge, before he could get hold of Maureen.

"Do I need to call the cops?"

Michael Jr. stood up in a rage, though it wasn't clear whether he was angry over his sister's sinfulness or his injured pride that lay flattened on the porch beside the broken screen door.

George stood between the brother and sister, Maureen behind him and Michael Jr. hitting George's hand away from his chest.

Michael Jr. pointed at Maureen, "If you don't leave here with me now, you are not my sister! I'll never talk to you again."

"Michael." Maureen lifted her head slowly and met his eyes.

She was frightened by the ultimatum but she was as stubborn as the rest of them—and she did not like the alternative. Go back to the motel, change dirty sheets and wait for a marriage proposal from some nice Irish boy. No. She couldn't do it.

"I mean it, Maureen."

And it's true. He did mean it. Even when the rest of the family reconciled, Michael Jr. stayed firm in his declaration. Even when Maureen had tried to embrace him as his eyes watered with the tears of mourning his mother, he had pushed her away.

"You are dead to me."

And now she contemplated calling him and asking him for help with Andreas. He worked in the district attorney's office. He had the influence they needed.

"It's not a good idea." Maureen was answering George. "If we let him know what's going on, there's a better chance he would use his power to hurt you, rather than help. Call Minos, instead."

The phone call was a good one. It bore the fruit they had hoped for.

Andreas was released after Minos provided the money for his nephew's bail. George knew what needed to be done, but whom could he trust?

He drove back to East End with Maureen at his side and Andreas in the back seat. As they passed along Main Street on their way to the restaurant, all three heads turned toward the yellow police tape across the front of the gas station so none noticed Kareem walking through the park on the opposite side of the street, holding the wallet that Andreas assumed he'd left in Bakus' car when he'd discovered it was missing.

Kareem bent down and picked up a dead tree branch lying in the grass. He passed through the play-area and walked between the swings on the swing set, batting wildly at the chains with the branch, sending them into a dancing frenzy as he continued toward the lake. Before getting to the tall willows that lay ahead of him, he took a moment to swing the branch down one more time—hard—onto the metal slide, sending a few sparrows higher into the air. Then he pushed the branch into the crook of his underarm and reached into his pocket to take the photo out, rage bubbling inside him with each new look at Sarah—completely naked. Exposed. He stared, unable to look away from the shining wet form, her expression difficult to read but Kareem could see everything—all of her, uncovered. As he passed by the lake, he threw Andreas' wallet far into the water and watched it sink and then he stuffed the photo back into his pocket and quickened his pace.

He knew Sarah would be just waking up. It was early. He hadn't worked out what he was going to say and if he'd stopped to think about it, he'd have seen how foolish he was acting. Hurt, yes—but outraged? She was not his girlfriend. That had always been clear to both of them.

But he had the die-hard unrealistic expectations as only a fourteen-year-old boy could have. The superhero always gets the girl and if he could have had just a little more time with her, she would have seen the real Kareem. But that photo spoke volumes to him. He'd been competing with the wrong guy. It wasn't that young Greek, Alexandros, at all. And she'd lied to him! That load of crap she'd given him about Andreas attacking her—when all this time she was screwing around with him. The photo was from Andreas' wallet—it was proof. Kareem rounded the bend and saw the boarding house, but he also saw the red car and he stopped dead in his tracks.

He still had the branch in his hand and he was thinking of his father in the hospital. He was thinking of Andreas, the criminal who put him there, and about Sarah's naked body and that Greek—the one who drove the red car, or was it Andreas' car? He didn't stop to sort out his confusion. Sarah was not the person he thought she was. That he knew for sure and he did not like the girl he had seen in the photo.

At first he whispered it to himself as he began walking toward the red car, "whore," quickening his pace to match the angry hammering of his heart.

"Whore!" He launched the word again from his mouth, hoping

to free himself from his thoughts as he took the first swing. The glass was crashing to the street as he continued swinging the branch watching it smash through each of the car windows, the pieces of glass flying haphazardly through the air until one hit just below his bottom lip, cutting into his flesh. He saw the notebook on the floor and reached into the car to grab it. As he picked it up, the torn cover ripped completely off and fell to the seat. He rolled the rest of it up and stuck it in his back pocket. Then he began swinging the branch again. The side mirror crashed to the ground as Mrs. Middleground came slowly down the steps of the trailer. The screen door at the entrance to the boarding house slammed hard against the door jam and Alexandros was running toward him, Sarah behind.

"Whore!" he screamed and he thrust the photo at Alexandros saying, "This is the bitch you're fucking!"

Sarah gasped at the cutting words coming from the one person she had relied on from the beginning, the person she'd thought had cared about her and then she realized what was in Alexandros' hand.

"I've called the police." Mrs. Middleground called from a safe distance.

Sarah found herself unable to breathe as she watched Alexandros look at the picture and then look at her.

Alexandros was not quite sure what the young Turk was saying but he understood the boy's rage. It was natural for him to be jealous, but he was a boy and Sarah needed someone like Alexandros — a man.

But the photo.

Sarah felt Alexandros slipping from her grasp as if she were trying to hold water in a net. But Kareem's twisted face and angry words were frightening her.

"I should have my father's gun, instead of a fucking branch."

He threw it to the street and looked up. His eyes met Sarah's.

"You! I hate you."

Faces were coming to the windows at the Hensen's place. People down the street were walking to the end of their driveways, asking each other what the commotion was, not quite sure if they should venture further toward it.

"I could blow all your fucking heads off! I'm sick of it. I was born here. In this town. Here! I deserve *you!*"

He was looking at Sarah and tears were streaming down his face, a police siren coming closer. Kareem ran toward Mrs. Middleground causing her to run back up the steps as she let out a quick high-pitched shriek. But he passed her by and disappeared into the brush around the lake.

The police car pulled up onto the dirt; the officer jumped out.

"Manny, he has a gun!" Mrs. Middleground called from behind her screen door.

"No!" shouted Sarah.

But the cherub-faced officer had his own gun drawn.

"Everyone get back. Ruth, close your door!"

Manny hadn't expected much more than a suntan and some lost tourists—maybe a fender bender here and there—when he'd been assigned to East End's station by the port. He certainly never thought he'd have to face down an armed criminal.

Kareem was on the dirt trail that had been worn around the lake and he was cutting through the park, just about to cross over Main Street, when Manny was on his car radio calling for reinforcements.

"Perpetrator is armed and dangerous," he was saying as Sarah yelled to him, "he doesn't have a gun!" and someone from across the street yelled, "It's the Turk's boy."

"Armed and dangerous—the boy of the gas station guy who got beat up." There was static on the radio and then the response, "Ten-four. Will send back-up."

"Oh God! What's wrong with them?" Sarah said it to Alexandros but he wasn't quite sure what she meant.

She ran past him, back into the house and grabbed her keys from the dresser, then ran to her car, got in and took off down the street, never looking back.

Alexandros watched her go, barefooted, no purse—just keys.

He looked at Eagle's car, the windows smashed. Then he went back into Sarah's room and grabbed a pair of her sneakers, ran back out to the broken car, got in and turned the key just as the squad car was pulling away, siren blasting.

And Oscar, with Karen Marie in the passenger seat, was just cresting the hill that led into the town of East End when he had to pull the car over to allow the police cars to pass—Southampton written on the side door.

CHAPTER 15

Kareem ducked under the police tape and went into the gas station office. He pulled the spiral notebook from his back pocket and laid it on the desk as he sat in the lawn chair. He began to turn the pages. He knew Sarah better than anyone in East End. How was it she had never shown him the spiral notebook. The first poem was dated from the year he started grammar school. This was not something she had just begun. He tried to read but the tears blurred his vision. He couldn't see it — any of it. He put his head in his hands and cried so hard that he almost didn't hear the police car pull up to the curb.

The officers got out of their car just as Manny pulled up behind them and got out with his gun drawn. He had thought it was a weapon in the boy's hand as he emerged from the office. It looked like a small handgun and when he fired he hadn't thought about the gas pumps.

Sarah had pulled over to let the police cars pass. She had to. But once they'd sped by, she'd gotten back on the road and had made it half way to Main Street before the vibrations hit against the car and a deafening blast slapped against her face through the open window. Her body went ice cold, the chill starting at the base of her spine, running up her back and stopping at the nape of her neck. She knew — without knowing — it was over. Nothing could be the same after this.

She pulled to the side of the road when she came to the line of police cars blocking the intersection and then she was walking with other onlookers when a cop with a walkie-talkie grabbed her elbow.

"Move back. Crime scene. Move back. C'mon, move!" He was yelling.

Sarah stood listening to the hum of conversation around her but not really hearing it. A hand on her shoulder startled her and she turned.

"Sarah." It was Oscar. She almost didn't recognize him, except that Karen Marie was standing next to him. The three embraced.

Alexandros had just pulled the car into the sand across the street. As he got out, he noticed the cover of the spiral notebook lying on the floor of the car without its pages. He grabbed it as he reached for the sneakers and he was running toward Sarah when he saw the other two putting their arms around her and it took him a moment, but he realized where he'd seen them before. The friends from her village — that photo she'd shown him when they were driving back from Astoria, though the boy had no hair and was wearing military fatigues. But she had told Alexandros that the boy was in the army. That was him — the boy — *the best friend*. Alexandros stood in the street watching them, the three embracing as one. Sarah's sneakers dropped from his hand.

"She deserves to be with an American," he thought, *"I'll only complicate her life."*

He backed away from the crowd and crossed the street. The three were still embracing. Alexandros looked at the notebook cover in his hand. He folded it neatly into a small square and tucked it into his shirt pocket. Then, he put his head down and looked at the sidewalk as he made his way to the restaurant, feeling the folded cover hit against his heart.

He was surprised to see Andreas standing in the kitchen with cousin Minos and George and he thought they were talking about the explosion; their heads were bent forward whispering. All of the staff was out in the parking lot or walking toward the rising smoke. The three men looked at Alexandros as he walked in. George looked at Minos and said, "How about him?"

*   *   *   *

Montreal. That was where they were going. Why not? Alexandros was done with New York, done with America. The only thing he'd wanted, he could never have. She was beyond his reach.

It was decided that Andreas would drive. When they got to the Canadian border, Alexandros should pretend to be sleeping. This was the first *getaway* any of them had ever planned and they agreed that Alexandros' broken English might cause suspicion.

"Whatever you do, Alexandros, don't open your mouth. Don't even look at anyone." George had one hand on his shoulder as he spoke to him.

"I understand," Alexandros said.

Minos had been leading the conversation as they stood in a huddle behind the steam table in the deserted kitchen. His sister's death weighed him down. If he could get her son safely away from an American jail, he hoped it would lighten the crush against his chest. And he was the only one who had experience with an illegal border crossing, from when he's done so as a young man with his first wife, an American girl. They'd driven into Canada, following exactly the instructions given to him by an older Greek. Minos was the sleeping *husband* as the young bride drove. She smiled and answered the questions of the friendly border guard in a hushed voice so as not to awaken her exhausted husband—for he'd been driving all day. At the American Embassy in Montreal, they submitted to a short interview and used the marriage license to fill out paperwork to get Minos his temporary green card and then they reentered the United States, the procedure having turned Minos into a legal resident. Minos had rushed to take his citizen test and then a few months later, once the divorce was final, the girl got her money and Minos was free to marry Roula and bring her over from Greece.

But Alexandros and Andreas wouldn't be reentering the U.S. They'd be staying in Montreal because that's where Minos' cousin, Costas, was—the one who'd be getting them the tickets to Athens.

As they left the dunes of East End and pulled onto the narrow road that would take them to the highway, Alexandros wasn't in the mood to talk to the degenerate who'd taken photos of the woman he loved. He remembered the shock of seeing them together, but also the look on Sarah's face when he had pulled Andreas from her. Sitting next to him now, Alexandros' hands closed into two fists as the memory of those moments took hold and he wished he had gone to Sarah first and helped her compose herself, rather than release his rage on Andreas' face, though there'd been a certain satisfaction in seeing Andreas cry, his tears mix with the blood from his nose as George pulled them apart.

"My Greek's not really that good," Andreas said in English. He was still reeling from the shock of losing his mother—again. If only this had been happening a week earlier. His mother could be there to welcome him and help him acclimate. It didn't occur to him that had his mother been alive, none of the present events would be happening—he couldn't see the connection. His only thoughts were of his own aloneness, and he was afraid. And he was driving with that lunatic right next to him.

"Your Greek stinks," Alexandros answered in Greek.

They were silent for the entire trip, except when Andreas said, "I need to stop for the bathroom." And when he emerged from the bathroom stall glassy-eyed and subdued, Alexandros realized it hadn't been a cigarette he'd lit up on the way in.

"I'm driving," Alexandros said.

Andreas leaned back on the passenger seat, lost in the moving images of the side window. Alexandros was looking at the scenery also, marveling at its beauty—such majestic mountains, so much green. It was beautiful. He wished he were driving with Sarah; he thought she'd have loved the landscape.

The car moved smoothly along the highway, in and around the high mountains. Just outside of Canada, after they'd descended from among several high peaks, one of which had a rocky façade that made Alexandros think of an animal's head—perhaps an eagle or an owl—the land became a little tamer and they stopped in a town called Malone.

"Okay, you understand?" Alexandros spoke broken English. "I sleep. You drive. I no talk to anyone."

He leaned his head back on the seat. It was of no concern to him whether Andreas went to jail or not—in fact, it would be justified. Andreas was a criminal. He had caused harm to another person. Alexandros thought of Exohorio. If this had all happened there, Kareem would have been able to avenge his father, possibly kill Andreas or at the very least give him a far worse beating than that which Andreas had given Amir, and not one soul would have intervened; police never would have been involved. But more than likely Andreas would have been dead long before that, unable to harm Amir at all, because of what he'd done to Sarah. Justice was meted out among those mountains without complication or the forgiveness of time. It was swift and final. But they weren't in Exohorio, though the same moral code that governed his life back home was also the one that compelled him to help his uncle in Andreas' escape. Above all else—written laws, emotional pleas—only the village code was final. Right or wrong, you protect your own kind.

Andreas held the steering wheel with one hand, his other lay limp as his elbow leaned on top of the open window, the wind catching the hair on one side of his head and blowing strands in little whirlwinds above his ear. He had the look of a relaxed driver, out with a friend for a simple drive on that sunny afternoon. But his heart pounded in his chest as the border grew closer. They passed under a giant green sign that said *Welcome to Canada* so he eased off the gas and coasted toward a string of booths, each with a person inside and a line of cars passing by the border guards. Silently, Andreas practiced his lines: *My cousin and I are just crossing over for a few hours to visit a friend,* and he thought he could see his shirt moving up and down at the spot on his chest where his heart pounded. His mouth was so dry, he wasn't sure he'd be able to form the words. He pulled up to the booth, carefully following the directions given to him down in East End, but the border officer was so disinterested in the two young men as George's old sedan came to a stop, he muffled a yawn. Andreas said his line, Alexandros opened his eyes and gave a friendly nod, and the officer simply waved them into Canada.

At the same time, Minos' wife, Roula, was making coffee down in East End for those who came to the house to pay their respects after hearing about Dina's plane. George and Maureen were among the visitors.

Minos wiped his eyes with a handkerchief he had taken from his pocket as he stood near the fireplace smoking a cigarette and talking to George.

"Are you sure you don't want to come? I'll close the restaurant." He put his hand on George's shoulder. "If it's the money, I'll pay your airfare. It will be helpful for Andreas to have you there at the memorial."

"No. It's not a good idea." George knew Dina's relatives would not be happy to see him. He'd be an irritant at a time when they were trying to mourn their loss.

The phone rang. Roula answered and began speaking Greek. She tucked the phone in the crook of her neck while she continued putting small ceramic cups onto a silver serving tray. Suddenly she froze with one small cup hovering in the air over the tray. Maureen took the cup from her grasp but the other woman's hand remained in the air, her fingers molded to the shape of the missing cup. Maureen walked around the house passing the cups out but she continued watching Minos' wife.

"It's got to be a call from Greece," she thought.

Roula slowly sat down in a chair at the kitchen table, the cord of the phone stretched tightly to its limit, creating a long taut line between them.

"Minos!"

He heard Roula call to him from the other room and before he had time to answer or to move away from the fireplace mantle she said his name again.

"Minos!"

It was in such a way that he and everyone else in the house ran to her. They found her trembling at the kitchen table as she handed the phone to him.

"It's your sister," she said.

CHAPTER 16

Minos' cousin, Costas, lived in Montreal—that's true—but he lived there in the same way Minos lived in *New York*. It was thrilling to tell the villagers back in the old country that he lived *in* Montreal, especially when there was no chance of their visiting him, though they would most likely have been just as impressed with the life he had sculpted for himself in a quiet suburb thirty minutes outside the city.

He had done well. At his young age of sixty, he had a savings from the sale of the aluminum siding business and an income from the house on Bank Street that he'd bought and turned into apartments. His first son was a successful architect, the other a teacher and his two married daughters had found Greek-Canadians for husbands after a few worrisome years of rebellion against his ardent attempts at matchmaking. It was the youngest, Angela, the unmarried daughter, who kept him awake at night, turning his ebony curls a silver-gray and making him light one cigarette too many. She was living at home, choosing the foolishness of a university rather than follow the correct path for a nice Greek girl, like her two sisters.

At first Angela had gone to the university as a way to avoid the wedding altar. Without knowing the reason, she knew that the idea of marriage—of relationships in general—frightened her. But slowly, as she sat in those classrooms she felt a comfort she had never known. She became soaked with a culture that seemed to have endless possibilities. The discussions and debates where others actually wanted to hear what she had to say, were inexhaustible. It seemed to her, she'd found the exact environment she'd yearned for during most of her youth, but it would take several more years for her to realize that it was that one particular person in those courses, a woman with whom she would later become inseparable, that satisfied her yearning. Her father would be long gone before she'd admit to anyone, including herself, that it was the love of this *best friend*, Claire, who brought her the peace her soul had longed for. She and Claire would buy a house together and live a more satisfying life than that which her father had searched for among the sons of his Greek friends.

At that time though, it was Angela, the unmarried daughter, who was standing next to the phone when the call came from East End. She picked up the receiver and heard the news from Minos. His sister — Cousin Dina — Andreas' mother, was alive!

Angela and her mother had prepared the table with an assortment of food for the guests. They weren't quite sure what Alexandros and Andreas would want to eat after driving all day, but they knew it would be a terrible insult not to have something prepared. So Angela hung up the phone and relayed the good news to the men as they came in the front door, her father having gone to meet them out on Route 21 so that they could follow him back to the house. They all cried with Andreas, but it was Angela who was embracing him as he wept.

"Thanks be to God!" Costas' wife, Vaso, exclaimed in Greek and gave her husband a hard look as she read his thoughts. He was looking from the young man in his daughter's arms to his wife, a smile stretched across his face. Costas hadn't been able to get airline tickets for a flight out, until the following week. Anything could happen. He met his wife's eyes with the look of innocence.

"For God's sake, Costas. They're cousins," she whispered to her husband.

"It's okay, third cousins."

Vaso locked his eyes as she gave his shin a quick kick with her foot and turned to her guests.

"Come in. Come in. Sit down — let's eat."

Costas recovered quickly from the pain in his shin and added, "Angela, go get the wine glasses. We have much to celebrate!"

A few hours later, more food was prepared and the aroma of it hypnotized Andreas as he and Alexandros were introduced to Costas' other two daughters with their husbands and their small children as they came to meet the visitors. The house was full of life and laughter and loud conversation. Vaso stood in front of the stove, the steam from a boiling pot dampening her face.

"Take these kids out in the back," she yelled to her son-in-laws as one of her granddaughter's set up some building blocks at her feet.

"Oh, ma," her daughter cried, "they're going to get dirty out there." She was standing next to her mother chopping onions. "And it's starting to get dark."

"Don't *oh-ma* me. Go get a soccer ball or something."

Andreas kicked the soccer ball around the backyard with the other young men and the children and he longed to be one of them.

"Kick it here, Uncle!" one of the little ones screamed at him when the ball was between his feet.

Uncle. He liked the sound of it.

"Come Alexandros," one of the sons-in-law called. Alexandros was sitting on the steps of the cement patio smoking a cigarette. He shook his head and inhaled the smoke, waved his hand and called back.

"Next time."

Alexandros was thinking of Sarah.

"Such a solemn young man." Vaso watched him closely from the kitchen window, but Costas stayed focused on Andreas.

When it was time to eat and everyone was milling around the dining room table, Costas grabbed Andreas' arm.

"You sit here," he said pulling the chair out next to Angela, and he watched them carefully all through dinner, throwing the conversation their way at each chance he got.

"Did you know that Angela teaches Sunday school, Andreas?"

"Dad."

She'd been through many uncomfortable matchmaking attempts disguised as *coincidental-dinner-guests*, but she'd thought she could relax with this one. After all, he was a cousin—and a criminal. But he was a Greek and she knew that took precedence over all else.

"She's also graduating from the university next spring," Vaso added, her eyes on Costas.

"What are you studying?" Andreas asked her.

She turned to him and smiled. "Art history. It's really fascinating. I'd like to—"

"Andreas, you lived in Greece for a while, didn't you?" her father interrupted her, saying it in Greek for emphasis, "a Greek woman with a strong knowledge of Greek art!"

"Dad."

"What?" Costas gave her his best look of innocence, but Andreas was lost in the switching between English and Greek.

"Actually, Andreas," Angela continued in English, and though she addressed her guest, she was looking at her mother for help, "*Greek* art is a very small portion of the degree."

"Yes," Vaso took over, "What was that you were showing me last night about the Egyptian display in the city?"

"Vaso, we need more bread." Costas turned his head toward Angela. "Remember when you danced in the Greek Independence Day parade? Oh, Andreas—that was something. She knows all the dances from our villages. This one," he put his hands out toward Angela, "she's a real Greek."

Vaso caught the last few words as she reentered the dining room with a full bread basket and Angela slipped comfortably back into the Greek language, correctly suspecting that her father's *Greek-wife-sales-pitch* was wasted on that American.

"What he means, Andreas," Angela continued in her perfect Greek-school Greek, "is, would you marry his unmarried daughter—that'd be me—and save her from the travesty of old-maid-hood."

Vaso noted it was the first time Alexandros had laughed, or even smiled for that matter, and Andreas followed along by smiling with the others who'd also found whatever Angela had said humorous but she'd used unusual phrases and words that confused him.

Alexandros continued the conversation, though Costas was visibly annoyed. "A good father finds a good son-in-law." He tried to smooth out his host's ruffled feathers.

"Yes! You understand. You're from the other side. These guys, they don't know. Life is short, my friend. It is a happier one when you find the right partner."

Vaso scoffed, "*Partner.*"

"I agree," said Alexandros.

Costas looked around the table at his family. "You stick with your own kind. You have a happy life, eh?"

He threw his hands out and motioned to his married daughters as if that were enough. Both were preoccupied with the complaints of the children around them and heard none of the banter — though their husbands nodded vigorously.

Alexandros continued.

"It's exactly what I plan to do," he said and Vaso thought, "*Hmm, so the young man does talk.*"

Alexandros told them about Aphrodite, the girl he'd been promised to, a lovely person, though they hadn't spoken much. But her father was an upstanding citizen of Exohorio, a good friend of his own father. And that's where he was headed, back to his village for the engagement. The men at the table nodded their heads in agreement. It was correct. It was the way things were done.

*   *   *   *

Though it was still dark in the guest room next to the kitchen, dawn was not far off as Alexandros lay awake staring into the darkness. He was relieved that he and Andreas were sleeping away from the other bedrooms as he lay silently, still shaken from his dream. There were only a few remnants of it as he struggled to retrieve the pieces still there but just barely visible, like cobwebs in the shadows of a room. Her hair — he could still smell it — that mixture of lemon and roses. Their bodies pressed tightly together. It had felt so real; he ached from the loss of it. He had whispered into her ear, a perfect language.

"I love you, Sarah."

The feel of her lobe on his lips was leaving him and all that was left was the faint memory of the village music — barely a whisper, though it had been loud and nearby only moments before when he was in the garden — at home, in Exohorio. Aphrodite was in her wedding dress, a smile painted on her face, her feet buried in the soil. He took his place beside her just as his mother called from the window. "It's time Alexandros. The priest is here. Where is your betrothed?" The feeling lingered like a bit of sand in his eyes—the obligation—the duty. And as Alexandros reached for her hand, Aphrodite disappeared, leaving nothing behind but some green sprouts pushing up through the ground where her feet had been. The relief was palpable.

But his mother's voice reached him again, "Where is she, Alexandros? The priest is waiting. Bring her here." And she was there—suddenly, Sarah, kissing his neck, nestled in his arms. And then his mother's voice again, intruding.

"Where is she Alexandros? The priest is waiting? Bring Sarah here!"

Sarah?

He awoke abruptly with a gasp and had found himself in that strange guest room, blinking up at the ceiling. He lay there, willing his brain to find the sweetness of the dream again, to have Sarah's body next to him, there under those sheets. But she was gone, and as hard as he tried, he couldn't will her back. He closed his eyes, looking for her but only saw darkness.

Alexandros slipped silently from the bed, not wanting to wake Andreas whose light breathing was coming from the bed across the room. He pulled on his pants and searched for the shirt he'd left on the floor and then remembered Vaso had taken some of their clothes to wash. So he fished around in his bag and found a tee shirt, pulled it over his head and slipped from the room with a pack of cigarettes and his lighter.

The glow of dawn was just peeking into the kitchen window as he passed by the refrigerator and made his way to the back door.

"Oh!" He was startled by Vaso's silhouette sitting at the kitchen table inside the large bay window.

"I'm so sorry. I didn't realize you were there," he whispered.

A small cup rested in her palm, the other hand held the tiny handle. She took a quick sip and said, "it's my favorite time of day. Peaceful. I enjoy it before the others wake up. Isn't it beautiful?" She gestured toward the large window where the sun was coming up over the trees filtering a soft light through the small square panes.

Alexandros nodded.

"Here, sit." She pointed to a chair. "I'll make you coffee."

She went to the refrigerator and poured a glass of juice, then brought it to Alexandros just as he was pulling out a cigarette from the packet.

"Cigarette?" he asked.

"Sure, why not?"

She let him light it for her and then went to the stove to brew his coffee. Alexandros felt her watching him as she stood there, the cigarette dangling between her lips, with one hand on her hip, the other stirring the liquid in the tiny copper pot. The coffee bubbled up to the rim of the metal, so she laid the spoon on the counter and pulled the pot from the flame just as a small drop spilled over the brim, dripping a brown line down the side of the pot. Vaso poured it into two small cups and put the cups on a small disc tray.

"So," she said as she took the cigarette from her mouth and put it between her fingers, "are you going to come back after you get engaged?"

"I don't think so."

"Really?" Her surprise seemed disingenuous. "You'd rather live as a shepherd on the top of some mountain, than to live *in* America?"

Vaso walked to the table holding the tray in one hand and her cigarette in the other.

"Well," Alexandros said, "I have to serve in the army first, and you know, it's a good life here but, well the language. It's hard. I like the mountains over there, I mean—not here. Well, actually they're beautiful over here too—the mountains, I mean. We drove through some kind of a mountain range on the road up. We saw—um, we went through some, ah—real high ones. Kind of reminded me of my area." He knew he was rambling.

Vaso put the coffee cup in front of him and an ashtray between them and took a seat.

"You know Alexandros, my husband is wrong." She looked hard into the young man's eyes. "Life is not short. That's something we old people say when we realize we've wasted it. Life is very long, Alexandros—especially when you marry the wrong person."

She pulled a crumpled paper from her pocket and put it on the table. It was the photo. She'd found it among his dirty clothes.

Sarah completely exposed, sat between them until Alexandros realized what it was and snatched it up quickly, embarrassed and relieved.

"It's not what you think," he began.

"You have no idea what I'm thinking."

"It's a girl I met down there. She's um, she's not Greek."

"She's also not clothed."

"Listen — it's not what you're thinking. She's not bad."

"That's not what I'm thinking."

"I, um I, it's, well complicated."

"No it's not. It's not complicated. It's easy, but we always seem to make it complicated."

Alexandros stopped and listened.

"My dear boy, I don't know what you were doing with her and I don't want to know, but I see your reaction now. Don't be stupid. You described your betrothed, what's her name? Aphrodite? You talked of her with all the passion of a stone. This girl, here, moves you. Give me that picture."

Alexandros shook his head slowly.

"Give it to me." Vaso extended her hand and looked hard into Alexandros' eyes.

He looked down at her hand and slowly placed the crumpled photo in it. Vaso ripped it in half and handed back the part that showed Sarah's head and shoulders. Then she ripped the other one into tiny pieces and cupped it in her hand.

"If I could find it mistakenly, then someone else could too. Now you can remember her safely. Your new wife will not like finding this picture but she doesn't need to see the rest. And don't be a fool, my boy. Just like this girl was naked with you here, your sweet innocent betrothed might be naked with someone else right now — but she's not stupid enough to use a camera."

Alexandros opened his mouth to speak but she put her hand up to stop him.

"Every Greek man marries a virgin but before he does that, he screws around with every girl he can find, in the dark corners during village festivals, up in the mountains in a hidden cave, under the cover of night behind the church during midnight service. You figure it out. Who are they screwing? Give me another cigarette."

He lit it for her and she drew in a mouthful of smoke. Alexandros waited as she pursed her lips and blew the smoke in a straight line over his shoulder.

"Alexandros, if you find someone, a person who loves what you love, a friend—a good friend—hold onto that person. Hold on for dear life. The road is rocky and twisted and life is long, Alexandros. Be sure you have someone you want to say hello to every morning."

The sun was up higher, shining in the window and illuminating the kitchen. They heard the stirring and shuffle of footsteps in the other room.

"Well, time to make Costas' coffee. He likes it burning hot when he walks into the kitchen."

CHAPTER 17

Sarah awoke and the dawn that hovered over the horizon in Montreal was also pushing through her open window shade. She was lying between Karen Marie and Oscar; the three had collapsed onto her bed after the turmoil of the day before. She'd felt relief at seeing Kareem alive, but also agony upon seeing him led away in handcuffs. And then shock at having her two best friends at her side at the very moment she needed them.

It would be impossible to talk to Oscar, to convey the happenings of the last eight months, of the turbulence in her heart, the trauma within her family and within her own life. Eons had gone by since they'd been together in her bedroom — the exact night when her father had set in motion the grinding of gears that seemed to have their own unstoppable momentum.

Like triplets crowded together in the womb, the three friends lay on her bed; arms were over legs, faces pressed together, one body indistinguishable from the other. Sarah peered into Oscar's half-opened eyes.

"Oh geez," she said with a grimace, "what did you do, take a bite of a raw onion in the middle of the night?"

It was so good to see him but she was surprised at how much she longed to have it be Alexandros waking up next to her.

Oscar blew hard into her face and smiled.

"Oh! Stop."

She pushed him away from her face, which started the mesh of body limbs in motion, and then Karen Marie grunted, "hey, what the — whoa!" Thud. Her body landed on the floor but one foot was still on the bed.

Sarah sat up.

"You guys — oh man, I'm so glad you're here."

Karen Marie scrambled to get up off the floor and said, "What's up with not returning my calls?"

"What are you talking about?"

"I called this place a hundred times."

"I didn't know."

"Some lady — she said she'd told you."

"She lied. I didn't know. She didn't tell me."

"Well how come you never called me? Your finger broken? Can't dial a pay phone?"

"Listen — I'm sorry. It's complicated."

"Okay, okay." Karen Marie wanted her annoyance at Sarah to be known but she knew it was nothing compared to what they'd come down there for and time was running out. Oscar would need to be on a bus soon, back to the barracks. So Karen Marie turned to Oscar, "We came to tell you something Sarah, right Oscar?"

Sarah was too entrenched in her own guilt to notice the seriousness in Karen Marie's voice. She wanted to enjoy the last few moments before she told them about Alexandros.

"Look at you," she smiled at Oscar and rubbed the peach fuzz that was growing on his head. "Mr. Military Man. You look cool." Her smile stayed unbroken. How would she tell him about Alexandros? She wondered and half worried that he might show up at her door before she was able to. It would hit Oscar hard but he needed to know. She just wasn't quite brave enough to possibly lose him, yet.

"Okay, what's going on?" She sat up and crossed her legs underneath her.

"You remember when your father found me in your room last summer?"

"Of course." She rolled her eyes. "I don't know what the big deal was." She thought of how innocent she'd been back then — barely a year ago.

Oscar swallowed hard and Karen Marie retreated to the corner of the room, leaning her elbow on the dresser as Oscar remembered that night, retelling the details of his conversation with Sarah's father. They were all back in Sarah's bedroom, together again in Owl's Head. Then they were standing with him in the hallway listening to Ron as the words spilled from his lips.

"Oscar," Ron put his arm gently around the boy's shoulder. It wasn't how Oscar had expected to be treated, having been caught in the bed of that man's daughter. It put him off-guard, so he hadn't quite expected what came next.

"You and Sarah, you cannot have this kind of relationship."

He thought he knew what the next words would be: *You're too young. You have no future. You're from a broken family. Your father's a loser so you're a loser. Stay away from my daughter* — so Ron's actual words did not quite penetrate for a few seconds.

"Sarah is your sister," Ron said. "Your mother and I, well — we uh — you're my son. And well — I want to make this right for both of you, but you have to stay away from Sarah for a few days. Just give me a little time — but," Ron continued talking. By then, the two were on the front porch, and Oscar wasn't able to recall any words after that. He only remembered the need to escape. But to where? To whom? Sarah had always been that person and suddenly she'd been taken away without warning. He'd wanted to run and never stop — to feel his legs burn with movement. And for him, not much was clear until he'd found himself in boot camp.

Sarah listened to Oscar and she heard it as Oscar had that night, the summer before, but the meaning bounced against the walls like a rubber ball gaining momentum until it smacked hard against her heart. There, in that room at the end of the hallway in the Middleground Boarding House as she heard it all for the first time, its force ripped through her like a blow to the chest. She was down, knocked out, pinned to the ground by this unlikely attacker.

Karen Marie and Oscar watched her carefully as seconds ticked by and then it was a small whisper that escaped her lips but they weren't sure of the question.

"What?" The whisper was almost undetectable, like vapor from a volcanic fissure before the eruption. She looked at Karen Marie who came toward her and sat at her other side.

"I'm sorry, Sarah." She put her arm around her friend and

continued. "Your mom's gone. She moved in with your aunt."

"Earnest?"

"He's with your mom and aunt."

"Oh my God." She sat staring at her feet, leaning forward with her head in her hands. "Oh my God." She fought the churning in her stomach.

"And Sarah—your dad, he um—" How could she tell her the rest? The words were stuck. Karen Marie looked at Oscar and he knew she needed help, but he couldn't do it. He couldn't tell her because he couldn't bear to hear it himself. Not again. The words wouldn't form. He wouldn't let them come from him.

Karen Marie was looking at him. Imploring. But he just shook his head slowly. No. He couldn't do it.

Sarah looked up.

"What?" she saw the exchange between the other two, "What?"

Karen Marie knew it had to be her. It was too cruel to make Oscar say it.

"Sarah—your father. He um—he," she hesitated.

"What?!" Sarah's eyes widened.

"Oscar's mother is living in the house with your father."

"Sarah." Oscar tried to put his arm around her but she pulled her shoulder away and looked at him. Logic was somehow blocked from her thoughts. She didn't think about how this information affected him, or the pain he must have been in for those months he'd known. He was her brother. She felt disgust. His face repulsed her.

And she blamed him.

"Don't touch me."

She jumped up from the bed and Oscar stood as she did. They were face to face when she hit him—hard, in the chest—so that he moved away.

"Sarah. What are you doing?" Karen Marie asked.

Oscar's hands were up, in defense. "It's okay, Karen."

Sarah heard him. *Okay?* She flew into a blind rage and all she wanted was to tear him to pieces.

"What do you mean it's okay?" And she struck him again and again in the chest, but he grabbed her arms and she fought wildly, her body flailing. Her family was gone. Destroyed. They'd left her blowing in the wind—alone. No one had come for her—except

Oscar. Her brother? The sight of his face was revolting.

"Okay? You say it's okay!?" Sarah was screaming. "Nothing's okay!"

Karen Marie came around from behind and was just grabbing her waist when the door flew open and Mack was standing there. He grabbed Karen Marie and pushed her aside.

"What're you people doing? What's going on?"

Sarah saw Mack's face and she stopped fighting. Her body went limp and she fell to the floor.

"What's going on?" Mack stood there, not moving, trying to assess the situation. He heard Sarah's meek voice below him.

"Oh God, Mack."

Karen Marie tried to take his arm, to lead him out into the hall where some of the other fishermen had gathered — craning to get a look at the scene inside the little room, but he shook her loose.

Again he asked, "What's going on?" Louder.

He sat on the floor next to Sarah and put his hand to her chin, pulling her face to meet his.

"What's happening here? Tell me."

Karen Marie turned toward the door and walked quietly into the hallway to address the fishermen who still stood waiting for Mack to emerge with an explanation. She pulled the bedroom door closed and walked toward them.

Inside the room, Mack tried again, "Tell me little girl; what's wrong?"

"Mack," Sarah whispered.

She seemed unable to say more, but she let him pull her to his chest and hold her as he rocked slightly back and forth, listening as Oscar told him the saga of their lives. He slowly laid out the broken pieces of their world, and some of them made Sarah twitch when they worked their way into the protective shell of Mack's arms. Mack held her tightly, thinking of his daughter, Belle, as he smoothed her hair with his big paw-hands. He thought of how he had hurt Belle and wondered how the events had unfolded for her that last time — the time he'd left port and never returned. Had there been someone to hold her when she'd finally understood his selfishness? Had her mother recovered enough from their breakup to be there for their daughter; had she been able to help Belle understand?

"Little girl." His voice was a wisp of air. "Forgive your father. He loves you very much. He's stupid and selfish and his pain will never go away because he can't undo what he's done. Forgive him."

Tears fell into the top of her hair as he sobbed softly — stopping Sarah dead in her sorrow. To see Mack, the toughest of the tough, brought to tears by her own sadness, shook her awake.

She looked up at his face.

"Please," he begged, "forgive him."

      *   *   *   *

Oscar stood on the train platform. He wasn't quite sure why Sarah insisted on staying in East End; he couldn't seem to convince her to go back to Owl's Head with Karen Marie, or at least to Malone. But why stay in East End? Why *there*?

"Go back with Karen Marie and be with your mother and your little brother. There's nothing here for you." But she would not listen.

Oscar hugged both girls good-bye and boarded the train at the East End station. He understood the pain in Sarah's eyes; he was dealing with it himself. But he had the army. It was a well-defined, structured family. He had brothers there that would protect him like no one else ever had. But what did Sarah have?

Oscar thought of his father — the man he'd always thought was his father. He was alone in Owl's Head. That man had never loved him, could barely even stand the sight of him. That had always been clear.

"*He must have known something,*" Oscar thought, "*He must have guessed.*"

At any rate, Oscar knew he'd never be able to go back and live in Owl's Head. His mother and Mr. Petit — he would never call him dad — their deception was unforgivable. Finally seeing his mother again, hadn't created the joy he'd thought it would, especially having her *there* — on Church Street with Sarah's father — his father. There was so much shame; Oscar's own embarrassment was reflected in every face he'd seen in that short time he'd been back in town. It had replaced pity and it felt far worse. No — he'd never live in Owl's Head again.

Sarah and Karen Marie watched the train pull out of the station, not realizing that would be the last either of them would ever see of Oscar. He was stepping over the threshold of a new life and even he did not realize it. His career in the military, mostly overseas, would be long and fulfilling and his marriage would provide him with the love he had long expected to be excluded from. His entry into that other world would be so complete that he'd never hear the door close. But that was several years away and at that moment, as Sarah watched the train pull away, she turned toward the car with Karen Marie. There was only one haunting question that filled Sarah's head.

Where was Alexandros and why hadn't he come to seek her out in those hours after the standoff with Kareem?

It had to be the photo. There seemed to be no other explanation and that is what she told Karen Marie as they got into her car. She laid out the drama of the days leading to the gas station explosion.

"We were together every day and now—" Sarah's voice trailed off. "It's the photo," she whispered.

"Listen Sarah. Maybe you're right, but how do you know? You have to talk to him."

"They have this warped sense of morality—these Greeks."

"But you said yourself, Sarah. He's different."

"I don't know. You didn't see his face. He was freaked out."

"You're right. You don't know. It was all the drama that probably freaked him out. I saw what was going on. The fire. The cops. It freaked *me* out."

"No. It was before that. It was for just a second. He looked at the picture and then he looked at me. His eyes."

"Oh, c'mon. He saw you in the hotel room that day. He knows you weren't posing."

"I don't know what he knows."

Karen Marie turned the key and started the engine of the car. She pulled out onto the road and turned to the direction of the ocean.

"Let's go. Put it to rest. Find out from him."

"Wait a second. Let me think. His English is not that good. How am I going to do this?"

"Somebody at the restaurant?"

"No way! This is too private."

"All you need to do is see how he reacts when he sees you."

"You're right."

Sarah was silent. She was lost in thought. She looked at Karen Marie.

"What if he hates me? Oh God, Karen. I can't handle that."

"He doesn't hate you. It sounds like he cares a lot."

Sarah was shaking her head, "what'll I do?"

"Relax. It's gonna be okay."

Sarah sighed and looked down at her hands in her lap. Her body was suddenly cold. With Alexandros, she could face the rest, but without him, she was nobody. Nothing. Alone. She could barely breath as they pulled into the parking lot of the restaurant.

"Is his car here?"

"He doesn't have one."

She saw Eagle's red car parked at the back of the lot, the windshield smashed, the passenger windows missing, and Eagle bent over it, brushing shards of glass from behind the windshield wiper.

"Pull up close to the back door. I don't want that guy to see me."

Karen Marie pulled so close to the building that she almost scraped her bumper on the brick wall. Eagle looked in their direction as Sarah opened the car door to get out.

"Do you want me to come with you?" Karen Marie asked.

"No."

Eagle squinted at her as she made her way to the kitchen door.

"He's not here," he called.

Sarah turned toward him.

"Where is he?"

"Back in Greece."

The words hit her like a punch and it took a second for her to recover.

"Greece?"

"Yeah. He left right after the gas station explosion. Didn't even say goodbye."

"What?" It just wasn't penetrating.

"Greece. Back to Greece."

"Why?"

Eagle shrugged. "I guess he didn't like it here. He probably would go sooner, if you're not here."

"Me?"

"Yeah, you. You're all he talked about."

"Really?"

Sarah's eyes were blurry but she didn't feel the tears that began to run down both cheeks. Nor did she register the discomfort in Eagle's face at seeing her cry.

"Yes. I thought you dumped him."

Sarah was shaking her head.

Eagle was baffled. "He was crazy. Every day asking me, how do you say this and how do you say that. For you. He loves you. I just thought you dumped him. Why did he leave?"

"I don't know." Sarah lied. Then she turned back to the car and got in beside Karen Marie.

"He's gone." Sarah swiped her arm across her eyes leaving her tears on her sleeve. "He's gone."

"Where'd he go? I'll drive you."

"No." Sarah whispered. "I want to go home."

But Karen Marie was not quite sure what she meant and before she was able to ask her, a woman knocked at her window and she rolled it down.

It was Maureen and she thought she knew the reason Sarah was upset.

"It's okay, honey." Maureen spoke past Karen Marie. "The Turk's son is home. They had nothing on him. In fact, they have a pretty good case against the police."

Sarah didn't answer.

Karen Marie said, "Okay, thanks. Good to know," and began rolling up the window. But Maureen wasn't satisfied. Her information hadn't had the effect she'd thought it would. She put her hand on Karen Marie's window to stop her.

"Sarah. The father's gonna be okay too. He's in the hospital, but they're saying he'll be okay."

Still nothing from Sarah as she sat looking at her hands in her lap, sniffing as more tears flowed.

"Sarah," Maureen tried again, "Andreas won't bother you anymore. He's gone with Alexandros, somewhere." She thought she was maintaining the secrecy around Andreas' fleeing.

Sarah looked up. "Why did Alexandros leave?"

"I can't say."

"You don't know?"

"That's right. I don't know."

Maureen thought, *"better to play it safe — as little information as possible."*

"Thanks, Maureen," Sarah said and then she looked at Karen Marie, "take me back to the boarding house."

CHAPTER 18

Two years. How much time is that, really? For some, it's the depth of a canyon carved by a mighty river, while for others, it's as insignificant as a drop of rain hitting the surface of a bottomless sea. An older person might feel a random two years over the course of a lifetime, as no more than the blink of an eye. Yet, for an infant those same two years take him from belly to feet as he pulls himself upright, navigating the world on wobbly legs. And in the world of nature, in the ten-year life span of the Adirondack Mountains' great snowy owl, two years changes the adolescent bird into an adult—a quantum leap.

For Alexandros, after returning to Greece, two years meant the end of his military service and the arrival back in the mountains of his hometown, Exohorio, to fulfill his promise to become a married man. He grabbed his duffel bag from the taxi seat, put his hand on the door handle and looked at the driver.

"Come up, Cocho. Park the car here and come up to the house."

It was only a few feet away but the car risked injury on such a rocky path. With Dina, two years before, he had made it up to her house but only after several crunching noises below their feet that caused him to cringe as the car inched forward. The road to Alexandros' house was not much further but it was narrower and rockier. He wasn't willing to risk it.

Cocho was now a friend of the village. It happened two years before, when he'd driven Dina and Yianni down to the post office to make the phone call to America. He'd been there with the others when they'd all heard the news together, Dina's missed flight and her escape from a horrible fate and it was Cocho who had prevented its happening. His taxi had kept her from making it to her flight in Athens.

But Cocho knew that it was not he who had kept her from harm. That was ridiculous; he had no such power. It was the silver pomegranate hanging from his rearview mirror that had saved her.

Dina's phone call began as nothing out of the ordinary. She was still upset at having missed the flight. Her intention was to make a quick call to her brother so he could arrange for a new ticket. She wouldn't stay on the phone too long. It would be too expensive. But as Dina held the telephone receiver to her ear, yelling into it, "I missed the plane. No, I missed it. What? Yes, it's me. What's wrong with you?" it began to look as if the call would be something more.

The others in the post office began their quiet chatter debating the reason she continued to scream her message into the receiver of the phone, a message that should have been a simple one, yet seemed to be so difficult to deliver.

"I missed it! I missed the plane!" Her voice was becoming louder.

"What? What are you saying? Stop crying. I don't understand what you're saying. Put someone else on the phone."

With each declaration Dina made into the telephone, her voice not only got louder but also higher-pitched which was a signal to those sitting in the cafes or those passing by the post office door, that another eruption was imminent—though somehow these Greek citizens were compelled to rush toward a volcano, rather than away from it.

"I'm here. In Greece!" She screamed into the phone as Cocho and Yianni looked at each other and back to her. And then like the rat-a-tat-tat of a machine gun, obscenities spewed into the air, "Oh my God! Virgin Mary! Holy shit!" until she pulled away from the phone and shared the news of the plane crash with the group in the post office who then turned and shared the news with those who had spilled onto the street and gathered outside of the post office.

As the word spread, so did the movement of hands as the villagers put their fingers together and tapped foreheads then chests, crossing themselves and looking toward heaven—and then toward the taxi driver.

That's when Cocho ran out of the post office to retrieve the silver pomegranate from the taxi. Dina was just hanging up the phone when he returned with it swinging on the thin red rope, the silver sparkling in the sunlight that found its way into the dusty post office windows and threw its rays against the cuts and angles of the pomegranate. Cocho explained how his mother had hung it on his rearview mirror when he'd bought his taxi, ten years before—and he'd been a lucky man ever since. Not one accident. No problems at all, smooth sailing ever since. The pomegranate's power was already well known in Exohorio, but Cocho reminded them all of its strength.

After Dina realized that Andreas would be coming home, she made a pilgrimage every morning to the church of the Virgin Mary down in the village to light a candle. But she also insisted on planting more pomegranate bushes around her garden—just for a little extra insurance for a safe return and her neighbors followed suit—especially those who had someone travelling, which in fact was almost everyone. Even more were planted along the mountainside as other villagers added them to the hills. And after the two young men had returned and Alexandros was whisked away to the army base, Maria, Alexandros' mother, planted more as she awaited his return. So in the spring of 1977, the large red flowers of the pomegranate bushes created a wall of color to greet Alexandros as he opened the car door of the taxi.

"Come, Cocho."

"No, no. Next time. I won't stand between a mother and her son. I remember when I came back from the army. My mother, well, you know."

Maria was already trotting toward the car. "He's here! He's here!" Her arms outstretched, several people following her, including Aphrodite.

Aphrodite, followed her future mother-in-law's lead, as she'd done on each of Alexandros' brief visits over the past two years. She fixed a smile on her face, provided hugs and kisses for her betrothed, and then took her place beside him, walking back up the hill with her arm folding into his. They made their way toward the house—the one she'd soon share with him and his parents.

But her head turned toward Dina's yard as they passed by. And there was Andreas coming to the stone wall to greet the returning villager, though his eyes were on her.

"Welcome back, Alexandros." He shook the young man's hand.

The engagement ceremony had been two years before, both he and Alexandros still reeling from jet lag as Father John had blessed the newly engaged couple—Alexandros and Aphrodite.

The week before, when Andreas' mother had learned that her little boy was finally coming home, she'd scrubbed the stones of the small living room floor with enough vigor to crumble them into sand. She moved the sofa out into the courtyard to make room for his bed—or more accurately, the one Yianni brought down from his home, a bed that he had not slept in for some years. Dina folded the sheets around the soft thin foam and smoothed them out with her hand. Then she took the pillow her mother gave her, punched it between her fists, trying to move the goose feathers around in it so it looked a little rounder—more American. She put it at the head of the bed, stepped back, looked and shook her head. Not quite right. She studied it as an artist studies a painting, and then she walked back to it and pulled it ever so slightly so that it was exactly in the middle at the head of the bed. Hm. Better. She opened the chest under the window and rifled around inside it until she found his little slippers, the one's her father had made out of goatskin. They were as small as two little morning roses. She placed them at the end of the bed, stepped back and looked once more at the work of art. Her own mother had been in the courtyard watching from the open window. She understood. How does a mother prepare for a reunion with her son? A small child who left with barely enough time to take one last breath of the mountain air, and now he returns as a man, a stranger. How would they bridge the years?

At first Andreas was like an American tourist visiting the northern countryside of Greece—until he made that last ascent to Exohorio—the final leg of his journey, a journey that brought him through the lower village, and tugged slightly at his memory.

There wasn't anything in particular, a slant of light against an old house, a twitter of birds in a lemon tree. He had a sense of familiarity without being able to place anything that was familiar. But as the two men took the end of the trail by foot, the crunch of the dirt beneath his feet and the heat of the sun on his neck, caused him to stop in his tracks, to look around at the valley below, to look down at his footprints in the dirt. He reached over and snapped off a sprig of thyme. Alexandros had continued walking and it took him a second to realize that Andreas had stopped. He turned around to see Andreas with his eyes closed, bringing the crushed thyme to his nose and inhaling deeply.

Alexandros had been an infant when Andreas had left the mountainside as a seven-year-old. He'd heard the story but he'd never thought much of it until that moment. Andreas' eyes opened and met Alexandros' — and Alexandros tried hard not to have sympathy for him.

Alexandros spoke to him in slow enunciated English, "You remember the place?"

"I remember something, but I'm not sure." He stopped again and looked behind, at the empty trail, then over the edge at the valley that had such perfect green squares of farmland that they looked like a drawing.

"I'm not sure. I'm just not sure. Do you have a cigarette?"

"You don't smoke."

"I need to light something and smoke it. C'mon give me one of your cigarettes."

Alexandros pulled the package from his front shirt pocket and slid two cigarettes out. He lit both and the two young men continued walking, the smoke circling their heads as they made their way home.

The first to see them was the postmaster as he walked his motor scooter toward them on his way back down to the village. He'd been delivering a package to one of the shepherds. He recognized Alexandros.

"Alexandros, welcome back." He leaned the scooter on the side of the mountain and came toward the two young men. "You're Dina's son, aren't you?" He addressed Andreas.

"Yeah." Alexandros answered for him and translated further as best he could. Andreas shook the postmaster's hand but was a little surprised when the older man pulled him close and kissed him on both cheeks.

"Your mother's been down in the post office every day this week, asking if anyone's seen you." He laughed. "Can you believe it? Today, she didn't show up. I waited all day because I figured I could send my mail up with her, but she didn't come. Figures, right?"

Andreas waited for the translation and then smiled shyly, "every day?"

"Whoa, yes! Every day. But not today and here you are." He laughed again.

"*Every day*," Andreas thought, "*she's been looking for me every day*." He felt a flutter in his chest and fought to keep his eyes dry.

The postmaster kept talking, telling them about the time Dina had threatened to kill her brother and the Americanos because she thought her little Andreas was hurt in America. He spoke as though Andreas were a celebrity and he, the postmaster with his coveted telephone, had been the one to provide that connection between Dina and the celebrity son, as though it had been he who orchestrated the homecoming between the two.

When they left the postmaster and continued up the trail, Andreas could barely hold the emotion that filled him with each inhale, and as he came around the corner and stepped into the path that led to a little stone house, he remembered. And he heard his mother's voice, a voice that he had heard over the telephone, a voice from his dreams, a voice that whispered late at night in the sleepless dark, and every ounce of longing was met with a promise. He was home; after seventeen years he was finally home.

*   *   *   *

It would be foolish to think that Andreas so easily stepped from the sidewalks of America and became a citizen of Exohorio without consequence. No — that would not be a reliable rendition of how his life on the mountainside unfolded after the emotions of the homecoming died away. The language kept him separate. His mother spoke to him with simple Greek words and a few words in English but her repertoire of English words was so small, it was almost pointless.

He began to feel lonely—a loneliness that rolled over him as slowly as an evening fog coming into the valley—so gradual that he didn't realize he hadn't spoken in several days until he heard his own voice answering a question. It was a small question that came from the bustle of women around him as they prepared the evening meal.

"Where's that cooking pot?"

She'd said it in Greek, but he'd heard it without conscious thought of any language. And his answer, "here," his voice, scratchy and small, emerged briefly as he handed her the black pot on the shelf near the cooking fire. One small word—*here*—it was sent from his brain as English, but it reached his mouth as Greek. And that's how it started. Slowly, like the first few pecks of a hatchling inside an egg, until he was adding a few words to the conversations that slowly became a few broken sentences. Peck, peck, peck—a few more shards of shell falling away—the light of the outside world coming into focus.

Dina had taken her son by the arm from that first moment he had walked with Alexandros into the yard. Even after the celebration had ended, she pulled his arm to bring him with her, to follow every step she took, to every chore she had, every visit she made. She feared he'd disappear if she didn't keep him in her sight. Her constant touch soothed him as she rubbed his arm while they walked side by side from the cooking house, suddenly brushing his hair back with her flour-filled fingers that left clumps of dough in the strands of his hair. Sometimes as Andreas sat in the courtyard helping Yianni with some meaningless task, she would just walk over to him and touch his back lightly or feel his ear lobe, and he would look at her and smile.

Yianni waited. Then after a while, he said to Andreas, "tomorrow you come with me up to the goats. Your people are herders. Your grandfather was a herder. You are a herder now too. You need to learn."

Andreas did not object.

The next morning, he followed Yianni further up the mountain to the goat shed. It took several days before the goats would let Andreas approach them without scattering and running from him as though he were a wolf. Andreas watched Yianni milk the goats, grabbing the long teats and going from one to the other with skill and speed. It looked easy enough but the first time he sat behind one and clumsily pulled her legs apart, her tail brushed his forehead and she turned back to look at him, her judging eyes saying: *novice*.

He grabbed each giant round udder of flesh in his hands and was stunned by their warmth. He hesitated. The goat looked back again and he met the challenge by pulling down on each long teat and spraying the milk onto his feet, into his crotch, and over his shoulder. Eventually though, he became quite an adept shepherd, milking the entire herd in the milking season, going from one to the next emptying the heavy udders, which made him a respected shepherd in the village.

And it seemed that Yianni and Dina were the last among their neighbors to notice Andreas slipping into Aphrodite's cooking house each morning in the early hours before going to the flock. When Dina learned of the liaisons she had too much sympathy for her son's lost years, to fault him. But Yianni felt the need to intervene.

"Andreas." He'd waited until they were alone outside the goat shed. "As you know, I am not a man of convention. Your mother and I live as man and wife though she is still married to your father."

Andreas realized where the conversation was going and looked at the older man carefully.

"But you know Aphrodite is promised to another." Yianni continued. "The engagement is as good as marriage."

Andreas stood up straight and met Yianni's eyes. "I love her," his words clear and strong.

"And she?"

"Yes — she loves me."

"Then talk to Alexandros when he returns from the army. I think he will understand. If he releases her from her promise, I will support you among the villagers."

And that is how Alexandros found himself as a guest at the wedding of his betrothed upon his return to the village. He walked with Minos to the celebration. He wanted to hear about the business in East End.

"Come back and work," Minos told him. "What's here for you? You were there legally; you had a visa. I can get you back. Just say the word."

"I thought I might go to Athens. I have a friend from the army. His uncle has a warehouse there."

"Athens? That's not a bad idea."

"So, how are things at the restaurant going, cousin?"

"Very well. The season will be starting soon, though. We could use your help."

"Are the same guys in the kitchen?" Alexandros danced around the question that he really wanted to ask.

"Yes. Same guys." Minos nodded.

"And the waitresses?"

"Yes. Same waitresses. There are always the college girls after May." He winked at Alexandros. "But the same two are there all winter."

"Same two?"

"Like light fixtures. They never change, just get a year older." He gave a little grunt, "like me."

"Sarah?"

"Oh, that's right—you and that young one. No she's gone. She never came back to work after the Turk's station went up in flames. The day after you and Andreas left, she didn't come into work."

"I see."

But Alexandros didn't see. He assumed Sarah had gone back to her mountain village just as he had. And he expected that she would have married that young soldier he'd seen her embracing. He wondered if her American wedding was like the one he was attending there in his village.

He sighed. He had always thought that he'd visit far off exotic places like those he'd seen in the movies projected on the white wall in the churchyard. He knew he would find work and make his fortune, and like his own father, he'd return to his birthplace to marry, build a house, and raise a family. He belonged to the mountain. What else was there? It was an unanswered question.

But his return with Andreas had not brought the relief he had expected. The engagement to Aphrodite had been a weight on a drowning man. His tour of duty, an act he had previously dreaded, had become a temporary escape.

Alexandros watched the married couple. Andreas was helping

Aphrodite navigate the folds of the long white dress around the chair as she took her place next to him at the feast. He recognized the look in the man's eyes and felt imprisoned by a fate more difficult to accept than the marriage from which he'd narrowly escaped.

He had helped Andreas flee from East End. It had been a quick decision and required speed. But in his haste to distance himself from his own pain, he had left his heart behind. He was adrift at sea, each foot in a different boat, sailing in opposite directions as he teetered in both, ready to fall between them, without any way to stay afloat.

And as he had suspected, Sarah, back in Owl's Head, was indeed preparing for a wedding. It hadn't been easy returning to the role of *child* in her father's house. But worse was the loss that no one would understand so she kept it to herself, and it slowly seeped into every bone in her body, like a parasite eating far into the marrow.

The ache was deep and painful as she longed for the impossible: to be back in time, sharing those moments with Alexandros. And to be back in time meant also to have her family again, before it was broken — or at least before she knew it was.

At first she'd gone to her old home, but living there with her father and his new girlfriend, Miriam, their former neighbor, the mother of Oscar, the wife of the guy a few doors down, *that home-wrecking bitch*, as her mother called her — it was all too strange.

Ron Petit had tried to reach his daughter when she first came back. There had been very little contact with her for almost a full year and then there she was, standing in the hallway — thin, pale and tearful. He had encircled her with his arms, the front of his shirt soaked with her tears as Miriam backed out of the hall and into the kitchen, not quite sure what Sarah knew of them.

Miriam listened to them as she stuck her thumbnail in the cracked countertop and picked at it silently, her feet stone still, planted on the worn linoleum as she listened to the murmur of Ron's voice and the deep sobs of his daughter. Her own tears escaped from the corner of her eyes and slid down the bridge of her nose. She wondered about Oscar. She'd only seen him for a few minutes before he'd left. The change in him was wrenching, his hair gone, the army fatigues. It was as if that angry young soldier had killed her son—both of her boys gone now, each from fighting his own battle. She thought of those last few moments with Oscar, there in that kitchen, a place more familiar to him than to her as he had played in that house so often in his youth and she'd felt comforted at seeing him with Sarah, part of a family— the kind she so desperately had wanted for herself and for her boys but had been unable to give them. Her fear of her husband, Paul, was so great. The first time she'd jumped the hedge to escape his temper had been when she was pregnant with Daniel. Oh Daniel—sweet, sweet Daniel. She was so thrilled to be having a baby. *"Children are a blessing,"* she'd been told. *"Oh yes, they light your life forever."* That's what the other women had said when they saw her heavy belly. None had shared the pain of delivery—or of recovery for that matter—the sleepless nights, or the life sentence that followed. It wasn't until she was one of them, with a baby on her hip, greasy neglected hair and one of Paul's old sweatshirts crusted with dried formula that she found herself inside the circle; she was one of them as they joked about the hardship and the fatigue, but it was not to be discussed among those outside that circle. Somehow it was an unwritten rule among the sisters of motherhood, a sort of genetic program for preserving the human species.

Those early years were the hardest—an angry husband and two small boys. She thought it would never end and now that it had, now that her boys were gone beyond her embrace, her arms ached from the emptiness.

Miriam had looked at Oscar, a soldier standing in front of her in that kitchen, only a few days before, and she opened her mouth to tell him everything, all of it, but one's children should never be told the truth. They don't deserve such cruelty. So instead she gave him a few simple lines that maybe had been in her head from a movie or some television show. They were worn out phrases like, "our destiny, you'll understand someday, I didn't ask for it to happen this way."

The words just made Oscar fidget with his hands and then when he heard her say, "you were a product of our love," a fire rose in his eyes. As his fist came toward her, she had only a split second to realize it was her son's and not her husband's before the blow to her head sent her back with such force into the chair, it fell over and crashed down onto the linoleum. The commotion sent Ron flying through the door to catch Oscar's arm before the second blow landed. Oscar's frozen eyes told them that he was as horrified as they to find himself hovering over his mother, his hand in midair as Ron grasped it hard enough to leave a red burn of fingers in his wrist.

Miriam tried to remember the words that followed but the memory was a visual one, no sound at all, though there must have been a deafening thunder of moving chairs and army boots and shouting as she cried and watched her son retreat and then disappear from the house. Miriam would wait all her life to see Oscar again, never knowing where he was, and it wouldn't be until she lay in a hospital bed, riddled with the same cancer that had taken her mother, an illness that had pushed their lives toward permanent change, that Oscar would return as an older man saying his goodbyes and she would know he'd finally created that family she had dreamed for him.

Long before that, though, before she stood in Ron's kitchen listening to him comfort Sarah, before she'd lost her boys, before the status quo of accepted routine had been shattered, Miriam had watched her own mother take her last breath. And that was the moment Miriam's brain shut down and an automatic pilot took over. After a few days of doing what was necessary—following the rules of bereavement—on her way to throw the trash into the cans at the side of the house, she'd gotten into the truck without a thought and put her foot on the gas pedal, barely feeling the movement of the wheels taking her away—to where? It never mattered, just *away* was all she wanted and she didn't even notice the bag of garbage she'd taken with her as it sat on the passenger side, never having made it to that trash can.

As she stood in Ron's kitchen and stared at the cracked counter, the cancer cells divided slowly deep within her body and though those microscopic changes would take years to appear, it was that same silent demon who had taken her mother. It was there, with those cancer cells that the blame for everything that happened afterwards would rest. Oscar was in high school by then, Daniel in the army, so she thought it would be okay for her to stay in her parents' home and care for Mama. But Paul didn't like it. He wanted her at home—he always seemed to have a problem staying by himself, and yet seemed irritated by the company of others. That time, though, Miriam defied him and he sensed that it was a moment—one of the few—that he should back off, so he sat with his vodka bottles and waited for her return.

It's not easy to watch a person die, especially someone who is loved as much as Miriam loved her mother. The last week was the cruelest. Mama lay on the mattress barely able to move or speak. Miriam held her hand and watched the older woman, small and helpless, sometimes shuddering beneath the sheets. And Miriam was unsure whether it was pain or cold or fear that plagued her mother. Occasionally there'd be a small sigh like that of a frightened child and Miriam would squeeze her hand. "I'm here, Mama. It's me—it's Miriam." Mama would return the squeeze with her pale hand, the skin stretched translucent over the tiny bones of her fingers, a squeeze with so much strength it was hard for Miriam to believe she had that much left.

"It's okay, Mama. I'm here."

At night, Miriam lay next to her mother so Mama could feel her warmth and know that she wasn't alone. Miriam's father slept on a cot next to them. He helped move his wife so she wouldn't get bedsores. She was so small and thin; it was like holding a child. Miriam could have moved her without her father's help, but Mama cringed with each movement and Miriam thought it might be causing her pain, but it was hard to know for sure. Mama's muscles tensed at the slightest of touches.

"I promise, I won't leave you," Miriam whispered and Mama seemed to relax. "*She hears me*," Miriam thought. But Mama hadn't talked in days. The last time her voice was heard, it was a tiny whisper, barely audible.

"I'm scared," she'd said and Miriam told her "Don't be afraid. I'm here." But Miriam was frightened too, maybe more so.

Sometimes Mama was there again, her eyes alive, staring straight into her daughter's soul and other times she was gone, an empty shell. Miriam didn't want to think about it, about what was happening to her mother, how the last minutes of life looked. But it was inescapable. Death blatantly sat beside them, waiting. The truth about life was in Death's hands and Miriam had barely thought about it until it was there beside her. Life ends—and this is what it looks like when it does.

One morning Miriam awoke and felt the dampness of the sheets and couldn't fathom how her mother could have wet the bed because she and her father had been cutting up some old flannel sheets to make diapers. Until that morning, they'd been pretty effective. Her mother had never been wet in the mornings before that one, and she wasn't drinking anything anymore so it was somewhat perplexing when Miriam felt the wet sheets around her. Mama's breathing had changed too. It came in short quick jumps, reminding Miriam of her boys when they were newborns. She got out of bed and prepared some clean sheets and a new diaper but when she reached down to brush the hair from her mother's face, she saw the beads of sweat all over her skin and felt an oily film. It was on her entire body and had soaked through her nightgown.

Standing there in Ron's kitchen, Miriam remembered mostly the smells and sounds of that morning in her parents' bedroom, probably because, as she gently washed the film from her mother's face, her own eyes were so full of tears she could barely see, though she still didn't understand that those were her last moments with her mother.

Miriam ran her thumb across the kitchen counter. She listened to the murmur of Ron's voice in the hallway as she thought of her own father, standing behind her as they watched the last breath escape from the woman they both would miss dearly.

"*It's so odd.*" Miriam thought, "*You know that the diagnosis is a death sentence. You watch the person dwindle to a whisper of her former self and then when she's gone, you just stand there in utter disbelief. That's it. Her life is finished and will never exist again.*"

Miriam knew there would be nothing else after life but she wasn't afraid as she said goodbye to her mother. Nor was she sad. She was angry — at that God she was sure did not exist and at her father who stood shaking with grief at the sight of her mother's lifeless body. Was he crying for his wife or for the fact that he would soon follow. She put her arms around him but what she really wanted to do, was to smack him hard across the face and scream at all his inadequacies, his limits as a human, the stupid decisions of his lifetime — all of the imbecilic choices he'd made from the day he was born until that very moment as they stood together next to Mama. A father is suppose to lay the path and guide his children down it, but there he was, blubbering away, and Miriam was still in *his* town with a path that looked painfully like his own and it was his fault and she hated him for it. In the days that followed she was the dutiful daughter. She put on her black clothes and walked behind the hearse as it made its slow descent through town toward the graveyard, but when the casket was lowered into the ground she knew she could not stay. Something needed to change. She thought of her husband, Paul, of her sons and then put a barrier between herself and those thoughts.

A few days later, two soldiers in full uniform brought the hand-delivered letter from the president to her front door, and she was laying Daniel beside his grandmother soon after that. Mama had had sixty years, Daniel twenty-one. Where is the justice in that?

She got as far as Ohio before the money she found tucked into the truck visor and the gas in the tank ran out. She lived out of the truck for a few days, and then got a job sweeping the floor in a bar she'd gone into, to use the rest room. A full week went by before she realized that wanting to escape and actually doing it were two different things so she called the only person she could count on — Ron Petit.

Ron got the call at the mill. The foreman told him he had a phone call and he'd thought it was Edith. They'd fought the day before, another stupid argument over a topic forgotten, and she'd gone to stay with her sister, Jackie. But when he heard Miriam's voice on the receiver he forgot about Edith. The secretary turned to her typewriter and seemed to be deeply concentrating on the keys under her fingertips as Ron spoke into the receiver.

"I've been worried sick about you. Yes, of course. Come back. We'll work it out. Yes, I promise. Come on, now. Stop that. It'll be okay. Don't worry. Hold on a second."

He looked at the desk and then around the room. The secretary continued to punch the keys of the typewriter. Ron bent and took a crumpled paper from the waste paper basket and smoothed it out on the surface of the desk. The secretary reached over and handed him a pen without looking up. Ron took the pen and spoke to Miriam as he held the phone in the crook of his neck and put the pen to the paper.

"Okay, go ahead," he said and he scrawled the address on the paper.

"Is there a number I can reach you at?" he asked Miriam.

She gave him the number of the bar.

He immediately wired Miriam the money for her return — well actually the secretary did the wiring after he hung up and asked her to. He had no idea how to do such things. Then he went back into the mill.

A man needs to keep his wits about him when working the saw or he could lose a finger or two, so Ron tried to concentrate on the work as best he could, but Edith kept creeping into his thoughts. They'd have to make some changes. The kids were old enough to understand. He had a hundred imaginary conversations with her but none real so he had only himself to blame on the day Edith came back to the house and found him with Miriam.

Miriam remembered the emotions that followed in those few seconds as she scrambled for her clothes on the floor while Edith lobbed items at them, and the most memorable was that of relief.

Now, Sarah was back — no one had bothered to consider how she would handle the new arrangements. Miriam continued to listen to Ron's muffled voice as he tried to comfort his daughter.

When Sarah pulled away from her father with the realization that she was finally *home* but *home* was unrecognizable, she immediately retired to her room, barely eating anything for two days. Ron was overcome with guilt at his daughter's reaction to the new family situation, believing that to be the only explanation for her descent into darkness. Then early one morning, out of the blue, Sarah came into the master bedroom before dawn and turned on the light, startling both him and Miriam.

"This is too awful," she'd said.

He thought he knew what she was referring to.

"I cannot stay here." She continued in a whisper, "I want to go back to East End." Maybe she would be able to contact Alexandros somehow.

"Okay. No problem." Ron answered her in a soft even tone, "But how about if you stay with your mom and Earnest at Aunt Jackie's for a week, first. Then go back downstate if that's what you want."

"Okay," she whispered.

She turned and went back to her bedroom and pulled the sheets over her head. And that's where Ron found her after getting off the phone with Edith. He had stood in his underwear in the kitchen whispering into the receiver with his estranged wife—Sarah's condition having produced a truce between them, both worried about the reaction she was having to their break-up.

Sarah took her place in the makeshift bedroom in Aunt Jackie's basement after Ron brought some wood from the mill over to his sister-in-law's house to construct a wall, making a division down the middle of the room, separating the washing machine from Sarah's area.

A few days later, Edith came down the worn wooden stairs of the basement with the intention of throwing a load of dirty clothes into the washer. The music coming from Sarah's stereo was pounding a beat into the wobbly wood panels of the new wall, so she swung around the corner into her daughter's space—ready to admonish her for the music. But she was struck by the image of Sarah lying on the unmade bed sound asleep, one hand rolled up under her chin and the other clutching the blanket to her chest, a very child-like posture, she thought. She walked slowly to the turned-over crate where the stereo sat, and she twisted the dial down slightly so the volume was barely lowered and Sarah undisturbed. Then she quietly placed the laundry basket on the top of the washer.

"*I'll do it later*," she thought as she ascended the stairs, craning her neck to get one last glimpse of her little girl, and then she disappeared into the kitchen.

At first she didn't see her sister, Jackie, at the refrigerator door, as her attention was so intent on closing the basement door quietly, holding the door frame with one hand and the knob with the other as she slowly fit the door back into its place. The look on Edith's face caused Jackie to close the refrigerator door without retrieving any of its items.

"What's the matter Edi?"

"God Jackie. What happened to us?"

"Whatta ya mean?"

"We were going to conquer the world. Remember when we were her age? Geez. Where'd it all go?"

Jackie came over to Edith and put her arm around her. "We're still here." She gave her sister a squeeze, then grabbed her cigarette case from the counter and pulled a cigarette out, put it in her mouth and presented the case to Edith.

"Here, take one." Jackie rustled her hand in a box of junk on the counter until she came up with a lighter. She lit the cigarette and offered her sister a light. The two sat down at the table.

"Look — what choice did you have back then, Edi?"

"I was so ignorant. He told me I wouldn't get pregnant the first time."

"We were all ignorant. Ron probably believed it himself. It's not like he got off scot free."

Edith looked at her sister and narrowed her eyes, "oh, please."

"Well, he had other plans too. Things happen. Stop beating yourself up."

Edith sucked in the smoke and looked at her sister. "I was going to be a park ranger. Remember?" A small laugh escaped her. "Protect the Adirondacks. Oh God — how many times did we climb Owl's Head Mountain?" Her laugh was a little bit longer, slightly louder. There was pleasure in it.

Jackie put her cigarette in the ashtray. "Let's go now. Come on." She pushed her chair away from the table and it scraped along the floor. "Get up, woman." She met Edith's eyes. The light behind the irises was dim but it was still there.

"Jackie, are you crazy?"

"Yes, I'm crazy. Let's go. Get up." She was reaching over the table as Edith pushed her chair back slightly, then stopped.

"Jackie I can't. Earnest will be home in a few hours. There's not enough time. It's too late."

"So, leave Sarah a note. Damn — you were a mother by her age. She can handle one little kid. God knows he's more mature than all of us put together." She smacked her hand on the table. "Come on!"

Before Edith could say another word, her sister was behind her, grabbing her under the arms and supporting her as she pulled her from her seat.

The two women sat on the back steps lacing up their sneakers, whispering and giggling like two young girls. They walked to the back fence and struggled over it, one helping the other, overcome with laughter when Edith's shoelace caught between the wooden slats and was left dangling as she tumbled to the ground, her sock sinking into the tall damp grass. But she picked herself up, replaced her sneaker and walked arm and arm with her sister toward the foot of the mountain.

*   *   *   *

Sarah slowly came back to life, realizing that Alexandros was gone. There'd be no way for her to find him. She settled into Aunt Jackie's house and took her cues from her little brother who had been a *kid-from-a-broken-home* for a longer time than she had. She watched with awe at his adeptness in bilking their father out of his hard earned money for guilt-gifts such as the new bike that sat on the front porch, the stacks of board games in his new room, the walkie-talkies that crackled with static day and night, and then the console for some kind of game that was played on a television screen, so naturally another television was needed.

But Sarah had her eye on one specific prize and it was soon apparent that her father would do whatever he needed to free himself from the shackles of guilt.

"I think Grandma Anne would have wanted me to have the store," she said to her father one day after she'd been in Owl's Head for about a year. He had come to take Earnest for his weekend visit and Sarah had decided to join them for dinner at the Howard Johnsons on Route 21.

"I have an idea for it."

Ron was thrilled to have her there at dinner, but even happier to hear her speak of a future.

"Like what?"

"I was thinking of a wine and cheese place."

"A what?"

"Wine and cheese. I went to a place downstate. It was really nice. I'd like something like that." Sarah thought she might be able to use wood and nails and hammers to recreate what she longed for.

"Well—uh, Sarah," Ron was thinking that it was a ridiculous idea to hand over a piece of real estate to an *almost-twenty-year-old*. But he said, "That sounds like a great idea."

"I'd need some money to convert it."

"Well—that's certainly something to think about." His voice was a little too high, which of course, did not escape Earnest.

"Why are you talking like that?"

"Like what?"

"Like she's a baby or something."

"No I'm not."

"Yes, you are."

Sarah broke in. "So, when do you think we could get it signed over to me?"

"I'll tell you what." Ron began, and he carefully watched the pitch of his voice. "Let me talk to the lawyer at the mill. Let's see what advice he gives us."

In the end, Ron did sign the store over to Sarah and he cosigned for a loan that allowed her to fix up the top floors for her to live in. The project kept her busy and lightened her heart with anticipation. After several months she was ready to begin renovations on the bottom floor for her wine and cheese place. She would need her father to write another check.

She stood with the carpenter, trying to explain to him her vision of the dining area. She closed her eyes for a second and saw herself sitting next to Alexandros under the dim Tiffany-style light. She inhaled deeply and opened her eyes to see the carpenter waiting for her to continue. He was the man who was going to give her back her life.

She swept her arms around the small space and said, "let's just tear this out, get rid of everything, gut the whole place and then," she walked over to the wall and brushed her hand along it, "put up like a little wall here and then a little wall here."

"Uh, Sarah." The carpenter interrupted, "You need some kind of a plan. I need to see a blueprint or at the very least a sketch. You know? Dimensions. Measurements. Stuff like that. The living space upstairs was easy because everything was there already. Your great-grandparents raised a family up there. This is different. It's all new."

"Hmm."

She put her hand to her chin and she was gone again—deep in thought. She looked around and then at the carpenter, nodding slightly. Yes, a plan—of course—it's stupid to go blindly forward without a plan.

"I see what you mean," she said.

The carpenter took out his wallet. "This woman is a good architect. She's honest." He handed her a business card. "She'll do right by you. See her first and then we can discuss my work and a price."

She took the card. Of course—yes, she wanted a plan, a blueprint—something that laid it all out. The carpenter was merely there to follow her direction. That's what she needed. Direction. That's what had been missing all along—some guidance—a well thought out plan. She had an architect. She had a carpenter. She had *herself* and that was something big. She had a vision of the future. Her vision. And she could face the future, with or without Alexandros. She saw that then, standing there in Grandma Anne's store.

Her store.

Ron had been trying to figure out a way to talk to Sarah about the loan. He'd been able to carry the payments for his daughter, but she was going to have to take them over soon. He wasn't *made of money* as Miriam put it. The girl needed to find work and carry her own weight. But Ron figured he'd wait until after Mike's wedding, the following month.

So yes, as Alexandros sat at the wedding celebration of Andreas and Aphrodite, Sarah was also contemplating a wedding.

It had only been a few weeks before that, when she realized she'd be going back to East End. This time it would be for Uncle Mike's wedding, but she wondered how it would feel.

"Will you be my date?" she asked Karen Marie, batting her eyes, "we could share a room. I'll show you around. It's actually a nice place."

The invitation from Uncle Mike's soon-to-be in-laws said that the reception would be at the Yacht Club and there was a block of rooms reserved for the guests from out of town—which meant Mike's family from upstate. So the wedding plans were underway and Sarah's return to East End was not far from her mind as she made an appointment with the architect and wondered as she looked at the woman's business card, what it took to have such impressive credentials.

CHAPTER 19

"Hi, This is Bob from the Yacht Club. Is Minos around?"

"Sorry, Bob." Maureen spoke into the receiver as she sat behind the desk in the Atlantic Palace Hotel office. "He's in Greece. He's at his nephew's wedding. Should be back in a few days. What's up?"

"Oh that's right. I forgot about that wedding. Well, you know we've got our own wedding next week. Bo Hoffman's daughter."

"Yeah. I heard about that."

"I'm kind of short on kitchen help over here. You think there's any way you guys could help me out?

"I'm sure we could. I'll tell George to get back to you."

"George didn't go?"

"No Bob. You know how it is between him and his ex. Why poison a wedding, right?"

"I guess so. Okay, tell George to give me a call when he gets a chance. Take it easy."

It was Eagle who was sent to help out at the wedding the following month, and if he hadn't gone out the kitchen door to smoke a cigarette in the fresh sea breeze just at the moment his old blue Impala pulled into the parking lot and drove past him on its way to the valet parking, he'd never have known that Sarah was one of the guests. And if he hadn't just spent the previous night with Alexandros at Main Street Bar, as Alexandros tried to acclimate to the time difference after arriving back in East End only a few hours before that, he wouldn't have felt more than a passing interest. But having listened to the regrets and lamentations of his friend as they shared a bottle of scotch and philosophized about the missed moments of one's life, he felt even more compelled to see if she was with someone.

He walked slowly around the building and came to the front, carefully hidden behind the shrubs, and watched as the bellhop opened the driver's door and there she was—Sarah, as radiant as the sun— emerging from the front seat in a flowing red dress that came just past her knees with a slit that went up the side of her leg and stopped at mid thigh. And from the passenger side came that girl, the one who'd driven her to the back of the restaurant on the last day he'd seen her, just as he'd told Alexandros the night before.

He'd been standing in the kitchen of the Atlantic Palace restaurant when Alexandros walked through the back door, having just arrived from the airport. Minos was with him. They stood talking with George and the cooks and then Maureen wandered over from the hotel. She greeted Alexandros and listened for a while as best she could within a conversation that lapsed between English and Greek. But when the topic turned to the day Alexandros had left with Andreas, and the aftermath of the gas station explosion, Maureen spoke.

"Poor Sarah. She was inconsolable no matter what I told her about the Turk and his son. She just wouldn't stop crying. Her heart was broken," Maureen raised her brows and looked at Alexandros, "I'm not sure from what, but she *did* ask for you, Alexandros."

With that, Eagle had nodded toward Alexandros, "Come back after my shift. We'll go out for a drink. We need to talk."

So—Sarah was not with another guy. Alexandros had been wrong and he'd already wasted two years. Eagle wanted desperately to get hold of him. He walked along the side bushes back to the kitchen door.

"Is there a phone I could use?" he asked one of the cooks.

"No, sorry man. There's one at the front desk, but the guests are starting to arrive. You really can't go out there now."

Frustrated, Eagle got behind the steam table but each time the door opened into the dining room, he craned his neck looking for a splash of red or any hint of Sarah. He decided he would find her after the celebration was over and make small talk, ask her how she was doing and *oh, what a coincidence — Alexandros is here too.* Just to see her reaction, to see if there was any interest. But when his shift was almost over, Bob came back and thanked him and handed him a wad of cash.

"You can leave. Thanks for the help. I really appreciate it."

"I can stay until the end. I don't mind."

"No — we're good. You can take off."

"Really. I feel like I should stay."

"We've got it covered. Don't worry about it."

So Eagle left reluctantly and Bob marveled at the Greek work ethic, wishing he had a few of them in *his* kitchen.

Eagle went straight to Minos' house and knocked at the front door, not realizing how late it was until Roula came to the door, disheveled and visibly upset.

"Oh my God! Who's dead?" She asked.

"No. No. I'm sorry." Eagle felt foolish. "I just wanted to talk to Alexandros."

"What's wrong with you Costas!" Minos' wife never used his nickname. "It's late. The kids are sleeping. You woke me up." She pulled the ties on her robe and pushed the hair from her eyes. "He's not here. He went somewhere with Minos. You want me to call the restaurant and see if they're there? Come in."

"No, don't call." He knew everyone was instructed to say that Minos had just left whenever his wife should call. "I'll go there."

"Do you want coffee, or something to eat?"

"No — really. I'm sorry I bothered you."

"Don't worry. It's okay — now that I know everything is alright."

On Eagle's way toward the restaurant, he did not notice Minos' car passing him, so he never did get to find Alexandros that night, but he promised himself he'd get up early and go back to Minos' house — but not too early.

Roula told Alexandros as he came in the door a few minutes later, that Eagle had been looking for him, so Alexandros made a mental note to seek him out in the morning — whenever that would be — for his body was so confused by the time difference, he had fallen asleep while sitting in the office waiting for Minos to drive him back to the house.

Hours later, with the wedding celebration finished and the moon hovering over the bay, Sarah and Karen Marie made their way to the hotel rooms with the last of the wedding party. They were all walking through the parking lot. Sarah looked toward the marina and could see the outline of some of the taller masts against the night sky.

"Let's go to the dock," she said to Karen Marie.

"What for? I'm tired."

"I just want to see something."

"Tomorrow," Karen Marie groaned as she bent her knee and took off one heel, and then the other, letting her bare feet fall to the asphalt. "Ah." She held the heels by the back strap, "or, I should say, later today – it's almost three."

Sarah was thinking of *The Hope* as she turned from the water and followed Karen Marie to their room. She'd never actually seen the fishing boat that Mack worked on but she knew he used to leave the boarding house as early as four, sometimes. She thought she might run into him, but there was no movement by the marina and three o'clock would be too early anyway. She thought of the boarding house and wondered if he were just hitting the button on his alarm.

She and Karen Marie found their way to their room. While Karen Marie took a shower, Sarah slipped from her dress and put on a robe, then went onto the balcony that faced the Yacht Club's docks. Those boats were very unlike the fishing boats in the marina, though some had expensive fishing gear with rods sticking straight up in rod holders. In the dark, the boats looked like sea creatures with antennae feeling out into the air. Sarah moved to the far corner of the balcony to see if she could get a glimpse of the fishing boats at the marina, but the building was constructed in such a way that it protected its guests from having to see any ungainly sights.

"Bathroom's free," Karen Marie called from the room.

Sarah went back in and Karen Marie was halfway to sleep – both girls' dresses were lying on the floor as if they'd melted and those were all that was left of them. Sarah kicked hers aside and went into the bathroom to use the shower.

By the time she was lying on the bed, facing the sliding glass window, the pink light of dawn was just peeking into the sky. She got up and closed the curtain. Then quietly, she found a pair of jeans and a tee shirt, dressed silently and left the room.

The sun wasn't up yet, but the early morning dimness was enough to see the bustle of activity along where the fishing boats were anchored. Sarah walked over and looked around. She nodded to some of the men who were loading crates on boats and calling back and forth to each other. The boat names were easy to read: Harbor Queen, Mary Louise, Midnight Water and Belle. But The Hope was not among them. It must be at a different port, maybe in Florida or Trinidad.

Sarah was remembering Mack's stories, how the captain liked to move between ports but she had thought East End was the summer port and was surprised that the boat was not there. They might have left for the day already. It was hard to know—she never had paid much attention to the time of day Mack had left the boarding house for the dock. She just knew it was early and sometimes she'd be coming home as he was leaving. Other times he'd still be at the boarding house, tinkering around the kitchen, when she was waking up to get ready for her hotel work. For someone she longed to see at that moment, she realized how little she had paid attention to him back then.

"Sarah?"

And there he was coming off of the boat that was named Belle.

"Mack!" The two embraced. "How are you?"

"Great. What are doing here? Are you back at the boarding house? Looking for a job on the boats?" He laughed.

"Just here for my uncle's wedding. He got married at the Yacht Club last night."

"Well, how are you doing, little girl? It's good to see you. You look happy—much better than the last time we saw each other."

"I'm good Mack. Everything's good. But what about you? I thought you'd never leave The Hope. That's all you talked about."

"I haven't." He made a sweeping movement with his hand, pointing to the boat behind them as though it were a prize on a game show. "This is The Hope—or was—I bought it. Captain retired—now I'm the captain. I changed the name, but it's still the same boat."

"Mack, that's great!"

"Belle!" He yelled the boat's name, looking on deck. "I want you to meet someone."

A young girl around Sarah's age walked off the gangplank and came toward them. She had the same intense eyes as Mack and her smile was his too. Her silky brown arms were long and skinny coming out from an oversized man's fishing vest and her hair was a mass of black corkscrews sticking wildly out from a floppy hat.

"Sarah, this is my daughter, Belle."

"Oh, I didn't realize—so that's the boat, the name of the boat." She took the brown hand that was extended to her and shook it.

"Nice to meet you." Belle said, "So you're Sarah? My father talks about you. I guess I should thank you."

Mack coughed nervously, "Well, you know." He didn't finish but both girls sensed that whatever it was Belle wanted to thank her for would cause him some embarrassment.

"It's nice to meet you too," Sarah said. "Your dad—he's a great guy. Has some fun stories too. Do you live here in East End?"

"No, just for the summer. I stay at the boarding house with my dad." She crunched up her nose and it was obvious that the boarding house was a necessary inconvenience, "but I go to college in Florida in the winter and then home to Trinidad on holidays. I guess I'm everywhere."

Mack beamed with pride, "Yeah—my Belle, she's a college girl." And he winked at Sarah.

Mack had a daughter. And she was a college girl living in Middleground Boarding house. And a fisherman on *his* fishing boat. The idea was so gigantic. It was hard to hold onto.

After they parted, Sarah headed for the blue Impala. She drove it down the hill toward the ocean and slowed, easing off the gas pedal as she passed the hotel and restaurant.

"Atlantic Palace Hotel," she said aloud. The sun was just coming over the roof of the office as she passed the building and continued driving toward the gas station—the waiter at the wedding said it had been rebuilt. She saw it in the distance so she pulled her foot from the gas pedal completely and coasted slowly past it. She could see that it had a large neon sign hanging in the middle of a giant window that went from the ceiling to the floor. The sign bellowed in bright orange: *open*. Sarah made a U-turn and passed by again slowly. This time she saw a man standing in the window, his head turning, following her car as it drove by.

She pulled into the empty IGA parking lot and turned around heading toward the gas station once more, but this time she pulled in and parked next to the building just as a young man came around the corner toward her.

He stopped and looked at her questioningly for a few awkward seconds.

"Oh—I used to know the owners," Sarah said, "uh, so—do you work here?

"Sarah. You don't recognize me?"

The young man was a foot over her and was sporting a full mustache. She heard Kareem's voice, but it was coming from the mouth of a stranger.

"Kareem?

"Yeah." He came toward her with his arms extended, but she took a step back, so his hands quickly shot down to his side as he stopped dead in his stride and just stood like a stone as he said, "how're ya doin'?"

"Uh—good. How about you?"

"I'm good too."

There was a moment of awkward silence.

Kareem still not moving, said, "Sarah, come and sit inside. I won't hurt you," and he laughed nervously.

"I know, Kareem," she said slowly. "It's just so weird to see you like this—you're a man! I mean, what is that thing?" She stepped in front of him and grabbed the side of his mustache.

"Hey—watch it. That hurt."

"Yeah? It was supposed to. That's payback for that canoe ride you took me on, remember?"

"Of course I remember. You were the only person I ever thought about back then."

Again—silence.

"Sarah, I'm really sorry about—"

"Kareem, don't. It's okay. I didn't treat you right either."

"I just want you to know. I just want—Sarah. I'm sorry. I know I destroyed your relationship with—"

"No, really Kareem. You did what you did and I did what I did. We were two dumb kids. Whatever happened, it was, well—because of my own choices. It's okay. Let's just erase that day."

"Yeah—wouldn't it be great if we could erase the mistakes we make in life?" he smiled.

"We can." Sarah put her hand up flat against the air and rubbed back and forth. "There. Done. It's gone. Erased."

They both smiled and the years fell away. They were Sarah and Kareem and there was so much they had to talk about. They went inside and talked until the seagulls flew over the dunes looking for their morning meal. Kareem told her about his father and how Amir was unable to work at the gas station alone anymore. After the attack, he had become afraid — an unnamed fear that kept him from being the person he used to be. He was physically healed but his psyche remained permanently damaged. Kareem spoke of revenge and Sarah listened, saying nothing. Though Kareem looked like a man, he was but a sixteen-year-old boy and she remembered the ignorant kid she'd been at sixteen.

At that moment she also remembered Grandma Anne, "*It's true,*" she thought, "*Everything changes, but nothing is ever different.*"

An artist's imagination is endless. The brush moves across the white canvas with unique strokes and an infinite mixture of colors. But the canvas, itself, is always the same. It was there before the artist arrived and it will be there long after the artist is gone.

They said their goodbyes as the sunlight began to pour into the station and illuminate the floor behind the large window. Sarah got back into the car and drove toward Atlantic Palace Hotel. She crawled past the lobby, looking carefully at the side of the restaurant and the guest rooms, looking for anything familiar. There was a maid's cart sitting at the back of the lobby. She thought of Teresa and thought she might stop by later, but she continued driving until she was past the hotel. Then she parked in the road with the wheels on one side of the car resting in the sand and the others on the street. She opened the door slowly and brought her feet to the sandy asphalt.

Tiny sprouts of beach grass pushed through the cracks in the broken pavement at her feet and she stared down at them for a few moments. Their tough little shoots of green managed to find a way to take root in such a difficult environment, not only to take root but to actually sprout healthy leaves that pushed their way toward the sun — such strength against odds.

She left the car and walked onto the cool sand at the base of the dunes. Then she climbed up, ignoring the grit as the sand filled her sneakers. She crested the first dune, inhaling deeply, letting the breeze blow her hair back from her face, tasting the salty air. She made her way across the rest of the dunes until she stood atop the last mound of sand, ready to descend to the beach as an early morning jogger ran past. He nodded at her and she smiled and nodded back, then closed her eyes and smelled the dampness of the sea.

She was back with Alexandros, sitting on the sheet from the hotel, holding a cold bottle of beer, watching him peel the label, drawing mountains and valleys in the sand. She felt a heaviness in her throat and swallowed hard.

"These are *good* memories," she told herself and smiled.

Then she kicked her shoes off and walked down the mound toward the surf. As she sunk her toes into the wet sand and let the foam of the waves wash over her feet, she did not know that Alexandros, still trying to adjust to the time difference, had been out walking around in the early morning. And at that moment he was running toward the blue Impala, having recognized it immediately. He looked into the windows with reckless abandon, going from one door to the next, trying each door handle, yanking at it hard until he came to the driver's side and pulled the door open. He sat inside and he could smell her. He was a wild animal—all of his senses focused and alert, searching for that which he needed, nourishment to keep him alive. He looked quickly from the front seat to the back and then to the dashboard, inhaling deeply and then he jumped from the car and looked around, turning his head quickly from one direction to the next, his neck swiveling back and forth, his eyes searching.

Where is she?

He ran to the top of the sandy embankment and squinted toward the horizon. It was her hair that he saw first, those wild strands of amber whipping around her face.

"Sarah!" he called and she turned toward him.

"Sarah!"

His body moved toward the surf with perfect symmetry, every muscle, every nerve called forward for one destination and suddenly he was there—in the place he had wanted to be since the moment he'd left. He pulled her into his arms and they held each other before their thoughts had time to doubt their instincts. And then Alexandros remembered Canada and Vaso's words.

If you find someone, a friend – a good friend, hold onto that person.

He held Sarah by the shoulders and looked into her eyes with such focus, Sarah knew he was seeing all of her. But when he opened his mouth, he hesitated. He had to get it right; the words had to be exact so she would understand.

"Sarah, my love, my friend, I want to wake up with you every morning."

Their lips met and it was the delicious fullness of a feast that had been imagined by those who were long starved. The embrace brought them so close together that when the person in room twenty-one looked toward the sunrise, he saw only one person standing in the surf.

Ithaka

BY C. P. CAVAFY
(circa 1911)

As you set out for Ithaka
hope your road is a long one,
full of adventure, full of discovery.
Laistrygonians, Cyclops,
angry Poseidon—don't be afraid of them:
you'll never find things like that on your way
as long as you keep your thoughts raised high,
as long as a rare excitement
stirs your spirit and your body.
Laistrygonians, Cyclops,
wild Poseidon—you won't encounter them
unless you bring them along inside your soul,
unless your soul sets them up in front of you.

Hope your road is a long one.
May there be many summer mornings when,
with what pleasure, what joy,
you enter harbors you're seeing for the first time;
may you stop at Phoenician trading stations
to buy fine things,
mother of pearl and coral, amber and ebony,
sensual perfume of every kind—
as many sensual perfumes as you can;
and may you visit many Egyptian cities
to learn and go on learning from their scholars.

Keep Ithaka always in your mind.
Arriving there is what you're destined for.
But don't hurry the journey at all.
Better if it lasts for years,
so you're old by the time you reach the island,
wealthy with all you've gained on the way,
not expecting Ithaka to make you rich.

Ithaka gave you the marvelous journey.
Without her you wouldn't have set out.
She has nothing left to give you now.

And if you find her poor, Ithaka won't have fooled you.
Wise as you will have become, so full of experience,
you'll have understood by then what these Ithakas
mean.

From *C.P. Cavafy Collected Poems*. Edited by George Savidis. Translate by Edmund Keeley and Philip Sherrard. Princton University Press, Princton, NJ.1975, 1992.

ABOUT THE AUTHOR

Linda Fagioli-Katsiotas lives on Long Island with her husband, Nick. She teaches English to newly immigrated English language learners at her local school district. When she is not teaching, she is often passing her time by reading a variety of books or writing on her blog, but her favorite activity, which is strictly seasonal, is lying on a beach in Epirus, staring out at the sea.

You can visit her at: www.truestorythenifi.blogspot.com

Independent authors often have quite a challenge in getting exposure for their work. I hope, dear reader, you will consider writing a review on Amazon or Goodreads.com.

AMONG THE ZINNIAS

Eighty-five-year-old Giovanna Boeri awaits the return of her daughter, Angelina, from a place in America called New Jersey. She cannot understand why Angelina has left from their small Adriatic island when anything anyone would ever want is there on Incompresso.

Angelina and her husband, Pasquale, are struggling to maintain a pizzeria in the small American town of Robin's Nest. Their son, Rocco, has just been released from an Italian jail at the age of twenty-five, after having served ten years for murder. Rather than have him return to their small island, they've bought the pizzeria in hopes of giving Rocco a new beginning. The pizzeria is supposed to be their catalyst to a happy life, though life rarely follows one's expectations.

Gina Ziti, an American customer, dealing with the grief of a parent and uncertainty about the direction of her marriage, finds herself several times a week visiting the pizzeria, enamored by the young Rocco.

In the meantime, back on Incompresso, Giovanna struggles to care for her ailing husband who is beset by memories of war and murder, one he himself committed and then realizes years later that it's his grandson, Rocco, who will pay the price. As Giovanna comes to terms with her husband's deteriorating mind, she throws away her age-old beliefs and realizes she cannot wait for others to decide her fate.

A MEMOIR

In Greek, the word "nifi" is used to describe a woman who marries into a family. *The Nifi* is, in part, the story of the author's journey in which she struggles to keep her identity in a culture that threatens to swallow her whole. It is also juxtaposed with that of her mother-in-law, Chevi, who gladly welcomes her into the family, though they speak no common language.

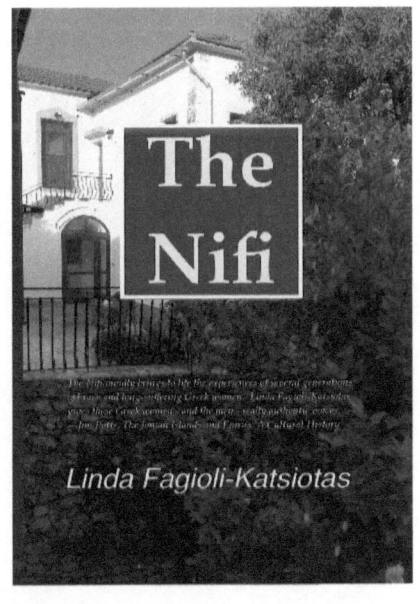

Chevi, through the translation of her son, and then years later as the author begins to learn Greek, conveys her story, a life which is rife with heartache and betrayal. She is no less than a heroine who quietly fights against the patriarchal society that dictates her every movement. Those stories which Chevi repeated often as though she feared they'd be lost forever, ultimately inspired the memoir, *The Nifi*.

The Nifi opens in 1983 in the village of Margariti in Epirus, Greece. In addition to a new unknown language, the author is faced with a lack of running water, poor roadways, no way to contact her family back in the U.S. and a mind-numbing culture shock. A month before, in a New York suburb she'd married her husband in an impulsive moment of passion after having worked with him at a local restaurant for a short period of time. With her inexperience and with mounds of unrealistic romanticism, she'd agreed to travel to his village and stay for an undefined period of time.

British author, Jim Potts, in his review of The Nifi writes: *The Nifi vividly brings to life the experiences of several generations of brave and long-suffering Greek women, as well as gives these Greek women—and men—authentic voices. . . It's a very honest and utterly convincing true story. It's a pity that there are not more accounts written by Epirote women.*

www.ingramcontent.com/pod-product-compliance
Lightning Source LLC
Chambersburg PA
CBHW031317170626
46807CB00002B/456